Actually YOURS

A SWEET ROMANTIC COMEDY

Actually YOURS

BELINDA MARY

Titles by Belinda Mary:

LOVE ALWAYS SERIES

Love, Lilly
Always, Amy
Ciao, Bella
Noticing Natalie

H&J Publishing

Cover illustrations by Elin Tan Art

Cover design by Philip Jiricek

1st edition 2024

ISBN: 978-0-6456942-9-1

www.belindamary.com

CONTENTS

PROLOGUE

Jake

Twelve months earlier

S HE'S HERE TO MEET MY brother.

The words reverberate around my brain and I stumble through the crowded restaurant, bumping through the rowdy after-work crowd, to get back to my dimly lit table where Steven, my best friend is waiting for me.

"Hey man, sorry I'm late."

I shake my head at him, willing myself not to look back towards the bar. Towards her.

"Jake? Are you OK?"

Am I OK? My world has just tilted off its axis and I'm unsure whether it will right itself again.

"I'm fine."

I manage to get the words out from my clenched jaw, my temples throbbing with the intensity of what had just occurred. This sort of thing doesn't happen to me. I'm never driven to act by emotion, by *need*. But that's exactly what had happened eleven minutes ago when I'd looked up and seen her walk into the restaurant. She'd appeared in the restaurant's doorway, the evening sun setting behind her, giving her an ethereal halo and making her red hair glow, and floated to the bar while the eyes of every man in the place followed her. Mine included.

And everything's been hazy ever since.

"Hey, isn't that your brother?"

Steven nods towards where I know Robby is now sitting with Amelia. *Amelia.* I let her name linger in my mind and stifle a groan. *I have to get out of here.*

"Yes." My tone is terse and my friend sends me a concerned glance. "He's on a date."

Date. I've never hated a word more.

Steven whistles. "He's got a beauty there. She's gorgeous."

I want to scream at him, "I know!" She's so beautiful it almost hurts to look at her. It's why when she'd sat down at the bar stool, my feet had taken me to her. Like they were guiding me to exactly where I was supposed to be. Only to find she's here to meet my brother. For a blind date, of all things.

"Man, your brother is a lucky guy," Steven interrupts my internal turmoil to state the obvious, sitting back in his chair and taking a long sip of his whiskey. "He's got no job, no ambition, no personality and he ends up with someone like her."

I feel every syllable from my friend's mouth like a bullet. And it's all true. Though he may be my brother and I love him, I also know that he's a spoilt, self-involved brat. And now he's dating Amelia.

No, scratch that. He's on a *first date* with her and after meeting the two of us at the same time (what are the chances?), she chose to be with him. And I let it happen, because that's the story of my life. I'm the giver in our relationship; the older brother willing to do anything to keep his undeserving younger brother happy.

Even this.

These thoughts sink like lead in my stomach as the leather seat behind me bites into my back, adding to my growing discomfort. "Can we just get out of here?"

Steven's mouth drops open. "But we just got here."

I fish a wad of cash out of my wallet—more than enough to cover our drinks—drop it on the table and stand up, not caring whether he follows me.

"Jake? What's wrong?"

Cutting the distance between our table and the exit, I wave away his question. It feels too ridiculous to even voice. "I just need to get home."

He follows, not asking any more questions, shooting me looks out of the side of his eyes. I ignore him, steeling myself to glance one last time at my brother. He's still at the bar, leaning forward, his face alight with laugher as he charms Amelia. Just like I knew he would.

I force myself to look away and step out into the rain, the bleakness of the blisteringly cold weather matching my mood. Frigid raindrop run over my face as I jog to my car, running away from the restaurant, away from where my brother is on a date with Amelia.

Amelia.

The woman I saw first.

The woman I now must forget.

CHAPTER 1

Amelia

Present day

H ERE ARE THE FIVE PLACES I'd rather be than standing up on this brightly-coloured, yellow-themed church altar:

1. At the dentist (root canal, no less)
2. Getting a Bikini wax (Brazilian!)
3. Doing my taxes (numbers—ugh!)
4. Doing a presentation in front of *people*
5. On a long-haul plane trip (surrounded by *only* crying babies).

Am I being a tad dramatic? Maybe. But as I look around, absorbing all the love and romance and gooey feelings of the people surrounding me, I believe I'm justified in feeling this way.

"I now pronounce you husband and wife."

A swell of joyous applause erupts around me as I watch my bestie, Bella Mancini-now Richardson, kiss the love of her life, her new husband Daniel. My traitorous eyeballs fill with tears despite my previous rebellious thoughts, and my hands clap vigorously. I can't help myself. They're such a beautiful couple, both inside and out. If I didn't love them so much, I'd hate them.

"You may now kiss the bride."

Danel leans all the way down and kisses the life out of a beaming Bella while the rapturous applause continues. I watch, happiness and dread fighting for pole position in my stomach, because once this overly-long, somewhat inappropriate for a church setting kiss ends, the spotlight will move to the bridal party. AKA, me.

Bella laughingly pushes Daniel away, earning one last peck on the lips from her besotted husband, before they turn hand in hand and face the congregation, all the people who love them the most. And here we are, this is it. The time has come, the reason for my earlier dread, the wishing to be anywhere else but here. Sweat drips down my back as Bella takes her bouquet of yellow roses from her smiling maid of honour and with her arm looped through Daniel's, the two of them start their married life with the short walk down the aisle towards the now open doors of the church. Following behind them comes the best man and maid of honour, Lucas and Amy Mancini. Another disgustingly in love couple, joining together and all but skipping in the footsteps of the bride and groom. And then? The other bridesmaid, Lilly, and her grooms-man husband, Oliver. *Another couple.* Linking hands and making their way out of the church.

And then there's…me. Just me. Only me. Apparently, Daniel has only two friends in the entire world and decided, quite rudely if you ask me, to pick Lucas and Oliver to be his groomsman, while Bella wanted all three of us to be her bridesmaids. And when you look at those numbers, well the math ain't mathing. Leaving me the odd one out. The one who has to walk down the aisle, behind the happy couples. Alone. All alone.

Deep breath, Amelia. No one is even looking at you.

Except they are. The faces of the hundred-plus congregation—how do Bella and Daniel know so many people? And again, how could Daniel not one person in this crowd to partner with me today?—follow my every step. And it may be that I'm *imagining* the pitying looks written on their faces as I sprint-walk down the aisle, as fast as my heels and the mermaid skirt of this gorgeous yet restrictive yellow dress will allow me. But it's like every furrowed brow and slight head shake is a sad indictment of my single status. Like I need that kind of reminding.

Just a few more steps and then freedom.

Except, what awaits me on the other sides of these doors is more couple time, more playing third—seventh?—wheel in this group of twosomes as we make a procession line to accept the hugs and kisses from all the well-wishers, waiting to share their glowing congratulations with the bride and groom. And the friends of the happy couple. Couple, couple, couple…and then one lone woman. Wishing I was anywhere but here.

"You must be the friend, the spinster." I'm startled from my internal panic at being the odd one out by Bella's aunty, who had travelled all the way from Florence, Italy to be here today. To insult me, apparently.

"Not spinster, Zia," Lucas, Bella's older brother, gently chides the confused-looking woman in front of us. He's standing next to me in this hellish procession line and has the privilege of witnessing my utter humiliation. "That's not quite the English word for what you mean."

The said aunty looks perplexed, and I mirror her expression. I get English isn't her first language—and being unable to speak anything beyond the tertiary Japanese I learnt in high school, I admire anyone who is bi-lingual—but come on! A spinster is a spinster in any language.

"You mean, *single*," Lucas clarifies with an embarrassed chuckle while my cheeks flame. "She means you're the unattached member of the bridal party," he continues to try to reassure me while making things worse.

"Ah, ok," I mutter, happy to see the baffled-looking aunty being moved on by another kindly family member, who is also shooting me a sympathetic glance. When did being single become so taboo?

"Smile!"

The bridal party turns in unison at the command of the tiny but mighty photographer, who according to Bella is the best in the business. She's working hard to move us into position and making us pose…all while looking natural. An oxymoron if you ask me.

"Are you OK?" Amy, Lucas's wife and Bella's new sister-in-law asks me through clenched teeth, as we continue to smile like maniacal evil geniuses. It's almost painful holding this smile in place at this point.

"Sure, I'm fine." I don't want any of the focus of today to be on me. This is Bella's day and I wish only the most perfect wedding for her.

"Don't take any notice of Zia Anna. When we last visited Bella and Lucas's family in Florence, she called me a young prostitute, when she meant to say young professional."

A loud chuckle bursts out of me as I picture the scene and Amy's giggles follow mine until we're both laughing uncontrollably. The rest of the group stop their enforced smiling for the photographer and turn to us, keen to be included in the joke.

"I'm just filling Amelia in on the troubles we've all faced with the Italian-to-English language barrier," Amy gasps out between snorts. "Aunty Anna just called Amelia a spinster."

Another laugh escapes me as I try to ignore the sting that word still has in its tail. It's just a silly misunderstanding. *Why am I letting it get to me so much?*

"Amelia, I'm so sorry." Bella moves away from the arms of her husband and wraps her own arms around me.

"Don't be silly," I mumble into her neck while pulling her closer, drawing comfort from her nearness. I've only known Bella for eighteen months, but it feels like we were always destined to be best friends. And given Bella moved from the other side of the world only to stumble into the hair salon where I work on her third day in the country, it makes finding her even more special. "It's fine."

She pulls back and frowns at me. That's the trouble with having a bestie who knows you better than you know yourself. She knows all my sore spots and she can see straight through my lies. She knows that my single status, after so many attempts at being part of a couple, is something that bothers me more than it should.

"Are you sure?" She says this under her breath as we make our way to where the shiny white stretch limousine is waiting to take us to the reception venue. I've seen the location, having visited it with Bella many months ago, and I know what awaits us: a beautiful white tented marquee, smothered in yellow ribbons and flowers, perched just by the ocean.

I squeeze her arm to my side and wobble a smile in her direction. "You know me, I'm working on being fine, being on my own. I do *not* need a man."

Her eyebrows draw down into an even deeper frown and I use my forefinger to push them back into place.

"Seriously, Bella. Today is all about you and that hunky man who is now your husband. My doomed love life is a discussion for another day."

She opens her mouth, no doubt to argue with me and is interrupted by her husband winding his muscular arms around her and pulling her back against him. "Everything alright, Mrs Richardson?"

I watch Bella melt into him and stifle the pang of longing I feel whenever I'm near them. Or Lucas and Amy. Or Oliver and Lilly. Three perfect couples. I could look at them and see what's possible, but after the disaster that has been my love life over the years, all I see when I look at them are my own failures. My inability to find what they've found.

"Everything is perfect, Mr Mancini," Bella teases her husband, turning to plant a soft kiss on his lips while he beams down at her. I know Daniel would go against tradition and happily take Bella's last name, if that's what she wanted. He's willing to do anything for her.

"Then let's get this party started!" This comes from Lilly, who's already in the limo, an opened champagne bottle in her hand. *Oooh, alcohol. Maybe that's the ticket to making it through the rest of the day?*

Maybe not.

I'm on my fifth glass of champagne and have almost given up looking for the numbing effects a good bottle of champagne can offer. Sure, after the first glass went down and the crisp bubbles went straight to my head, things had been looking up. But then we'd arrived at this magical venue, the marquee lit with fairy-lights and candles, and filled with the light fragrance of vases upon vases of yellow roses, adding to the sensual vibe Bella was hoping to achieve, and I had halted at the seating arrangements of the bridal table.

Here's what it's like: you know when you go to a dinner party that has just enough room at the table to fit the invited guests? Say, in this case, three happy couples? And then someone brings an extra stray person along, so the hosts have to find a fold-out table, stick it on the end, slap on a tablecloth and hope no one will notice where the real table ends and the add-on table begins? Well, that's where I am today, at the end of the table, the extra part that's not supposed to be there. I feel like my mere presence is making everything lopsided and slightly wrong. And I *know* I'm being overly sensitive and this perception of my role today is most likely all in my head, but I can't get over the notion that my being here without a partner is throwing the entire bridal party off.

"Aren't they the most beautiful couple?" Lilly's slightly slurred words draw my attention away from my unhinged internal monologue about seating arrangements and direct it back to the dancefloor where the bride and groom are sharing their first dance. The haunting notes of Etta James's "At Last" fill the air and goosebumps pop up along each of my arms as my attention is glued to the two of them gliding across the floor, lost in each other's gaze, their utter devotion to each other palpable.

I swallow hard. "They are."

"Do you want to get married?"

My head turns sharply to look at Lilly, wondering where this question came from. Since becoming friends with Bella all those months ago, I'd been adopted into her friendship group, which comprises Amy and her best friend Lilly, who is also Bella's business partner. We'd spent enough time together for Lilly to know that love and romance are not a popular topic of conversation for me.

"What about me makes you think I'm the marrying kind?"

She tilts her head, narrowing her eyes at me like she's attempting to peer into my soul. And it's working. Her intense inspection of me has my hands sweating.

"I think you're totally the marrying kind." She nods her head firmly after she says this, like the decision has been made.

"Lilly," I start, keeping my voice firm like I would if I were talking to an unruly toddler. "You know I don't want a relationship, that I've given up on love."

Her expression softens as she looks from the happy couple back to me. "Maybe you just haven't met the right man yet?"

I snort. "Well, I've met enough wrong men to know when to give up. It's just not in the cards for me."

"You haven't met anyone who you'd want to settle down with?"

A pair of emerald green eyes flash in my mind without permission, and I promptly shoo them away.

"Nope. Not a single one."

Lilly opens her mouth—to argue? to console me?—and is interrupted by the MC of the night, a role taken seriously by the fire station captain from where Daniel works. His deep commanding voice makes him perfect for the job, asking for the members of the bridal party to join the newlywed couple on the dance floor.

What fresh hell is this?

My mind races as Lucas leads Amy to the dance floor, followed by Oliver and Lilly. *No, no, no. This can't be happening!* I'd been prepared for the awkward walk down the aisle, the uncomfortable photo shoot, the uneven numbers of this seating arrangement, but this? This is too much.

I'm rooted in my seat, staving off a panic attack, when my blurry vision stumbles on a large figure coming towards me. Daniel, the groom.

"Come dance with us," he says with a dimpled smile and an offer of his hand. "We're all dancing together."

It's only now that I focus on the dancefloor. I can see the six of them in a circle, arms around each other, dancing as one. Not as three separate couples. My breath rushes out of my lungs and those pesky tears tremble on my lashes.

"You know Bella would never do anything to make you feel left out," Daniel says as he tucks my hand into the crook of his arm and walks us to where our friends are waiting. "I know you've been dreading being the 'odd number' today, but it's just that, we could never have had our wedding without you being right by our sides."

My insides flood with warmth; Daniel isn't typically very effusive with his words. Except for when he's with his love, Bella. With her, he's a walking love sonnet.

"Thanks, Daniel." My hand squeezes his arm as I'm filled with affection for the people in front of me. So what if I'm alone, the spinster of the group? Who needs a boyfriend when you have friends just like these?

A boyfriend wouldn't be the worst at a time like this.

This thought is playing on a loop in my mind, as I find myself several hours later, after the festivities are over, hobbling down the gravel path away from the magical fairyland wedding reception venue, towards where a car was supposed to be waiting for me. The rest of the bridal party had all left in groups of two (very Noah's ark of them), only leaving me alone once I'd given them several dozen reassurances that I had a ride home. And I thought I had, except now it's dark and my feet really hurt and the silver Subaru, licence plate TKO065, is nowhere in sight.

"Come on," I mutter at my phone, which is refusing to find 4G (or is it 5G now? Or is that the bad G that is trying to take over the human race?). "How am I supposed to order an Uber without the internet?"

My phone remains stoic in its non-answer and I huff out a breath. Which I can now see in front of me. Thank you, frosty spring nights in Melbourne. The day had been so blindingly sunny, that I hadn't given one single thought to bringing a jacket. Or a shawl or anything to cover my naked shoulders, left bare thanks to the flattering deep sweetheart neckline of this strapless lemon-coloured bridesmaid's dress.

"It's going to be OK." I say this into the darkness because the only person I'm reassuring with these words is me. And I'm not doing a great job at it, if I do say so myself.

With a sigh that I feel from the depths of my soul, I force my tired, aching feet to walk back up the hill to the reception venue, where, hopefully, there is a phone I can use. *Surely these places still have landlines?*

"Are you able to order me a taxi?" I ask the first person I stumble upon, who is busily clearing the tables we'd just vacated.

A blank stare greets this request.

"Do you have a phone?"

Nothing.

"Do you speak English?"

A slight shake of the head. *Great.* My night keeps getting better and better. I reach into my impractically small clutch purse and pull out my phone. Holding it up and pointing to it, I ask again in a loud voice, "Do you have a phone I can use?"

Now, I know speaking louder will not get her to understand me, but my tired, slightly intoxicated brain is working off fumes at the moment, so I'm hoping this will excuse my culturally insensitive behaviour. Just this once.

"Here." My new non-English-speaking friend hands over her phone and with a grateful smile, I take it from her, happy to see her service provider has granted her network privileges, and use it to call for a taxi. A taxi that will take thirty-five minutes to get to me. *Wonderful.*

"Thank you," I say, this time keeping my voice at a normal decibel, as I give her back her phone, hoping that she can understand the gratitude on my face and in my tone, if not my words themselves.

"Welcome." She gives me a timid smile and gets back to work, leaving me alone. Again. *Geez, talk about a theme for the entire day.*

The blister on my right toe takes this opportunity to burst, and this is my cue to take the sparkly, so pretty, silver torture devices off my throbbing feet and brave the walk back down the gravel path to the roadside, to wait for my taxi. Leaving a small trail of blood in my wake, I limp away from the warmth of the building into the night.

"Ouch," I hiss, walking on my tippy toes and debating with each step into the stones coating the pathway whether I should put my shoes back on. This is just a perfect end to what has been a really trying day.

Reaching the end of the driveway, I sink down into the grass, wincing at the grass stains I'm inevitably inflicting on this beautiful dress and blink furiously. I've made it through the day without giving in to the tears that have had my throat tightening every fifteen minutes. I'm not letting one little (enormous) blister and a missed Uber ride break me now.

A partner to share some of these burdens wouldn't be the worst thing.

I'm too emotionally spent to squash this annoying voice in my head that always seems to pop up when I'm feeling at my lowest. I hate this voice. It makes me feel weak and useless, like I can't be a fully-fledged, fully-functioning person without a boyfriend. But then, at times like these, when all my friends disappear into the night as couples, entwined and happy, I can't stifle the idea that things would be easier, *better even*, with someone by my side.

"You are a strong, independent woman, who doesn't need anyone to get you through this life. You have the tools to be successful and whole, all on your own."

I repeat this mantra out loud because there's literally not a single person nearby to hear me, until the taxi driver approaches, offering me a way to bring this day to an end. A ride home to bed. To sleep and then start tomorrow without this sense of loneliness dripping over me.

"Miss? You need a taxi?"

I slowly bring myself up to a standing position and gingerly walk to the car.

"Yes, that's me."

"You ready to go?"

Am I ever! "Yes, I'm so ready to go."

I sink gratefully back into the soft leather car seat, letting the rambling, running sentences of this particularly chatty taxi driver wash over me, only inserting the occasional "aha" and "yep" when it seemed appropriate.

"This is you, Miss."

I open my eyes, wondering if I'd actually fallen asleep and see my apartment building through the fogged-up car window.

"Thank you." I pay the exorbitant fare—*geez, my savings are taking a hit with this one taxi ride*—and, looping my fingers through the straps of my shoes, I walk the final few steps through the front door of my building.

"Stupid staircase!" I curse this older, elevator-free building, as I do daily, and gripping the handrail tightly, I pull my heavy legs up the one, two, three flights of stairs, summoning the last of my energy to trudge down the final hallway to my apartment. 3F.

"What in the mother of all that is holy is this?"

I say this out loud, out very loud, as I stare at the note taped haphazardly to my front door.

"Oh no, not today, Satan!"

With a burst of energy that would have seemed impossible to find a mere thirty seconds ago, I wrench the note off my door, crumple it in my hand, throw it down on the floor and using my foot—the bleeding one—I stomp on it.

"How dare he!?"

My angry words bounce off the walls in the silent corridor and when no answers are forthcoming, I use my phone to order an Uber (thank you, 4G) and run—no *sprint*—back down the three flights of stairs, to wait for it. It may be one o'clock in the morning, and this may be an overreaction, but this is not happening. Not today.

The car I ordered has barely screeched to a halt when I vault inside, telling the driver to step on it. He shoots me a startled glance in his rear-view mirror before doing as I ask and taking off at high speed. The force of this pins me back against the back of my seat and it's only after I've found my balance again that I'm able to look at the crumpled piece of paper in my hand. It's from my ex-boyfriend Robby. The ex-boyfriend who dumped me unceremoniously six months ago and then disappeared without a trace. And the note has the nerve to say:

"I miss you and I want you back."

I. Don't. Think. So!

Oh Robby, you're in for a world of pain. And I'm so in the right mood to inflict it on you.

CHAPTER 2

Amelia

"ROBBY!" I SCREAM, BANGING MY fist on the hard wooden door loud enough to wake the dead. But not Robby, apparently. After my Uber driver—turned would-be therapist who listened to me rant for the entirety of our fifteen-minute journey together—dropped me at the front door of the note-writing-douche-bag, I've been standing here for what feels like hours (probably less than two minutes) waiting for my ex-boyfriend, Robby the Ridiculous, to open the door. With absolutely zero luck. It's like he's not even home.

"I know you're in there!" I continue to scream at the un-answering timber door in front of me. "I'm not leaving, so you'll just have to open up and face me."

My heart races and a trail of sweat trickles down my back even though the middle-of-the-night air around me is verging on icy cold. I'm in such a state that my anger is keeping me warm, even as my toes are getting frostbite. *I really should have stopped to put on sneakers before charging out into the dead of night,* I think as I ponder my sore, sorry bare feet.

"Robby!" I give the door one more, most likely futile, thump, before stepping back to assess the situation. My loser-ex-boyfriend had left an impassioned note on my door after six months of silence and then doesn't even have t courtesy to be home when I want—no *need*—to respond!

"Amelia?"

The deep baritone of a man's—*his*—voice startles me and I stumble backwards, away from the house I'd just been desperate to get into.

"Is that you?"

I scan the man standing in front of me, taking in his dishevelled appearance (pyjama pants only, and a large expanse of bare, bronzed chest), messy jet-black hair, square jawline covered in what looks like designer stubble but is unlikely to be anything but natural, and tired emerald green eyes. *Oh boy, those eyes.*

"Where is he?" I go on the offence, demanding answers while willing myself to not take off running. "I know he's in there!"

The half-naked man in front of me gives me what can only be described as a look of pure bewilderment, before reaching up and putting on his glasses. *God save me from this man in glasses.*

"Robby? You're here for Robby?"

I push past him, my shoulder bumping his biceps as I flounce into the house, determined to complete my mission. My mission to find Robby and then kick him in the butt for being a gigantic jerk.

"Who else would I be here for?"

I turn to see him staring at me, pale like he'd seen a ghost.

"But, he's not here."

The air deflates from my lungs and I only just hold myself back from slumping to the ground. *He's not here.*

I rally. "Don't you cover for him, Jake Johnson. I know he lives here."

My breathing speeds up and the anger that only a moment ago had been downgraded to simmering is now back to boiling again. If I don't get to unleash it on somebody soon, I'm going to explode.

"He does live here," Jake, Robby's older brother and roommate, tells me, his voice slow and deliberate. Like he's explaining the laws of physics to a six-year-old. "But he isn't here *now*."

For reasons I will examine later, I decide not to believe him. "Robby?" I take off down the hallway away from the open plan living room and kitchen area, towards where I know his bedroom is. "Get your sorry butt out here!"

"Seriously, Amelia." Jake's voice is right behind me, following so close I can feel the heat from his body on my back. And for some strange reason, I want to stop and sink into it. "He just left. He's taken his new girlfriend and gone on tour with the band."

I screech to a halt for a variety of reasons. The words *girlfriend* and *band* being the most obvious.

"What?" I spin on the heels of my feet and come face to face with Jake's chest. Or face to chest, as the case may be.

"Are you OK?" The concern in his voice has me looking up and then up some more into his worried expression.

"Robby—what?" I can't find the words to continue and instead allow myself to be led by Jake's gentle hand on my upper arm, guiding me back to their beige overstuffed couch.

"Was he supposed to be here?"

I sink down into the couch cushions, the narrow skirt of this bridesmaid's dress (*how am I still wearing this thing?*) crinkling as I do.

"Hmmmph." I've run out of words. This day, all the good and the bad of it, has officially left me speechless. How is Robby not here when I desperately need him to be so I can tell him to get lost?

"Want to tell me what happened?" Jake is crouched in front of me, so his eyes, worried behind the lenses of his trendy black glasses frames, are level with mine.

"He's really not here?" My voice sounds as defeated as I feel and I startle when Jake takes my hands in his much larger hands, squeezing them like hs offering comfort. And also trying to get me to concentrate.

"No, he's really not."

We sit in silence. Me trying to gather my thoughts. Jake trying to read them.

"So, again, what's this all about?"

He asks this at the same time as letting go of my hand (*shame*), rising and walking to the kitchen where I watch through a haze of tiredness, as he puts the kettle on.

"Melbourne breakfast tea? One sugar and a splash of milk?" *How does he remember the way I take my tea?*

"Sounds perfect," I sigh. "Absolutely perfect."

Melbourne Breakfast tea is the cousin, the superior cousin in my opinion, to the more popular English Breakfast tea. The two are very similar, except as with all things made in Melbourne, our version is better.

"Here." I open my eyes, which I don't remember closing, to a steaming cup of tea in front of me. And Jake, with a long-sleeve navy blue Henley shirt on. *Did I fall asleep?* "Drink this."

My hands are shaking slightly as I take the cup from Jake and absorb the heat radiating from the ceramic cup. Now that the initial surge of energy that had driven me here, urging me on, has diminished, I just feel cold. And oh-so-tired.

"Amelia?"

I blow on the steaming teacup in my hands and avoid his gaze. My thoughts are muddled enough without having to look at that face.

"What happened?"

Well, I think, *it started when I met your brother and was stupid enough to actually date him for six months. And then he ghosted me, only to leave this stupid note on my door out of nowhere.*

The note!

I pull the crumpled piece of paper from my tiny golden purse and throw it at Jake, wishing I was throwing it at Robby's head instead.

"What's this?"

"The reason I'm here." My voice sounds as exhausted as I feel and I lean back against the couch cushion, taking a much-needed sip from my cup.

"I miss you and I want you back," he reads out loud, his voice confused with a tinge of something else. Anger? Disgust? "This is from Robby?"

Huh. I'd never stopped to question if it could be from anyone else. There's been no one in my life for so long; that it had to be from Robby was clear as day in my mind.

"Look at the handwriting," I say, my eyelids drooping shut. "That childlike scrawl is unmistakable."

We sit in silence as I absorb the darkness of my closed eyelids and Jake presumably absorbs the idiocy of his younger brother.

"But...why would he leave this? He has a new girlfriend."

I shrug. "Who knows why Robby does anything?"

"I'm sorry, Amelia. He shouldn't have done this." The sincerity in his voice has me prying open my eyelids to look at him. And then wishing I hadn't.

"Don't you feel sorry for me, Jake. I didn't come here to take him back."

Jake's cheeks flush, and he gets up to pace the room. Back and forth, I watch him prowl, like an animal in a cage. It's quite a sight to behold. The buttoned-up and normally restrained Jake, all angry and growly.

"Of course you wouldn't take him back."

Good, we agree.

"But the whole thing makes no sense. You haven't seen each other in six months."

So Jake has been paying attention.

"I know this. Don't ask me. Ask the man you share DNA with."

"Humph."

More silence. This time I'm more alert, fascinated by this display in front of me. During my time with Robby, I'd only seen Jake on a handful of occasions and our interactions had never been more than polite small talk, so seeing him all huffy and annoyed is quite delightful indeed.

"When did he leave the note?"

I shrug again. "I haven't been home since Friday. Bella got married today." I sweep my hand along the side of my body, hoping this will explain my appearance i this oh-so-fancy lemon-yellow dress. "So I've been staying with her the last two nights."

He gives me a soft look, his eyes unfocussed as he takes in my dress and what remains of my elegant up-do, before shaking himself slightly. "That means my idiot brother put this note on your door and then promptly took off with his girlfriend."

I snort at the absolute absurdity of it all. And then I chuckle, and when I can't hold that in, I just let it all out. I laugh until tears run down my face and a stitch form in my side. *Who does that? And why do I attract only the type of men who would do something like that?*

"Millie?"

My laughter stops abruptly at the use of this nickname.

"Yes?" My voice quivers and I hate myself for it.

"Are you really OK?"

Jake sits back down. This time he's right next to me, so close that I'm absorbing the heat from his thigh pressed against mine.

"Nope."

I let my one-word answer sit between us as I examine the painting on the wall. It's a Melbourne city landscape, and it looks familiar.

"How can I help?"

I turn my head, alarmed to find his face close to mine. So close I can see the flecks of gold around the irises of his startling green eyes, and the smattering of grey hair at his temple. Jake is seven years older than me and Robby and is very much a grown-up in every sense of the word. Grey hairs and all.

"I don't need help." The lie falls easily from my lips, having repeated it so often over the years that it comes naturally to me. Maybe one day when I say it, I'll actually mean it. "Tell me a bit about this tour Robby is going on," I say when it looks like Jake is gearing up to call me on my bullshit.

He grimaces and lets out a dismissive-sounding snort. "I use the word tour loosely. He got a call from that band he sometimes gigs with, 'Raging Inferno'. Apparently, they have a few venues booked for over the summer and they asked him to come along."

I recall Robby had sometimes played with these guys when we were together, and that they weren't very good at all.

"People are going to *pay* to see them?" Scepticism drips from my voice.

Jake laughs, his deep chuckle warming my belly. "No, don't be ridiculous. You've heard them. They're awful!"

A memory of exactly how awful surfaces and I wince. Like a fool in love, I'd attended several of their 'jamming' sessions and, after the first time, had smartly taken to wearing earplugs.

"So, they're just playing for free?"

Jake runs his hand over his stubbled jaw, a rueful gesture. "I tried to talk him out of it, but you know Robby. He thinks it will be his big break."

"But…what?" *The whole thing makes no sense. Maybe my tired brain is just not processing it all properly?* "You're telling me the band is going to play gigs for free and Robby thinks this will lead to something…more?"

Jake's lips tip up at one side, giving me that lopsided grin that I'd tried to avoid looking at when I was dating his brother. "And get this…" He pauses to build the anticipation.

"What?!" I demand.

"Robby is the back-up drummer! He's only going to play if something happens to the actual drummer."

A gleeful laugh bursts out of me and I'm filled with the kind of joy that comes only when bad things happen to bad people.

"He's not even the real drummer?" I gasp out between chuckles. "And he's gone with them, anyway?"

He sighs and runs his hand through that thick mop of black hair. "You know Robby…always chasing a dream."

My laughter abruptly stops. Again. This impulsive behaviour, the 'always chasing the impossible dream' mentality is what had drawn me to Robby in the first place. To all my boyfriends, now that I think about it. They all seem to have a boyish enthusiasm for life, but it's really just masking an inability to actually grow up and get a proper job. It's a pattern that I've identified and am determined to break. If I ever decide to give dating another go. Which, let's face it, seems pretty doubtful.

"How are the two of you even related? You're so different." When I'd first met Robby, I'd thought that maybe this was an insult to Jake, that he was merely stuffy and boring, but once again, my terrible judgement had led me down the wrong path. Straight to the guy who'd ultimately be careless with my heart.

"I'm the older brother," he shrugs. "My parents expected more from me. And they spoilt Robby. We all did."

That had been very clear since the early days of our relationship. Robby was always a child in the body of a man. And treated as such by his family, who adored him.

"Well, good luck to him." I run my hands over my satin-covered thighs, summoning the energy to get up off this marshmallow-soft couch and find my way home.

"What are you going to do about this?" He holds up the crumpled note, his eyebrows drawn down into a frown.

"Nothing. Robby's had six months to contact me. That note is just part of some twisted game to him."

He squashes the paper in his hand, flattening it like a pancake. "You just came here to tell him to get lost?"
There's a hint of something in this question that I can't quite place. It sounds like hope, but that makes no sense. *Why would he want me to reject his brother?*

"I actually came to kick his butt." This earns me another lopsided smile and I look away. "But essentially, yes, I came to reject him. And I'm bummed to have missed the chance."

"I'm more than happy to pass on the message," he says, his voice serious and gravelly. Like he'd relish the chance to tell his brother that I was rejecting him. "He shouldn't have done this to you. Any of it."

I agree and am grateful he's taking my side on this. Come to think of it, although our paths barely crossed during the months I was with Robby, he always managed to have my back. "I just feel sorry for his new girlfriend."

Jake rolls his eyes. "Don't. She knows exactly who he is, and she's with him, anyway."

My hackles rise, and I huff out a breath. "Do you think I should have seen Robby and known he'd hurt me? That I deserved what I got?"

The blood drains from his face. "Amelia, of course I don't." He sounds so sincere, so tortured I believe him. "I could have killed Robby for the way he treated you."

These words echo between us, and the air fills with tension. *Time to go, Amelia. You do not want to get caught up in any of the warm and fuzzy feelings this man evokes in you.*

"Good. I'm glad we're on the same page. Your brother is the jerk in this story." My words are snarky, but my tone is not. Jake doesn't deserve my anger. He's not the bad guy here. He never could be. He's just not built that way.

"He is."

Again, the complete sincerity in his voice has me longing to lay my head on his broad shoulder and have him tell me that everything is going to be OK. And this has me jumping to my feet.

Time to go, Amelia.

"I'd better go." I smooth down the front of my dress and try to hike up the top at the same time. It's been almost sixteen hours since I put it on this morning (or was that yesterday now?), and I'm dying to take it off.

"You have no shoes."

We both look down at my bloodied toes.

"Excellent powers of observation."

"You came here with no shoes on?"

I point to where I'd dropped my stunning, but torturous strappy heels by the door. "They hurt."

He takes off his glasses and rubs his eyes and I feel bad. The poor guy has to work tomorrow, and I've kept him up with my childish ranting and raving.

"I'm sorry to have woken you." I say these words now, feeling terrible for not saying them sooner. "You've got work tomorrow, right?"

His lips twist into a smile. "It's Monday tomorrow, Millie. Everyone has work."

"Not me!" I point out. The hair salon where I work is closed on Sundays and Mondays and I can't wait to spend the entirety of my day off tomorrow in bed, binge-watching *Gilmore Girls* to soothe my battered soul.

"That's right, Mondays are a day off for you," he says like a person who knows my schedule.

Strange.

"Yes," I mutter, flustered, but unsure exactly why. "But I'd better let you get some sleep. You probably have a big court case or something tomorrow? A closing argument to the jury, perhaps?" When I'd learnt that Jake was a lawyer, I'd imagined his daily life to be like that of Matthew McConaughey in *A Time to Kill* or Gregory Peck in *To Kill a Mockingbird*, filled with courtroom drama.

"I'm not a trial lawyer, Millie," he reminds me, effectively crushing my fantasy. "I spend my days filing motions and negotiating across a boardroom table."

Ooof. Maybe I was right? That sounds boring.

My thoughts must have flashed across my face because he gives me an amused look and ruffles my hair, like I'm a six-year-old child.

"Too boring for you?" he teases. "Not as glamorous as, say, a drummer in a band?"

I laugh. "An under-study for a drummer in a band! You can't get more glamorous than that."

"You know how to pick the good ones." This douses my merriment and has the pesky tears threatening to re-emerge. It's *definitely* time to leave.

"I've got to go." I half stumble away from him, seeing a flash of regret on his face before I turn away.

"I'm sorry," he says, his voice urgent. "I didn't mean to upset you."

"You're fine," I lie. "I just need to get home."

"Let me drive you," he offers, trying and failing to catch my gaze. "It's too late to be calling an Uber."

I limp to where my shoes are waiting for me. "It's how I got here."

"Well, I'm here now." His words hit a spot in me, stopping my forward march to the front door. "Let me drive you home. It's the least I can do...you know, to apologise for my brother."

I look at him. He seems upset and genuinely remorseful—for what? The actions of his brother? Or his own words, which were like a knife to the gut?

I decide to accept his offer. It's just one ride home after all, and then we won't have a reason to see each other again.

Huh, a strangely sad thought.

"OK."

"OK?" he repeats, like I've given him a gift instead of just accepting a ride home. "Wait here."

I watch his long legs take him towards his bedroom and chastise myself silently. *Get a grip, Amelia.* This is Robby's much older, more mature, out-of-your-league BROTHER. You can't be having any feelings for him.

"Here."

A soft-looking grey sweater is waved in front of my face and I take it before it drops on the floor.

"Put that on. It's freezing outside."

He doesn't need to ask me twice. In addition to my frost-bitten toes, my arms are also covered in goosebumps and the cold is making my bones ache. I long for a hot bath and my softest, most comfortable pyjamas.

"Thanks." I pull the sweatshirt over my head, laughing when it reaches the tops of my knees. At five-foot-four inches, I'm not miniature like my tiny friends Bella and Lilly; I never need to have the hem of my pants taken up. But wearing the clothes of the six-foot, three-inch giant next to me makes me feel like a kid wearing her mum's clothes as dress-up.

"Better?" The throaty quality in Jake's voice forces me to look up and then I immediately look down again. The heat in the way he's watching me wearing his clothes must be something I'm conjuring up in my sleep-deprived, alcohol-ridden, desperately lonely state of mind.

"Much."

We stand in silence; me looking at my feet, Jake looking at the top of my head, if the burning sensation in my skull is anything to go by.

"Then let's get you home."

I follow him to the front door, picking up my shoes as I go.

"You're not putting them on?" He's frowning at my shoes and then my bare feet, where they're peeking out from under the hem of my dress.

"You could offer me a million dollars to put them on, and I'd still say no."

He frowns some more. "You can't walk outside without shoes."

I stomp my foot. "I can and I will."

We stare at each other. Another stand-off. Which is broken when Jake bends down and swings me up into his arms.

"Problem solved." He cradles me against him and, without even a hitch in his breath to show that he's carrying a whole other human being in his arms, he walks us out the front door.

What is happening? And why is there not one single thing in me that wants to make it stop?

"Um, Jake?" I tug on his sleeve to bring his attention down to me, regretting it immediately when I see his green eyes closer than they've ever been. "Whatcha doing?" My voice is breathless and I'm not the one exerting any energy. This is not good.

He stops and smiles down at me. "I'm taking you home, Millie. So just hang on and enjoy the ride."

I do as he asks, guilt-ridden by the knowledge that I'm enjoying the ride just a little too much.

He's your ex-boyfriend's brother, I repeat in my mind in time with each footstep Jake takes. He's off-limits.

He's your ex-boyfriend's brother.

CHAPTER 3

Jake

S*HE'S YOUR BROTHER'S EX-GIRLFRIEND*, I repeat silently as I try to ignore how amazing Amelia feels in my arms.

Your brother's ex-girlfriend!

"You saw her first," a pesky little voice argues back, and I shut it down. Thoughts like these do nothing to help the reality of the situation: that she's not mine and she never will be.

"You can put me down now." Amelia's husky voice pulls me out of my head and I see that I'm in front of my car and have seemingly just been standing still. Holding her.

"Sorry." I let go of her legs and keep my arms around her shoulders to hold her steady.

"Thanks for the ride," she says, her voice soft, her gaze on the ground between us.

What made me think picking her up and carrying her like a caveman was a good idea?

"Let's get you home." I hear the defeat in my voice and I try to rally. Amelia showing up on my doorstep in the dead of night has shaken me to my core, but she doesn't need to know that. She needs to remain oblivious, as always.

I walk away from her, stopping myself from helping her into the passenger seat and buckling her in like I so desperately want to. Instead, I make my way to safety, all the way over to the other side of the car.

"Ready?" I ask after we're both settled into our seats.

"Yup." She gives me an uncertain look, like she's trying to figure me out.

Good luck. I can't figure myself out when she's around.

"Are you still at the same address? In Richmond?"

She throws me a shocked glance. "How do you know where I live?"

Act cool. "Robby must have told me. I have a pretty good memory." I tap my head for good measure and start the engine. *Time to wrap up this brief reunion.*

"Oh, that makes sense. You're also pretty observant."

"You need to be, in my job," I tell her, lying because I'm actually not usually an observant type. She's just easy to pay attention to. Like right now, in the dim light of the passing streetlights, I can see how tired she is, how drawn her features are, how upset Robby's note has left her. And how beautiful she looks. How beautiful she always looks.

"For all your non-courtroom negotiations?"

She's teasing me, but I could see the disappointment on her face when she'd learnt just how boring my job actually is. Most people think lawyers lead a fa-paced, main-character-in-a John-Grisham-story kind of existence, when in reality, I spend my days reading and writing dreary documents. Compared to the men she dates, I'm old, dull and lifeless.

"And don't forget the writing of contracts. That can get pretty tense."

She laughs and my stomach clenches. Amelia's laugh has a smoky quality to it, a sexy sound that I've been trying to forget for almost twelve months now.

"It can't be more exciting tha cutting and colouring hair for a living. That's really living on the edge."

Having seen some of the hairstyles and colours that Amelia has created, I want to argue, but that would once again reveal just how much I know about her. Not a rabbit hole I want to go down.

"Tell me about Bella's wedding." I'd heard a bit about her best friend over the handful of times we'd talked, and I know Amelia loves her like a sister.

"It was a beautiful day."
Her words are sincere, but her tone is sad. *What happened here?*

"Did it all go smoothly?" I frame the question like a lawyer, not asking her directly what I want to know, which is why the wedding of her best friend has made her look so defeated.

"It did. It was perfect."

We're stopped at a traffic light, and my gaze is drawn back to her. She's wearing my sweatshirt and I will my thoughts away from the body that was shown in such a perfect way by the daisy-yellow dress underneath. There had been too many curves on display for my peace of mind.

"The light's green."
I press my foot on the pedal and we lurch forward. Apparently, in Amelia's presence, I don't know how to drive. *Wonderful.*

"So, the day was perfect..." I prod.

"It was..." she trails off, her voice wistful. "Bella looked beautiful. Her vision of a yellow-themed fairyland came to life perfectly. It's just that..."

She stops again, and I bite my tongue, hard, to stop from asking more questions. If she wants to share, she will. It's not my place to probe any deeper.

"It's just…now that Bella's married, things will be different."

"Different how?" I slow my speed down, just a touch so Amelia won't notice, trying to prolong our time together.

I'm pathetic.

"I don't know." She sounds frustrated. *With herself? With me for asking too many questions?* "We used to do everything together, and now she's someone's wife. And I'm alone…"

Ahhh. So that's it? She's lonely?

"Bella sounds like a wonderful friend. I'm sure things won't change between you."

I feel her gaze on the side of my head, and I keep mine facing forward. Now is not the time to get lost in her big brown eyes.

"You think?" Her voice is both hopeful and doubtful.

"People get married all the time and don't lose their friends. You'll be fine."

When she doesn't reply, I hazard a quick look in her direction, seeing she's nodding while staring out her window.

"Seriously," I continue, wanting to make sure she's feeling better before I drop her at her front door. And say goodbye. "My best friend got married a few months back and now I can't get rid of him. He's at my place all the time…I think he's trying to get away from his wife, nagging him to pick up his socks."

This pulls a laugh from her and I feel ten feet tall. Cheering her up, making her smile. It's a minor victory for me, but one I'm happy to claim.

"Steven? Your best friend got married?"

I start. *She remembers my best friend? Maybe I wasn't the only one paying attention.*

"Yeah, he and Jasmine got married in June. A winter wedding. They wanted a winter wonderland theme, and they got it. The day was freezing cold, so cold that the bride could have been her own 'something blue'."

She laughs again—*victory!*—and asks me to tell her more. I oblige, telling stories of lost rings and drunken speeches gone wrong.

"But through it all, Steven and Jasmine were oblivious. They were just thrilled to be husband and wife."

"That's how it should be." Her voice is wistful again. "The wedding is just one day. It's the relationship that comes after it that counts the most. My parents didn't have the best relationship..."

She trails off again and I leave her words to sit between us. Silently willing her to open up to me.

"My dad left when I was sixteen." Her words drop like a heavy stone. "For most of my life, he travelled for work and was away more than he was at home. My mum raised me pretty much on her own anyway."

I say nothing, my stomach clenching at the bitterness in her tone.

"I could never understand why my dad loved his job more than me, why he chose his career over his family." She stumbles on the word career and a few things fall into place. Namely, her attraction to men like Robby, who wouldn't know a career if it bit him in the face.

"So, what happen?" I prompt into the silence.

"Well, one day, he didn't come back from his trip. And pretty soon after that, he started another family with another woman, had a couple more kids and I became an afterthought."

My heart hurts at the pain I hear in her voice and I'm inextricably angry at this man—her father—for ever making her feel this way.

"Anyway, that's it. My sad story. It's not even that unique really, just another tale of a man who can't keep himself from straying ..."

I want to argue, to tell her there are men out there who would cherish her and protect her heart. Men—a man like *me*, who'd do anything for a chance with a woman like her. But I don't. Because I'm not the man she wanted, the one she chose to be with all those months ago.

"I'm sorry that happened to you. And your mum."

From the corner of my eye, I see her wipe away tears, and it takes every ounce of willpower not to pull over and take her into my arms. To offer her comfort. But I'm merely a stranger to her. That's not what she'd want from me. *Right?*

"It was a long time ago," she shrugs, pulling herself upright and back together. "I'm over it. I should be over it..."

We are silent for the remaining three-minute drive home. A mere handful of seconds that fly by all too quickly.

"I'm sorry for waking you up," she says again as I park the car in front of her apartment building. "And for yelling at you. And dragging you out in the dead of night."

I shake my head at her. She has nothing to apologise for.

"It's me who's sorry. For having such a knuckle-head for a brother."

Her smile in response is sweet, her plump lower lip tipping up and making that single dimple in her left cheek appear and then just as swiftly disappear. *How had I forgotten that dimple?*

"It's not your fault."

"Maybe not, but when he gets back from his 'tour'"—we both laugh at the over-exaggerated inverted comas I gesture as I say the word—"when he's back, I'll be having a word with him about how to treat people with respect."

"I wish you'd had that conversation with him a year ago. Save us all this trouble."

I nod my agreement while quietly disagreeing. Even with all the angst their relationship had caused, it still meant that I got to know her. And I can't ever regret that.

"Well, you've moved past him. Onto someone better, I hope?" I hold my breath as I wait for her answer. The sense I've had from her over the past hour has been one of loneliness, but maybe that's just wishful thinking on my behalf.

She laughs, a small, bitter sound. "There's no one. After Robby, I swore to take a break from men. And the break seems to have become a full-on break-up. Me and relationships do not go together. Just ask my dad."

I wince, taking in her expression, filled with determination, and don't argue. If she wants to stay away from men, that suits me fine. I know this makes me a selfish jerk, but I can live with that.

"Well, goodnight, Jake." She opens her door and I can't think of a way to stop her from leaving. "Thanks for the ride."

"It was nice seeing you again, Amelia."

She pauses with one leg out of the door, turning back to me, her small front teeth biting her lower lip and I hold my breath in anticipation of what she might say.

"Good to see you, too."

My lungs deflate and I sit silently as she steps out of the car, taking her coconut-filled fragrance with her. I watch her walk slowly—*damn those bare feet*—to her lobby and up a flight of stairs. I continue to sit and watch the space long after she's out of my sight, wondering what to do with all the emotions seeing Amelia tonight have woken inside of me. And how I'm going to find the strength to push them all down again. One more time.

The drive home flies by in a blur of deafening silence and self-recriminations. It's been months since I'd thought of that woman, the one whom my brother was lucky enough to call his own, and I'd been doing so well to put her behind me when they'd broken up. And then one stupid note and a knock on the door had her barrelling back into my life. In bright colours, just like she had that first night. When she'd just been a stranger in a bar.

"Don't go there," I mutter out loud to stem the flood of memories threatening to surface. "Just get home, go to sleep and lose yourself at work. It's how you got through it last time. Just do it again."

I agree with myself as I park in my driveway, a feeling of utter exhaustion washing over me. My tired legs drag as I open the front door and trudge to my bedroom, taking my glasses off and rubbing the grit from my eyes. Once my legs hit the edge of my pillow-top mattress, I allow gravity to do its thing, falling backwards and landing with a little bounce, willing myself to sleep.

But sleep won't come. I toss and turn, trying to shut out the memories of the woman who had unknowingly just upended my carefully curated life.

"Screw it."

I give up on attempting to sleep and pick up my phone. Feeling guilty, I open my Google Play store and re-install the Instagram app. It has been a few months since I deleted it, thinking it best to get rid of the temptation, and now here I am. Giving in. They really should make it more difficult to access this site, for people like me who know that no good can come from it.

I type in my username and password, and a few notifications go off as I open my profile page. Which is empty. I don't use my account to show the world how amazing my life is. I use it for even more depressing reasons.

My stomach churns as I search her name. Not difficult, given she is one of three people I follow on here, and I can't help the smile that grows on my face as I take in her latest posts. For someone who seemingly had mixed emotions about her friend's wedding, Amelia sure has a lot of happy photos to document the day.

There on her grid are at least a dozen photos of Bella and her new husband, both looking radiant and glowing with happiness. There are also several shots of the bridesmaids and their respective husbands, and then there's one I was hoping to see. One photo of Amelia. By herself. She's smiling at someone just off to the side of the camera and she's so achingly beautiful, my heart hurts just looking at her.

She's wearing the yellow dress, the one she'd still been in when she'd flopped on my couch only an hour ago. The pale yellow colour brings out the warmth in her brown eyes and somehow makes the smattering of freckles across her nose pop. I silently thank whoever did her make-up for not covering those adorable spots, even though I know Amelia hates them. Her hair, which had been a bright, fire-engine red when I last saw her, is now a golden, honey colour, worn in some sort of elaborate bun, sitting low in the nape of her neck, a few tendrils out around the front, framing her face. I don't know how anyone at that wedding had looked at the bride with Amelia standing next to her; in that yellow dress, she looks like a goddess.

"This isn't helping." I close the app and put my phone face down on my bed. No good can come from having Amelia back in my life (or on my screen, as the case may be), and I need to remember that. I harrumph out loud and pick the phone back up again, deleting the Instagram app and the temptation to spend the few night hours I have left scrolling through her feed. Once done, I close my eyes and let the events of the night play on repeat through my mind. After not seeing Amelia for over half a year, I'd thought maybe I had put her in my rearview mirror.

Turns out, just like the warning on the stickers they put on car windows, objects are closer than they appear. And Amelia is back to being front and centre in my mind. Just like she's always been.

CHAPTER 4

Amelia

*B*ELLA'S BACK!

The thought flashes through my mind before I'm even properly awake. It's been ten days since the wedding, which means it's been ten days without my bestie around to debrief with. To vent with. Instead, I've been alone with my thoughts. Not a pleasant place to be, as it turns out.

AMELIA: Welcome home, B! Are you working today??

I send this message, ignoring the fact that the sun has barely risen and the newlyweds are probably still asleep. If it makes me seem desperate to see my friend, then the truth is out there. I am desperate to see Bella. Her absence has made me acutely aware of how few people I have in my life who I can turn to in times of distress.

BELLA: Yes! Come by for a coffee, I can't wait to see you!

Bella's almost immediate response warms my insides and I lie back down in bed, instantly feeling soothed. I'm scheduled to work the afternoon shift at the hair salon today, so I have all morning to spend hanging out with my bestie while she works.

AMELIA: I'll be there as soon as you open. Tell Lilly to have the brownies ready for me!

Lilly and Bella work together in Lilly's café, *Love, Lilly*, which they recently expanded to include a small art gallery to display the works of local artists, Bella included. They're both so driven that this joint venture is already a resounding success. I couldn't be prouder of them if I tried.

With my plans for the morning locked in place, I slowly make my way to the kitchen and put the kettle on. Taking down my box of Melbourne Breakfast tea, my mind flashes back to that night with Jake, as it has done hourly in the days since then. The whole encounter was a tangled mess, starting with that note.

That damn note, which I'd burned in a ritual cleansing ceremony a few days ago, very *Practical Magic* of me. I'd thought if I could rid myself of the bad juju associated with the note, that maybe I'd be able to move on, put it all behind me, but alas, it didn't work. Probably because I'm not really haunted by the note itself. Instead, it's the images of Jake without his shirt on, Jake with his glasses on (or off, either works for me), Jake carrying me to his car, which are keeping me awake at night. It's maddening that, after six months of not seeing him, not thinking of him (much), he's crept back into my thoughts. Like that song in your head that you just can't shake. *What's that called again?*

The kettle whistles and I pour boiling water into my cup with one hand while Googling with the other.

An 'earworm', that's it.

"The sticky music syndrome whereby music memories repeat uncontrollably in your head." I read this out loud while taking my first sip of tea. Otherwise known as the best sip.

"That's what that night with Jake has turned into, a memory that repeats uncontrollably," I say to my cactus plant, Callie, who sits in a prime position on the kitchen windowsill. After several attempts at cultivating a small garden on my balcony, each with disastrous results (read: many, many dead plants), Bella gave me what she termed the "unkillable plant" and we've been happily co-habituating ever since. As it turns out, Callie the Catus is an excellent listener. Not judgemental at all.

"Maybe I should Google how to get rid of an earworm?"

Callie doesn't respond (*fair*), and I force myself to put the phone down and walk away. This sort of behaviour is bordering on crazy-town. All I need to do is see Bella, hash it all out and put it behind me. It was just one night, not even a night, really. Ninety minutes of madness, tops. *Why is it bothering me so much?*

Ignoring that I know the answer to this internal question, I head to my small but practical bathroom, to get ready for the day. Once I see Bella, I know things will feel better. She'll talk me down off this ledge that I've made my way onto in her absence and everything will go back to the way it was. Me hating each and every man, the way it always should be.

"Millie!"

Before I'm even through the front door of Love, Lilly café, the little bell above the door still ringing as it closes behind me, I'm enveloped in the arms of my best friend. I breathe her in and wrap my arms around, instantly better.

"Never leave me again."

Bella laughs, like I'm joking, and squeezes me tight. "I missed you too."

I shoot her a disbelieving look, because she just spent ten days on a tropical island with her hot firefighter husband. There's not a chance that she even thought of me.

"I did," she protests at the look on my face.

I pretend to believe her because it feeds my neglected ego.

"Come sit. Lilly has the brownies waiting for you. Though I'm going to say it one more time, brownies should not be a breakfast food."

I start to argue this incorrect statement, but Lilly does it for me. "Brownies are an every-food. Suitable for any and all occasions."

I grin at her, loving that it's 8 a.m., and she's already a chaotic mess. This is Lilly to a tee. She's beautiful with her wild dark curly hair and big blue eyes, but she's always on the wrong side of dishevelled. Take right now: she has flour in her hair and on her apron. And *on her shoes?* And she has a chocolate moustache, making me think she's been out the back sampling the goods. And the best bit? She doesn't have a single care about any of it. Lilly is just comfortable in her skin; it makes me wonder how she got that way.

"Amelia! Sit, eat!" Lilly pushes me into one chair at what she deems her best table. It's by the front window, perfect for people watching but still close enough to the counter for chatting while they both work.

I happily take my seat at the VIP table, slicing into my still-warm-from-theoven-brownie with the fork she's shoved into my hand.

"So good!" I exclaim as the chocolate flavour explodes in my mouth. I don't know what she puts in these brownies, but I do know they are the best I've ever tasted.

"Bella, you sit with Amelia and catch up. We're not too busy now, so take advantage."

We watch as Lilly skips away, humming under her breath as she goes, the very picture of contentment.

"She's the best boss," Bella says, sipping on her cup of coffee. "I'm so lucky."

"You are," I agree.

"So, tell me, what have I missed since I've been gone?"

This is it, the moment I've been waiting for. The chance to unload all my woes on her, and yet now that it's here, I don't know where to start.

"Ummm," I start and then stop. *What's wrong with me?*

"What's wrong?" Bella sits up straighter in her chair. "What happened?"

Wishing I hadn't been so hasty in burning that note—it would have come in handy as the perfect prop in this moment—I open my mouth to fill her in when the bell on the front door trills. Distracting me.

"What...?" Only one word comes out as I continue to be a stuttering mess, but this time with good cause. Because the ringer of the bell, the man who had just walked in the door, is none other than the man who's been walking through all my thoughts.

My earworm has entered the building. Jake.

Bella follows my gaze and looks back at me with a confused frown. "You know Jake?"

WHAT?

"*You* know Jake?" I screech back at her, so loud that the man in question turns to look at both of us, his small smile growing as recognition flashes in his eyes.

"He's coming over," I hiss at Bella, who continues to look annoyingly baffled by my behaviour. "He's coming over!"

"Hi Bella," he greets my best friend in that deep voice of his. The one that causes the back of my neck to sweat. "Amelia."

"You two know each other?" Bella looks between the two of us, eyebrows raised so high they may just fly off her face.

"Yes," I mumble, looking down at the table between us to avoid looking into Jake's green eyes. Which somehow looks lighter today, more jade green than emerald. "He's Robby's brother."

Bella's expression turns from bemusement to disgust in a millisecond. Out of all my rubbish boyfriends, Robby's the one she hated the most.

"Oh." Her flat response has a strange anxiety dancing in my belly. I don't want her to feel this way towards Jake, and I also don't want to examine exactly why I feel this way.

"By that 'oh', I understand you've met my brother," Jake interjects before I can come to his rescue. Which is good, because there's no legitimate reason he'd need rescuing in the first place. As far as I know, he's just a customer here. Bella doesn't need to like him.

Except that she does.

"Jake's nothing like Robby," I blurt out before my mouth catches up to my brain.

His face lights up at this, like I'd handed him a gift. "Thank you, Mille."

Bella gives me a disbelieving look, like I'd betrayed her, and then glares at Jake, not convinced that he's completely innocent in all of this.

"Seriously, Bella. It's not his fault that his brother's a douche."

"True story," Jake agrees, putting both of his hands up. An act of surrender.

"Your brother is *non buono*," she tells him, slipping into her native Italian as she does when she's distracted or sad...or fuming mad.

"Absolutely, *non buono*," he says, biting his lip to stop the start of a smile. "I agree."

She continues to look at him, a long, hostile look that reminds me of her hot-blooded Italian nature and after a full sixty seconds of glaring, (I counted) she relaxes. A bit.

"Good, then you can continue to come here and eat."

The matter seemingly settled, Jake gives her a funny little bow and walks to the counter to order his coffee and breakfast, from the sounds of it.

"Does he come here often?" I ask, keeping my voice low, acutely aware that, at this time of day, before the morning rush of people, our conversation can be heard by anyone interested in listening.

Bella leans in, like we're two spies devising a plan. "He's been coming here almost every day for..." She leans back to think. "About six months."

Huh? That's right around the time that I broke up with Robby. Weird.

"It's strange that you haven't bumped into each other, given how often you're both here."

That is *strange.* I watch Jake from under my lashes, my spot at the VIP table giving me the perfect viewpoint from which to ogle him. I mean, objectively run my eyes dismissively over him.

"You never told me how hot Robby's brother is." I shush Bella and her not-so-soft voice, my attention glued to Jake's back.

"He's my ex-boyfriend's *brother*," I say, explaining the obvious, while letting my gaze drift over the way his suit jacket hugs his broad shoulders just so. *I wonder where he finds the time to build up those muscles.* From memory, the Jake I'd known worked ridiculously long hours.

"So?" My friend's indignant tone pulls my attention back to her. "That doesn't mean you have to be blind. My husband is a gorgeous specimen of a man and I can still appreciate all that Clark Kent goodness going on over there."

I groan, my cheeks heating, well aware that Jake can most likely hear every word that is coming from my not-so-subtle best friend.

"I'm not talking about this with you right now." I tilt my head in Jake's direction, hoping she will take the hint and shut the heck up. All this talk of Jake as the hot Superman counterpart will not help me get rid of this pesky earworm, now, will it?

"Fine." She heaves a sigh. *Dramatic, much.* "Then what are we allowed to talk about?"

From the corner of my eyes (*OK, from the front and back of my eyes, that's how close my attention is on this man*), I follow Jake's progress at the counter. He takes his freshly heated croissant and take-away coffee and walks it to the table…right next to ours.

"Nothing," I mumble, well aware that I can't update her on all things related to the note and what happened thereafter. "I'll tell you later."

Not picking up on any of the cues I'm putting down, she persists. "You wanted to tell me something. Sounds like it was important. On the night of the wedding, you sent me a garbled text message about a note. What was that all about?"

"I sent you a message?" Confused, I pull up my text messages and scroll back ten days, and there it is, in all its nonsensical glory: AMELIA: A note! After all this time I get a note?!?

"I tried calling you back, but it went straight to voicemail. And then I had to leave for the airport the next day," Bella explains while I put my head on the table and bang it, just a little, to knock some sense into it. "What's going on?"

I take in her worried expression and, keeping my voice as low as possible, barely above a whisper, I outline what had happened the night of her wedding.

Bella, on the other hand, was not keeping her voice below a whisper. "He did WHAT?" In fact, her heated cry had every person in the café looking at us. Including Lilly from behind the counter. And Jake, whose face is the picture of contrition. Like this is somehow all his fault.

"Shhhhh," I hiss, gesturing in Jake's direction. "It's all good now. I burnt the note, did a cleansing ritual. It's all behind me."

"Amelia," she said, keeping her voice at a suitable decibel. Just. "What he did was so wrong."

"I agree," Jake's voice chimes in, making it abundantly clear that he's been listening to this entire conversation. "I'm going to kick his arse when he gets back."

"Can I join you?" Bella asks, her cheeks red with rage.

"Absolutely!"

Before the two of them can bond any further over their tactics to beat up my ex-boyfriend, I put a stop to it.

"No violence is necessary here." I give them both a hard look. "Let's just move on."

Bella huffs and looks like she wants to argue.

"Please, Bella. I just want to put the whole sorry thing behind me."

She breathes out and relaxes her posture, no longer ready to charge into battle. "Yes, let's put him right behind us. In fact, let's not think of him ever again."

I nod, sparing a quick glance in Jake's direction, my gaze darting back to my friend when I see he's still watching me.

"And you know the best way to get over someone..."

"I'm over him!" I interrupt, not liking where this is heading.

"Is to get under someone else," she continues like I hadn't spoken.

"No."

"Yes."

"No." I shake my head and stomp my foot under the table.

"Yes." She bangs her fist and spears me with a no-nonsense look. "It's time."

"I don't want to. You know how I feel about relationships." I look nervously in Jake's direction, really wishing he wasn't here listening to every miserable word I'm saying. "I'm terrible at the whole thing."

Bella is quiet for a moment, like she's mulling over my words before a smile grows on her face. A smile, which, quite frankly, is terrifying.

"Then let us help you."

"No."

She pats my hand like I'm being an unruly child and soldiers on, not listening to a word I'm saying. That word being 'no'. Said repeatedly.

"You've just gone for the wrong guys."

"You can say that again."

My head swivels to look at Jake. *Did he just say what I think he said?*

"Excuse me," I ahem at him. "We're having a private conversation."

He flashes a grin that he thinks is disarming, but is actually...OK, it's very disarming. "Sorry, but it's true. You dated my brother. Who's an understudy for a drummer in a not-very-good band. I mean, that's not a great endorsement of the men you choose to date."

The tips of my ears heat and I'm glad I wore my hair down over my shoulders to hide the evidence of my shame. It's true, I somehow end up picking the guy most girls would run from. *I wonder what my therapist would say about this? If I actually went to therapy, that is.*

"And before Robby was that guy, Jeremy. What did he do for a living?"

I roll my lips between my teeth and refuse to answer. This is getting humiliating.

"He was a mime!" Lilly yells through her laughter from her spot behind the counter.

Bella does her Marcel Marceau impression and I let out a chuckle. *Oh boy, Jeremy.* Not only was he a professional mie artist, if that even is a profession, but he wasn't even a good one. *What a dud.*

"And who came before him?"

I let the silence drag out, refusing to partake in this trip down my nightmare dating memory lane.

"Alan! That's it. He was a…." She trails off, her brow scrunched up in concentration.

"A dog-walker." I give in and tell her, knowing that she won't let it go. "There's nothing wrong with being a dog walker."

"There is when he combined it with being thirty years old and still living in his parent's basement."

She's right. He had been a bit of a no-hoper, but he'd seemed so nice and caring. At the start. Before he inevitably turned into a jerk. *Why do I attract these types of guys?*

"You've picked some real stinkers," Lilly says, sitting down and joining in, adding an extra sprinkle of humiliation to the conversation.

"What you need is someone with an actual job," Bella announces, again loud enough for the whole café, block surrounding suburb to hear.

"What does a job have to do with being a suitable partner?" I argue, because I feel like I should. Choosing a man based on his career feels all kinds of superficial and elitist and just plain wrong.

"Nothing," she admits with a conciliatory smile. "But it's more like breaking a habit. If you were to date an accountant, or a barrister or a carpenter…maybe things would work out different?"

A laugh escapes me. "You're just listing the ABCs of careers. There's no validity in anything you're saying."

Lilly hums under her breath while she demolishes the cupcake in front of her, and Bella, well, she's being too quiet for my liking. I can almost see the wheels turning as she watches me closely.

"Maybe that's it."

Uh-oh. Bella's got an idea. A trickle of doom makes its way down my spine.

"We can make a game out of it."

A game? Oh, I like games!

"What sort of game?" I'm intrigued, but still sceptical.

"You can make your way through the ABCs of professions. As a fun way to look for Mr Right."

I'm shocked into silence. Gobsmacked. Bella's gone mad.

"Ridiculous idea," I sputter out.

"I don't think so," Lilly chimes in while licking buttercream frosting off her fingers. "You've had little luck dating the traditional way. And what do they say is the definition of insanity? Doing the same thing, the same way repeatedly and…" she trails off, searching for the rest of her point.

"And expecting a different result." This is from Jake, who has now turned his body completely in our direction.

"You shush." I point my finger at him and give him my fiercest glare. He does not need to be a part of this. "And you two, this is a terrible idea. Why can't I just go back to dating like a normal person? You know, with all the fun dating apps out there?"

Lilly gives an adamant shake of her head. "Bad idea. Been there, done that, would not recommend."

I smile slightly despite myself. Before Lilly had married Oliver, she'd dipped her toe into internet dating, only to find herself on a terrible blind date with a man who'd ended the evening by stealing her purse. She's been very anti-online dating ever since.

"It was one bad egg, Lilly," I tell her as we all share a laugh. "Not everyone you meet online is a kleptomaniac."

"You met Robby online." Again, this was the not-so-helpful voice of Jake chiming in, reminding me of this very unfortunate fact.

"Hush, you." I glare at him again and motion with my hand for him to turn all the way back around and out of our private conversation.

"Just think about it," Bella says, putting her hands into a prayer position and giving me her best puppy dog eyes. "You don't even need to take it that seriously. We can just find some nice, fully employed men to set you up with and see what happens. If you don't like the As, then we move on to the Bs."

When she puts it that way, it doesn't sound terrible. *But even so, why are we even talking about this? I don't want a relationship. Do I?*

"We can keep it light-hearted," Lilly add, sensing my resolve weakening. "You go out on one date, then we all catch up to get a report. It can be a fun thing for the entire group!"

Great. Humiliation with an audience.

"I don't know…" I waver.

"Come on, what do you have to lose?"

Without thought, I look in Jake's direction, startled at his expression as he stares back at me. I don't know what it means, but it makes my stomach flip. And starts my butterflies dancing. And my heart racing. All those good things you feel when you meet someone who you think could be the 'one'.

I flick my gaze away from him and bite the bullet.

"OK, fine. I'm in."

The girls cheer and I watch, a lump forming in my throat, as Jake looks down at the table in front of him, his shoulders slumped ever so slightly.

What have I signed myself up for?

And how do I make it stop?

CHAPTER 5

Amelia

"I'M SO ON BOARD WITH your dating plan!"

I sigh loudly and take a big gulp from my wine glass. It's been three days since the decision was made to help fix my love life—with a *game* no less—and I'd been hoping that maybe, if I wish hard enough on every star and all my fallen eyelashes, perhaps it would all go away.

No such luck.

"Amy," I begin, hoping to appeal to the one rational person in our group of book clubbers (that's what she calls us! So maybe not as rational as I need her to be?). "I still think this is a terrible idea."

She ignores me—*fun!*—and turns to the group, comprising Lilly, Bella and our other two book-loving (and wine-loving) friends, Madi and Sammi. We meet every few weeks at Amy's place under the guise of discussing whichever book Amy has chosen for us, when in reality it's just a great excuse to get together and catch up. Or bully a friend into doing something she really doesn't want to do, as the case may be tonight.

"I've put together a folder of potential suitors, all cross-referenced with their careers. See, I've even added different coloured tabs to help us keep track." Amy's cheeks are glowing with excitement. Whether it's about the dating plan or the elaborate use of her stationary, it's hard to tell.

"Amazing work, Amy." Bella takes the folder from her sister-in-law and starts flipping through it. "We can make a group decision on which lucky guy will get to date Amelia first."

"Explain the plan to me again," Sammi asks, biting into a Love, Lilly cookie, her face promptly contorting in ecstasy. "Lilly, these are SO good."

"I know," Lilly says, taking a cookie for herself and nibbling on the edge. "So, the basic premise is based on the notion that Amelia has been dating all the wrong men. Agreed?"

They all nod in unison, making me feel fan-freaking-tastic.

"When we dived into the past few disasters, we found a pattern. Not only are all her past boyfriends dead-set losers, but they also don't have proper jobs."

"None of them?" Madi, our resident career-woman, asks, her eyes wide in dismay.

"Not a single one of them," Bella confirms. "And we're not saying a man needs a job to be a good partner..."

Amy and Lilly both nod their heads in solidarity. We wouldn't want to appear snobbish in any way.

"But that's what they all have in common. So, Amelia decided she needs to break the pattern."

"Amelia decided no such thing," I interject. And am promptly ignored.

"To help with this, we've devised a fun way to get her out into the dating world." Bella picks up the folder, raining glitter down on the carpeted floor in the process (*Glitter? Really?*). "And that's where this comes in!"

The five of them gather around Amy's bedazzled handiwork, a hush coming over the group.

"*The ABCs of Dating Amelia*," Sammi reads out loud, a smile in her voice. "I love, love, *love* it!"

I snatch the book from my best friend and in horror see that the folder is, in fact, labelled *The ABCs of Dating Amelia*. In purple-coloured glitter pen.

"Is this really necessary?"

My friends all gape at me like I'm being a party-pooper. Which, to be fair, I totally am.

"It's a way of keeping track," Amy announces, taking the folder back from me and cradling it protectively against her chest. Like she's worried I'm going to do something to her precious creation. "And it's fun!"

"Here. Have another drink," Lilly says, filling up my now-empty wine glass and then pushing me into the nearest seat. "This is going to happen, so you may as well get on board."

I take a sip, a small one this time to remain sober and somewhat in control, and motion for them to continue. The sooner we get on with this, the sooner we can move away from focusing on my love life.

"Right," Bella calls the 'meeting' to order. "Let's begin."

The girls snicker at the absurdity of this moment, only stopping when they see Bella glaring at them.

"I get that this is a bit of fun," she lectures them, squinting, making her look alarmingly like a school teacher. A mean one who gives out detentions freely. "But we are also trying to ensure that our friend Amelia doesn't die alone."

OUCH.

"Geeze, Bella. Dramatic, much?" Sammi comes to my rescue, sending me a sympathetic smile. She and Madi are also single and perhaps sense that this sort of treatment heading their way. Possibly sometime very soon.

"Sorry, Millie," Bella reaches over and squeezes my hand. An apology. "But I just want you to be happy."

My smile is weak. "I am happy."

I'm fooling no one.

"OK, happ*ier*?" This is from Amy, who despite her passion for her newly decorated 'love manual', can understand that being with a partner doesn't equal being happy. Before she and her yummy husband Lucas got married, they went through a lot of turmoil, leaving Amy as the most realistic in this group in matters of the heart. She knows that a happily ever after isn't always guaranteed.

"Sure," I agree to keep the peace. "Happier."

"Right." Bella claps twice to get our attention. "Let's start at the beginning." She opens the folder and flips to the first tab. Careers that start with the letter A.

"This is so ridiculous," I mutter under my breath.

"But it could be fun," Sammi whispers back as the others debate over the names on the list.

"I vote for accountant," Lilly says, raising her voice for no reason. It's not like anyone is challenging her. "Oliver has a guy at work who would be perfect."

They all look at me expectantly. *An accountant? Boring!*

"Numbers? Really?"

"Yes, we're deviating from your normal type, remember?" This is Bella, who is shooting daggers at me from across the room for turning down the first suggestion. *Uh oh, I definitely don't want her angry at me.*

"Um, OK. Tell me more."

Lilly's pretty face lights up and she picks up her phone.

"His name is Tom, and he's twenty-eight years old," she reads off her screen. "He runs the accounts department where Oliver works. He's never been married. Apparently, he likes to cook and is training to run the Melbourne marathon next month."

"He sounds great!" Amy enthuses while the rest of the ladies all nod along happily.

"How do you know all of this?" I ask, dread taking up residence in my stomach.

She shows me her phone, where Oliver had typed a message for her with all the relevant details. It's like his friend is applying for a job; all his credentials are laid out for me to decide upon. "Did you tell Oliver about this ABC plan?" I ask, placing my wineglass on the table in front of me and then picking up a couch cushion to scream into. *This is mortifying.*

"I just asked him if he knows anyone who would be worthy of you," Lilly soothes while Bella takes the cushion off my face, preventing my self-suffocating attempt. "And he came up with loads of guys who he thinks would die for a shot to date you."

This makes me feel a little better.

"OK, so the accountant. What do we all think?" Bella puts it to the group for a vote, cutting me out of the decision-making process.

"Who's behind door number two?" Sammi asks, now firmly on board with the plan.

Bella reads the profiles of a few more candidates. *Who knew so many men in our orbit have a job beginning with the letter A?*

"So that's a no for Ted in advertising?"

The group all nod.

"And we're vetoing the architect?"

"He's too old," Amy shouts, the wine making her more boisterous than usual.

"And the 'automotive engineer' is getting bumped because of a technicality?"

"He's a mechanic trying to jazz up his job description," Madi points out, being all logical and acting like the rules in this plan are more than what we just made up on the spot. "We can revisit him when we get to the letter M."

My whole body shudders at the thought as I sing the ABC song in my head, counting on my fingers as I go. If I have to revisit Lachlan the mechanic, that means I'll have gone through thirteen other letters before him. Thirteen dud dates to get me to the letter M.

No. Thank. You.

"Let's park that one for now," Lilly says, reading the panic on my face and attempting to course-correct. "I think we have a winner in our midst."

My five friends look at each other with matching grins.

"Congratulations, Amelia. You've got yourself a date with an accountant."

Brilliant.

When I get home later that night, I'm consumed with a sense of relief. I had only just survived Book Club. After my friends had decided that my perfect match may just be Tom the accountant, Lilly had promptly texted Oliver to let him know to set something up and now I have a date with a stranger next Saturday night.

"How did I let this happen?" I ask Callie, the cactus.

When she gives me nothing in response, I do what I always do in times of stress. A beauty treatment. In my bathroom, I take my time deciding on what will best soothe my frayed nerves, settling on a hair mask that promises to add both shine and volume to my hair, in only one hour.

With Taylor Swift blasting in the background—I'm in my *Reputation* era—I carefully apply the lotion to my hair, starting at the roots and working my way down. Once I've applied a thick layer, I place the pink cap that came in t box on top of my head and sit down to let it work its magic. Given I'm someone who changes their hair colour on a dime, it's important to make sure I give my hair some love.

"Now what?"

It's only 9 p.m. and I don't have work in the morning. This treatment needs to stay on for another fifty-five minutes, so...I should probably call my mum.

Calling my mum is a weekly chore I'm eternally finding reasons to put off doing. Each week I find creative ways not to call her until I've run out of hours. If I don't call her tonight, she'll make her displeasure known. In her own creative, passive-aggressive ways.

"Mum first, then *Gilmore Girls* as my reward."

I press on her contact on my phone, holding my breath while it rings. Once, twice, three times. *Maybe she won't—*

"Amelia."

Groan. Internally, so as not to set her off.

"Hi Mum."

"I was wondering when you were going to find the time to call me."

And we're off. The guilt trips. The backhanded insults. The making me not want to call again.

"It's been a busy week," I get in as she draws breath. "With work and...stuff." I don't tell her about Bella's wedding; she won't want to hear it. Like I'd told Jake, my mum was once burnt, forever shy. She doesn't want anything to do with relationships.

"You're not seeing someone, are you?" She sounds suspicious and annoyed. So, normal, then.

"Not right now." It's the truth. I'm seeing Tom…later.

"Well, just remember what I've always told you. Find a man who is…"

"Not married to his job," I finish her sentence, having heard it a million times before. She's nothing if not consistent with her bitterness.

"And don't expect whoever it is, not to cheat."
My stomach drops at this. *How is she so OK telling her* daughter *this? To expect a man to treat her badly just because that is all either of us has ever known? Shouldn't she want more for me? Shouldn't I want more for* myself?

The dating plan is becoming more and more attractive the longer I stay on this phone call. *Maybe I do need a way to break the toxic cycle I've been in…forever.*

"Well, anyway, Mum. It's been nice talking to you," I lie. "But I think I'm heading off to bed." More lies. I have a date with Rory and Loreli that I'm dying to get to. A mother/daughter dynamic so different from my own, it's like an aspirational dream.

"Come and visit me soon," she demands. "You know the holiday season is hard for me."

Another silent groan. Every year when December rolls around, Mum gets more depressed. Then her sadness turns to anger and we both get bogged down by it. Fun times ahead.

"I will," I promise, knowing she only has me to rely on. A heavy burden. "I'll see you soon."

"Love you," she says as an afterthought. I grab onto it, holding it close so that I won't dread the next time I have to call her.

"I love you too, Mum."

We hang up and I sigh. A painful sigh that tries to purge all the negative feelings that rush to the surface when I'm speaking with her. My duty done, now I get to indulge.

Gilmore Girls it is.

Patting my haircap—still another forty-five minutes left on my treatment—I grab a box of Tiny Teddies from the pantry and make my way to the living room. Once there, I flop down onto the couch and settle into a comfortable position, stretching out length-wise with my feet elevated over the arm of the couch and carefully drape myself with two plush blankets, using the couch cushions to create a cushion fort around me.

"There," I say into the silence as I turn on Netflix and skip to the season where I'd left off. *Oh goody, season five. The one where Luke and Lorelai* finally *get together.*

"Oh Luke, you're such a big softie," I tell the TV through a mouthful of chocolate chip teddies. "How Lorelai waited so long to let you in is beyond me."

With my heart in my eyes, I watch my two favourite characters on their first date.

"Do you remember the first time we met?" Luke asks a luminous-looking Lorelai and then goes on to describe in great detail what he remembers from their first encounter. He loved her from the start.

"Have I ever had that feeling?" I wonder into the empty living room. "Meeting someone and everything being just, right?"

My mind, against both my will and my better judgment, takes me away from Stars Hollow and transports me back to the only time I've ever felt anything close to that feeling. Of being in the right place, at the right time…with the right person.

It was just over twelve months ago, and the night had started like any other night. Having just watched my best friend Bella fall deeply in love with her roommate Daniel, I'd decided it was time to dip my toe back into the dating pool again. Still a little bitter after the last heartbreak, I'd carefully scoured the online dating apps, looking for one that would bring the right sort of people—men—into my life. Given the many times I'd been swayed by a pretty face in the past, I'd settled on a dating app modelled after one of my favourite reality TV shows, Love is Blind, where candidates aren't allowed to upload pictures and instead the technology in the app chooses potential perfect matches based on shared values and personality traits.

"Are you sure you want to do this?" Bella had asked me over the phone, the night of my first blind/blind date. "This feels super risky."

I'd just pulled up in front of the restaurant where I was meeting my potential soulmate. It was too late to back out. Besides, the guy I'd chosen to go out with seemed super cool. And he was a musician. I had a good feeling about the whole thing.

"I need to give this a try," I'd told her, chewing on my bottom lip, my nerves threatening to overwhelm me.

"OK but send me an SOS message if you need saving. I'm on standby."

This had made me feel better, so after I hung up with Bella, with many assurances that I'd be safe, I made my way inside. And stopped dead in my tracks. *How am I supposed to find this guy when the entire experience was blind?*

"Can I help you?" I looked up to see the hostess staring at me expectantly.

"Um, I'm meeting someone?"

She gave me a knowing smile. "You're using the LIB app?"

"Yes!" I was so relieved that I wouldn't need to explain just how blind my blind date was.

"I suggest you wait at the bar and see if the two of you can find each other." She winked at me, and I smiled gratefully in return. At least I wasn't the only one dabbling in this crazy experiment.

On shaky legs, I made my way to the bar and hoisted myself up onto the bar stool. With nothing else to do but look around and wait, I ordered a glass of white wine, my gaze constantly roaming the surrounding area.

"Hi."

Ohmigod. That voice. That has to be him.

I turned slowly on my stool and came eye to eye with the most perfect-looking specimen of a man. Tall, a head taller than me, sitting on this stool, with thick wavy black hair that my hands itched to run their fingers through. He had an olive complexion and a long straight nose that looked to have never taken a punch. But it was his eyes, behind the most perfect pair of black glasses frames, that immediately captured my attention. Green, a deep shade like a polished emerald, with the smallest fleck of gold in the centre. They were the sort of eyes I could get lost in for the rest of my life.

"Hi," he said again, a smile causing a dimple to pop in his cheek and the skin around his eyes to crinkle.

"Hi." My one word came out sounding breathless, and I felt my cheeks heat.

"Is this seat taken?" He gestured to the empty seat next to me and instead of grimacing at this cheesy pickup line, I nodded. Eagerly.

"Yes."

He frowned at me. *Disappointed?*

"I mean no!" I yelled, like the lunatic I was. "I mean, please sit down."

His eyes crinkled at me again, like he found me cute, and I watched with a lump in my throat as he sat down. Next to me. *This has to be my blind date. Right?*

"What are you drinking?"

My brain blanked at this, the simplest of questions. *What was I drinking?*

"Umm." I stopped. *C'mon, Amelia! What's in your glass?*

"She's drinking white wine," the helpful bartender said, coming to my rescue.

"I'll have the same," he said with that heart-stopping smile. I looked at the bartender, whose nametag labelled her *Sally*, wondering if he's having the same effect on her.

Sally winked at him and wandered off to get his drink, while I continued to sit, frozen, staring at him. Even blinking seemed impossible.

"Hi," he said again, like we hadn't already covered this particular greeting. The side of his neck heated, and I wondered if he was feeling as nervous as I was. Probably not, given he could still form words.

"Hey," I breathed out the word. *Yes! I'd finally found a word.*

The wonderfully handsome stranger said nothing in return; instead, he just stared at me. I ran my hand over my hair, wishing it was a more normal shade than the fire-engine red I'd dabbled in last week, and searched for something to say. *If he's my match from the LIB app*, I figured, *surely, we'll have heaps to talk about.*

"Do you come here often?" The minute the words were out of his mouth, he grimaced. "Ignore that," he muttered. "Terrible question."

I watched with my heart in my mouth, my eyes and my stomach as he rubbed his large hand over his stubbled jaw. He seemed so awkward it made me like him even more. It's like he'd never met a girl at a bar before.

"I've never been here," I told him, putting us both out of our collective misery by finding my ability to converse again. "But I've heard great things."

He had lit up. "Me too! I've been wanting to come here for ages but never had the time."

This comment was weird, given his profile had him as a musician, but maybe he was a really successful one, who was too busy making music to check out the latest, trendiest restaurants in Melbourne?

"I'm Jake," he said, causing me to frown.
Jake? That wasn't right.

"Jake?"
We both turned in unison to find a younger version of the man who'd just captured all of my attention. *Wait, what?*

"Robby?"
Robby! That's it. That was the name of my match. Uh oh, this can't be happening.

I watched, my heart sinking from its residence in my eyes, my mouth and my stomach right down to the soles of my feet. The handsome stranger wasn't my match for the blindest of blind dates but instead seemed to know him. Somehow?

"What are you doing here?" This was from Jake, whose previously delicious bronze complexion had taken on a greenish tinge.

"I'm here on a date," Robby said in a voice that wasn't as deep or as smooth as Jake's. "A blind date."

"With Amelia?" I finally chimed in, wanting to put an end to this.

Robby swivels his head in my direction, wearing a cheerful grin. "*You're* Amelia?" His tone signalled that this pleased him and this silent approval made my sinking spirits pick up. Just a bit.

"You two? Are on a date?" Jake frowned at both of us, his eyebrows ruffled, his jaw clenching.

"Do you two know each other?" This is from Robby, and my temples throbbed at the absurdity of it all. The three of us were standing there, looking like the very embodiment of the Spider Man pointing meme. It was so ridiculous that even other people standing nearby were laughing.

"Let's start from the beginning." I hopped down off my stool and Jake followed suit. The two men dwarfed me, even in my highest heels, and I leaned back to look them both in the face. "I'm Amelia." I pointed to myself, clocking the way Jake's eyes narrowed at this. "And I'm supposed to be on a blind date with someone named Robby."

"That's me!" Robby raised his hand for a high-five, his enthusiasm clear.

"Yes," I agreed, watching closely the way Jake's cheek muscle twitched at this piece of news.

"And you two know each other how?" I motioned between the two of them, though the answer was as clear as day. They had to be related, with Robby the younger, paler, less formidable version of Jake.

"He's my older brother," Robby clarified, emphasizing the word *old.*

"Ah."

Jake silently continued to watch this all unfold, his expression growing darker with each second.

"Do you two know each other?" Robby asked, perhaps finally picking up on the palpable vibe within our little threesome.

I stared at Jake, wondering what he was going to say. We'd only exchanged a handful of words, most of them nonsensical, so the chances were he would not say much of anything.

"We just met," he finally conceded, looking pained.

"Yes," I agreed. "Your brother was just keeping me company while I waited for you."

I don't know why I said this, though in reality, it was true, but it caused Jake to stare at me. And his expression was…wounded? *What?*

"Well, I'd best leave you two to your date." His words had a bite to them that should have baffled me but didn't. Because I didn't want him to leave me with his brother. I wanted *him* to be my LIB perfect match.

"Thanks, bro."

I watched as Robby took the seat vacated by Jake and attempted to rally. The people and the algorithm at LIB Proprietary Limited had matched me with Robby, so I needed to see this through with him. *Right?*

"Have a good night," Jake said, looking like he was wishing us anything but. "It was nice to meet you, Amelia."

The way Jake said my name was like a warm blanket being draped over me on a wintry day. It offered me inexplicable levels of comfort, and I wanted to hear it come out of his mouth again and again.

"Bye, Jake," I said in place of what I wanted to say. Which was, *Stay and talk to me. Be my date. The algorithm got this one wrong.*

"How funny, you meeting my brother tonight," Robby said, bringing my attention back to him, back from where I'd been hungrily watching Jake walk away. Walk away with only the one backwards glance. "He barely ever has time to do anything social. A real work-a-holic, that one."

This immediately popped the enamoured bubble that had been forming around Jake since the moment he'd said hi all of ten minutes ago. A man who worked all the time and barely did anything for fun? That sounded an awful lot like another man I'd known, the one man who'd crushed my heart. The one man I should've been able to count on to never hurt me that way.

"Let's not talk about your brother." I turned my full attention back to Robby. My date. "I want to know all about you."

And for the next hour, that's what I did. I learnt Robby was the fun-loving, boyishly charming person I'd been hoping to meet. And that he ticked all the boxes I'd firmly put in place for the sort of partner I desired, someone who'd put me first, above his career, above all else. It was a shame that it had all been an illusion and that he'd go on to hurt me, just like all the men who'd come before him.

I shiver at the intensity of my memories and blink back to the present to see Luke and Lorelai on my TV screen on their way to their own happily ever after (though boy, that was a bumpy ride).

"Nothing good can come from thinking about Jake," I lecture myself, my words loud and firm in my silent apartment. "We had a moment at the start, and then one moment the other night. And that's it. They're just two moments in time. Focus on your upcoming date. With the accountant. Your first date with someone with a proper job. Keep your eye on the prize."

I nod. Once. Twice. Three times for good measure. This is a good thing, a healthy step in the right direction. Of not becoming my mother and of finally finding my Mr Right after dating way, way, way too many Mr Wrongs.

CHAPTER 6

Jake

A BLOODY DATING PLAN.

It's been ten long days since I left Amelia with her friends at that café, making plans to find her a new guy, the *right* guy, and I haven't been able to get any of it out of my mind.

"Jake," my best friend Steven nudges me in the ribs, causing me to spill the beer in my hand. "I've lost you again."

I look around me, taking in the chaos of Friday night after-work drinks at this particularly popular sports bar and wish once again that I'd found an excuse to get out of being here. An excuse that my annoying best friend would accept, that is. I had tried the old "too tired," "have to stay back at work" and "I don't want to," but none of them were valid enough. According to Steven, it's his job to get me out and about in society at least once a month. The good news is that, after tonight, I can look forward to four weeks of peaceful bliss ahead of me.

"I'm right here." I sigh and take a sip of craft beer which will hopefully take the edge off what has been a rough week.

"You're physically standing next to me, but I can see you're all up in here..." He knocks on my forehead with a smirk. "What's up?"

I glance up at the giant TV screen above the bar, hoping that something on there will distract him so I can wallow in my thoughts. Alone.

Cricket. Great. I know it's almost sacrilegious to be an Aussie bloke and not like cricket, but come on! A test match of cricket can last for five whole days, and more often than not, will end in a draw. *What a complete waste of time.*

"I just have a lot on my mind."

A table away from the crowd opens up and Steven and I rush to grab it. Any table here on a Friday night is prime real estate and we know we've lucked out nabbing this one.

"Want to talk about it?"

I really don't.

"There's not much to talk about."

He gives me that look, the one that reminds me we've been friends since we were five, and that he's like a brother to me, and that he knows when I'm not OK.

"It's nothing really," I tell him while trying to attract the attention of the passing server. This conversation needs both alcohol and a big bowl of nachos. "I saw Amelia last week."

Silence follows this statement. Well, as silent as a noisy Melbourne bar can be on the most hectic night of the week.

"Robby's Amelia?"

I wince at his description, hating that those two names will forever be linked. Amelia should never have been Robby's any-thing.

"Amelia, Amelia." Childishly, I refuse to repeat him. Refusing to say their names in the same breath.

"Where? What? How?"

Steven is the only person who knows about the spark of attraction I'd had with Amelia for those brief five minutes when she was just the gorgeous stranger at a bar. I'd accidentally told him all about it after a few too many drinks, a few weeks after she and my brother started dating, and apparently, he's going to hold it against me.

"My idiot brother left her a note, telling her he wants her back." My hand clenches around the beer bottle I'm holding, so tight I'm surprised it doesn't shatter.

He frowns. "Doesn't Robby have a new girlfriend?"

"Yes." My response is clipped as my blood boils with anger. It's not enough that he treated Amelia so poorly when they were a couple, but now he's going out of his way to mess with her after they've broken up.

"I'll never understand how the two of you are related." Steven shakes his head.

I nod in agreement. Robby and I are as different as night and day. Or eternal darkness and eternal light, if you want to be extreme about it. Robby was a surprise addition to our family, born almost seven years after me, well after my parents had given up hope of having another child. And as a result, he's been pampered and spoilt every day since. A fact that turned him into a complete and total narcissistic selfish prick (my official diagnosis).

"He's just so selfish, you know?" I grind out through my teeth. "He's got a girlfriend. What would possess him to contact Amelia after all this time?"

After six months, three days and a handful of hours. To be exact.

"Well, he'd be an idiot to not try to win her back. Amelia is an absolute catch." My very married, happily committed best friend's face flushes as he says this.

And who can blame him? Amelia has that effect on men. On everyone, really. She's the only one who doesn't see she has this power.

"He had his chance. He needs to leave her alone."

Steve watches me closely, for so long I feel like a fly trapped under a microscope.

"What?" I finally break down and ask. "Spit it out."

"You just seem pretty worked up about something that has very little to do with you." He says the words gently, like he's coaxing me towards some sort of realisation.

"It has a lot to do with me when that stupid note causes her to come knocking on my door at two o'clock in the morning. Wearing *that* dress."

He laughs, a big booming sound that has heads turning in our direction.

"Stop. It." I grit this out, annoyed at his amusement. There's not one single thing funny here that I can see.

"Tell me about the dress." His sly smile has the tips of my ears pinking up and I realise too late my slip up.

"It was yellow," I sigh, unable to stop the image of Amelia's curves looking like they'd been poured into that dress from flashing through my mind.

"Sounds delightful," he replies, his eyes twinkling. *I need to get new friends.*

This torturous conversation is interrupted—*thank God*—by a server finally coming to take our order. Just in time for me to have lost my appetite.

"So, she turns up in the yellow dress. Robby isn't home. Then what happens?" Steven is leaning in, his attention locked on me. This may be the most entertainment he's had all week. All month, perhaps? I'm assuming married life contains very little of this sort of excitement.

"Then, nothing," I lie, repressing the memory of Amelia on my couch, Amelia wearing my sweatshirt, Amelia in my arms. "We talked for a bit and then I drove her home. She was spitting mad at Robby, though." This brings a smile to my face. At least I know she hasn't stayed under his spell this whole time.

"And that's it?"

He's disappointed.

"Well..."

He perks up.

"Well?"

"I saw her again. At that café, the one I told you about?"

"The one you saw when you 'accidentally' happened upon her Instagram page?" He makes a big show of putting quotation marks around the word accidentally and I only just refrain from throwing a corn chip from our piping hot bowl that had just been delivered.

"It was an accident," I clarify. "It's not like I went looking for her information. Robby had his phone open, and a notification had me glancing in its direction."

He gives me a look and I refuse to buckle. We both know what I'm saying is a complete lie, but I'm sticking to it. The alternative makes me seem like a pervy stalker, and that's not a role I want to be cast in.

"So, you 'bump' into her at the café you 'accidentally' found out about." Quotation marks galore. "And then what?"

More scenes from that morning flash across my mind. Amelia looking gorgeous in her black leather pants and fire-engine red tank top, her caramel hair piled on top of her head in a careless bun. Amelia and her friends discussing how they plan on finding her a boyfriend, a decent one this time. Amelia *agreeing* to their ridiculous plan.

"She and her friends were talking a lot about Amelia's dating history," I start.

"You were listening to their conversation?" Steven's eyes continue to sparkle in delight, enjoyment written all over his face.

"I was at the table next to them. I couldn't *not* hear what they were saying." I defend myself with vigour, once again to avoid the label of stalker. This time with eavesdropper added to it.

"Did Robby's name come up?"

It's my turn to give him a look. "Of course it did. Right under the category of who *not* to date."

"So? Then what?" I watch as he heaps a corn chip with guacamole, sour cream and salsa, only just fitting the concoction into his mouth.

"Her friends decided she needs to break her pattern of dating 'losers'." My turn to use quotation marks.

Steven gives me a look that says 'duh' while chewing his food, motioning with his hands to continue.

"And they made a plan for her to date men with proper jobs." Even as I say the words, my stomach clenches. It's not that I don't want Amelia to find a good guy…OK, it is exactly that I don't want Amelia to find a good guy. Or any guy. Just until I'm over this little inconvenient crush, that is.

"Well, that's perfect," my friend gushes, spitting the remnants of his corn chip crumbs on the table between us. "You have a proper job."

I blanch at the suggestion that I'd ever be in the mix. That I'd ever have a chance with someone as amazing as Amelia.

"That ship has sailed. I'm not an option for her." I look to the left as I say this. A big fat lie from my end. But obviously not from hers.

He takes a chug of beer, wiping his mouth with the back of his hand before answering.

"Why not?"

I tick the well-rehearsed reasons off my fingers as I list them for him. "She's my brother's ex-girlfriend. She's seven years younger than me. She's gorgeous and feisty and clearly attracted to a different sort of man."

"Pfft," he snorts. "That's a whole heap of nonsense."

"And," I continue, ignoring his interruption, "and she chose Robby."

This hits home with Steven, stopping the next words out of his mouth. It's the ultimate stumbling block. When we'd met that night at the bar, when I'd felt sparks literally flying between us, she wasn't dating Robby. She didn't even know him; their date was the definition of blind. At that moment, if she'd felt even a tenth of the connection with me that I'd been feeling with her, she could have chosen to spend that evening with me. Or, at least, given me the same chance she'd given Robby. But she didn't. In fact, she dated my brother for six months, so clearly that initial attraction between us was all in my head.

"People change," Steven says finally, gearing to rally again. "We don't know why she made that decision that night. But she may have regretted it ever since."

It's a thought that's tickled my mind over the last year whenever I allow myself to think about her. But it's all redundant in the end. She picked Robby and now she'll always be my brother's ex-friend. Forever off-limits.

"Enough talking about this," I plead with him to drop it. "Let's focus on you and Clare and all this baby talk I'm hearing about."

My friend's face pales at this, like literally loses every ounce of colour and I let out a chuckle. *Not so much fun with the shoe on the other foot, is it?*

"She's got the baby fever," he tells me in a hushed voice. It's like if he says it out loud, it makes it real. "Lots of talk about ovulation and fertility windows."

I grimace. Too much information.

"But there's also a lot of fun to be had along the way," I remind him.

He grins at this and then steers the conversation away from baby-making and dating plans, towards something more manly. Like sports. And beer. And I dive in with him, ready to forget all about Amelia and her mission to find 'the one'. Determined to not give any of it another thought.

I'm not giving Amelia another thought.

It's several hours later and I'm sitting on my couch, my head woozy from the beers I'd consumed. Thinking only about Amelia.

"Craft beers. Taste better but have a higher alcohol content." I say this to myself out loud, as a reminder for next time (at least four weeks from now) as I scroll through the Netflix homepage, struggling to find something to watch amongst the millions of shows on offer.

"Ooh, a new season of *Alone*. Sounds fitting for my current life situation."

I stop muttering to myself and press play. It's a new season, set in the wilds of Patagonia and I lean back, sinking into the comfortable depths of my couch, ready to lose myself in the struggles of the men and women attempting to survive for as long as possible to win half a million dollars. This sort of show is right up my alley.

"Shelter," I tell the young woman on my screen who is currently wasting way too much time looking for the best spot to set up her tent. "You're going to need a better shelter than that."

I watch, annoyed as she continues to ignore my advice and my attention wanes. Drifting to where I'd vowed it shouldn't go. *Maybe I could just message her? See how she's doing?*

I have played this battle out in my mind more times than I can count in the weeks and months since she'd become my brother's *ex*-girlfriend, but I'd never given in. Until now.

JAKE: How's the dating plan coming along?

I press send and then lob my phone face down onto the rug in front of me. Like that's going to somehow stop whatever it is I'd just put into motion.

"I blame the beer." I pick up my phone and oh-so-casually look at my notifications. Nothing.

OK, that's that. Back to the wilderness engulfing the contestants competing in *Alone.*

"Don't eat the berries!" It's been twenty-three minutes and fourteen seconds since I'd sent the errant, ill-advised text to Amelia. And in that time, one contestant had tapped out, another had fallen into the icy lake near her tent and now this woman is about to eat a berry. Origin unknown. Oh, and also, there's been no response from Amelia.

"Told you," I tell the screen, where the berry lady is now throwing up violently. "Basic survival 101, never, ever eat something that may kill you."

I'm mulling over this sage advice when my phone lets out a *PING*, scaring me half to death. It's so quiet in my house with only the lonely contestants on my screen to keep me company, that the sound of an incoming message, the hope of which I'd let go of ever hearing, has me jumping. A manly jump, that is, barely a centimetre off the couch.

AMELIA: I've got a date tomorrow.

AMELIA: With an accountant.

This news makes me wish I'd never sent the text message in the first place. And also, how does she know the message is from me? I've never, ever texted her before.

AMELIA: I didn't know you had my number.

Huh. She's clearly grappling with the same realisation as me. We'd both had each other's numbers but had never had a reason to use them before.

JAKE: I'm sure Robby shared it with me at some point...

This is an outright lie. Because I'd specifically asked him for it in the days after they'd broken up. Under the guise of needing it 'just in case'. It had been a weak excuse at the time, one that Robby hadn't cared enough to question.

AMELIA: Same.

(*Interesting. Here Robby was, giving our numbers out willy-nilly, presumably not thinking we'd ever really use them*).

JAKE: So, are you looking forward to your date with the accountant?

(*Do I really want to know the answer to this question? Why am I torturing myself like this?*)

AMELIA: No!

(*Ahh, that's why. For that answer. And yet, she's still going out with him, and it still may turn into something*).

JAKE: Then why not cancel?

I hold my breath as three dots appear and disappear for several minutes. And then there's nothing. I'd overstepped my boundaries and offended her.

(*Well done, Jake*).

JAKE: Sorry, if that last message was too nosey.

(*There, that should fix it*).

More dots, then nothing. Then more dots.

AMELIA: You're fine. I didn't respond because I didn't have an answer. I want to cancel, but I also want to see this through. You know? Break the bad habit and all that?

I can hear the confusion ringing through these three simple sentences and instantly feel like a heel. Just because I don't want her to find someone doesn't mean she doesn't deserve to. Someone as incredible as she is.

JAKE: You should do it. What have you got to lose?

AMELIA: You're right.

AMELIA: What have I got to lose...

I end the conversation there, unable to summon the energy to be her cheerleader in this endeavour. Turning off the TV, leaving my new friends to survive the rest of the night in the wild alone, I make my way to bed.

AMELIA: Goodnight Jake. I'm happy you texted.

I read this message just before I give in to sleep, a smile stretching across my face. She may never be mine, but for tonight she's happy I reached out. And that's going to have to be enough. For now.

CHAPTER 7

Amelia

T HE MINUTES TICK OVER, HURTLING me towards the end of my shift at the salon, inching me closer to my upcoming date. My upcoming date with the accountant. I'm currently keeping my anxiety at bay while sweeping away the remnants of my last haircut of the day, waiting for my mentor and boss to finish with her last client, so she can make my hair look presentable.

"Millie, honey. I'm almost done here. Why don't you finish up and then take a seat?"

I nod my thanks to Andrea, aka the best boss in the world, and busy myself with putting away the broom and cleaning down my workstation. Anything to keep my mind off what's happening tonight.

"OK, spill."

I look up to see a worried frown on Andrea's face. She's been my boss, and more, since I started here at her salon over five years ago as an apprentice. It's because of her I love coming to work every day, that I'm actually good at my job and that I have a shoulder to cry on whenever I need it.

I blow some wayward strands off my face and puff my cheeks out. When I tell her what's on my mind, I'm guaranteed she's going to mock my dramatics. Dating for her, even in her fifties, is fun. She can't understand why it's such a chore for me.

"My friends have set me up on a date tonight." I hold my breath and wait for it.

"Yay!" she claps in delight. "That's exciting."

"That's one way to describe it," I mutter under my breath as she leads me to the sink, wrapping a towel around my shoulders when we get there. "It's a date with an accountant."

I close my eyes and let her magic hands soothe me as she washes my hair, complete with a deep cleaning scalp massage.

"There's nothing wrong with accountants," she chastises me. "My second husband was a whiz with numbers and also a whiz in bed!" Her booming laugh coaxes a smile from me and also from the few lingering clients scattered around the salon. "What's the actual problem here?"

With a towel wrapped around my head, I walk back to my chair and flop into it with a weary-sounding sigh. There isn't any real problem with going out with Tom the accountant, it's just that he may not be the one I want to be going out with.

"I saw Jake last week."

Andrea's brightly painted mouth drops open, and she immediately gets a faraway look expression on her face. She'd only met Jake on one occasion, when he'd visited the salon during the time I was dating Robby, to drop off my phone that I'd left at their place the night before. My boss had taken that opportunity to fall head over heels in love with him.

"Jake is back in our lives?" she asks, her tone reverent. Like she's praying for it to be true.

"I wouldn't go that far," I hedge. "I happened upon him—twice—and then he texted me last night out of the blue."

Her dark brown eyes bore into mine and I wonder if my hair will ever get done at this rate. *Maybe I should have saved this information for after my blow dry?*

"Tell me everything." She sits in the chair next to me, pulling me close to her, so that we are only inches apart. "How did he look? Is he as yummy as ever?"

Was he ever!

Wait—where did that thought come from?

"He looked the same," I tell her, my cheeks flaming from my errant thoughts.

"So, still like Clark Kent?"

My mind flashes to his face, which had been so close to mine as he carried me to his car. His stubbled jaw, his dimpled cheek, his arresting green eyes. *He's even better than Clark Kent.*

"He's the same!"

"Methinks you protest too much," she sing-songs at me, standing up to get to work on my dripping hair. *Finally.*

"Anyway, how did we get here?" I'm confused as to why we're talking about Jake when it's the accountant I should be focussed on.

"Because you started talking about your date and you mind magically ended up on Jake. I always knew there was something between the two of you."

It's true. From the brief five minutes she'd observed of me and Jake together, she'd sworn that he was the man I should be dating. Completely ignoring the fact that his brother was my boyfriend.

"You know, it was never like that. I'd never cheat on a boyfriend. Not even Robby."

She bobs her head at me, knowing that after what my dad put me and my mum through, I'd never, ever do that to another human being. Even someone as douchey as Robby.

"That doesn't mean there wasn't a little spark there. A baby ember perhaps?" she says, her voice loud over the hair dryer as she works on twisting my hair into natural-looking beach waves down my back. "Instead of dating the accountant, you should date him."

My long-ago eaten lunch takes a dive in my stomach at this thought and I promptly banish her words into the deep recesses of my mind. I can't acknowledge the attraction I felt for Jake that first night and then again, a week ago, because that would make me the worst type of person. A person just like my dad.

"Drea." I use my sternest voice. "I can't go after my ex-boyfriend's brother. It's not right."

I watch her shake her head in the mirror. "Honey," she uses her motherly voice, and I want to sink into it.

Andrea has been more of a mother figure to me than my own mum for the past half a decade I've worked for her, and I value her dearly. Except when it comes to men; that's when she's usually steering me in the wrong direction.

"If you were to give in to the feelings I know you have for that young man," Andrea continues, "you'd be doing nothing wrong. You were a loyal girlfriend to that no-hoper Robby. You stood by him and never once looked in another man's direction. Just remember, he dumped you." I wince at this harsh reminder. "And it's been six months, and he has a new girlfriend. What you decide to do next has nothing to do with him. Even if who you decide to do is his brother."

She laughs loudly at her little pun and after a minute, I join her. Even if I have no intention of following her advice and, um—doing—Jake, it's nice to know I have her blessing. Because in my mind, it still feels like a betrayal. It still feels wrong to have any of these thoughts about this particular man.

"Enough about Jake." I jostle in my seat to dislodge all thoughts of him. "What should I wear on my date tonight?"

Andrea purses her lips, deep in thought. "Something that will knock his socks off. Something that shows off all of your skin!"

And just like that, we're focussed on pulling together an outfit is sexy but not overly slutty, an outfit that could be the one to bowl over contestant number one in the dating plan. Causing me to have a small sprinkle of excitement about what's coming.

Bring on the night ahead!

Or maybe not.

It's the night of my big date, the first from my dating plan, and my hand is currently tucked under the fancy linen tablecloth, holding my phone and blindly typing the following message to any and all of my friends:

SOS! HELP!

I've been enduring this date for over an hour now and things are getting desperate. *Where are my friends when I need them?*

"Amelia? Are you listening?"

My head jolts towards Tom—aka, the accountant—and I send him what I hope is a conciliatory smile.

"Sorry, I missed that," I say.

"He was just getting to the best part of his story."

This sharp rebuke is the reason I'm frantically texting my friends under the table. Because the person who's chastising me for not listening to the most boring of all boring stories is…Tom's mother.

That's right. *His mother.*

The date had started off well. I'd met Tom, the accountant, for a drink at a local bar close to where we both live. After getting my hair done in sexy, tousled waves, I'd gone home and settled on an outfit that is classic with a bit of an edge—a little black dress paired with black combat boots—and I'd arrived feeling positive and ready. Tom had shown up looking handsome in a button-down blue shirt to match his eyes and black jeans, and he'd been…pleasant. So pleasant that when the time came to move forward with the date, to eat or not to eat, I'd seen no red flags urging me to walk away and so I'd followed him to the adjacent restaurant, to have dinner. To find his mother waiting for us.

At first, I'd thought she was just there in case our date had bombed; you know, to keep him company. To console him, perhaps. But then she stayed. And monopolised the entire conversation. And Tom just let her.

WHAT. IS. HAPPENING?

"Sorry, Mrs Walker," I mutter, hanging my head. Yes, she demanded I call her Mrs Walker. "Please continue, Tom."

Not needing any further encouragement, the accountant launches back into his story about filed taxes that went awry. I laugh along in all the appropriate places, following his mum's cues, not wanting to risk another lecture.

"Isn't he funny?" Tom's mum asks in an eager tone the second her son's story ends. "He's so smart and funny. Any girl would be lucky to have him."

I nod, too scared to do anything else, while scanning the room to catch the attention of the server. She'd seemed to pick up quite early what a train-wreck this date was and had been filling up my wine glass like clockwork. Last drop, top up.

"Will you excuse me?" I address the mother/son team in front of me. They're even sitting on the same side of the booth; I feel like

I'm on a job interview, for goodness' sake. "I'm just going to use the restroom."

Not waiting for an answer, I take off for the toilets, like the demons of hell are chasing me, only slowing down once the door of the bathroom has slammed shut behind me.

"Lilly, you are in so much trouble." I dial her number, tapping my foot impatiently as I wait for her to pick up.

"Amelia?"

"I'm going to kill you!"

Only silence greets me and I check my phone to see if she's hung up on me.

"Are you there?"

"We're all here!" The voices of Lilly, Bella and Amy sound through the phone, bringing me instant comfort. "We're having a wine night and waiting for you to call with an update. How's it going?"

How's it going? Shouldn't they have gleaed this from my SOS text messages?

"It's awful," I whisper, my attention focused on the door in case Mrs Walker follows me in here. "Why haven't you rescued me?"

"Did she text you for help?" Lilly's voice is fint, like she's holding the phone away from her mouth and I hear a muttering of voices in response.

"Ladies!" I snap at them to get their attention back to me. "I texted you all, *SOS!*"

"Nope, I didn't get it. I only got some random letters that I thought was a butt dial." This is from Amy.

"Me too."

"Me too."

I groan and pull up my text message thread. True enough, my blind texting spree had just been a jumble of gobbledegook. *Perfect.*

"Well, I'm telling you now. I'm sending a big SOS. In smoke signals and written in the sky. Get me out of here!" That last part comes out as a yell and I once again I check that Tom's mum isn't in here to hear this.

"What happened?" Again, this is Lilly. The one who is responsible for this entire ordeal in the first place.

"He brought his mum on the date."

Nothing.

Silence.

Then barking laughter.

"He did what?" Bella gasps out through her giggles.

"He. Brought. His. Mother. On. Our. Date." I punctuate every word so they can absorb the full effect of what I'm saying. "And she's not even nice."

"I'm sorry, Millie. That's awful." The laughter has stopped and, in its place, comes the sympathy.

Finally.

"It is. And I need you to fix it."

I stay on the line and listen to them discuss ways to get me out of here. Lilly suggests calling in a bomb threat (*no*). Bella suggests calling me with a family emergency (*maybe?*). And Amy, the ever-logical Amy, suggests I just tell them I want to leave.

"Like, just tell them the truth?" I'm gobsmacked at how easy she makes it all sound. "Isn't that rude?"

"It's not ruder than bringing a third person, unannounced and uninvited, on your date," she points out while the other two murmur in agreement. "Just pay for your meal. Tell them it's been nice to meet them and bounce. Come to my place and drink wine with us instead."

The mental image of the three of them hanging together is infinitely better than the prospect of sitting back down with Tom and Mrs Walker, being forced to listen to another one of his 'hilarious' stories.

"OK. OK, I'm going to do it."

The girls cheer me on from the other end of the line and I'm buoyed by their support. Hanging up, I take a minute to re-apply my cherry-red lipstick (completely wasted on the likes of that man waiting out there) and square my shoulders.

"You're a strong, confident woman. You can do this."

"Are you talking to me?"

I startle, whirling around to see that I'm no longer alone in the bathroom.

"Sorry," I smile at the young woman who's edging away from me, like she's worried I'm about to go off the deep end. *Fair.* "Just gearing myself up to get out of a terrible date."

Bathroom girl laughs, her shoulders relaxing. "Well, in that case, good luck, girl!"

We fist bump—*strange*—and with a spring in my step, I strut back to Tom and his mum. I leave my money on the table and wish them a pleasant evening. And then I bolt to the Uber I have waiting for me, unable to feel my legs as I go but still elated to put this awful night behind me.

"You owe me cookies." I say this to Lilly as she opens the door to let me into the house Amy shares with her husband Lucas. It had been a short Uber ride from my date from hell to my friend's place and I'd spent every minute stewing over what a disaster the whole night had been. "And brownies."

"Free cookies and brownies for a month." She puts her arms around me and pulls me in for a hug. A tight, warm, comforting hug.

"For a year," I counter-offer, a smile on my face to tell her I'm only half-serious.

"It can't have been that bad." This comes from Bella, who is lying on the floor, her head on a cushion, her feet up on the couch. She's drinking a cocktail from a straw and I'm pretty sure she'll end up sleeping through the night right where she currently lies.

"His mum lectured me about how unsuitable my boots are with this dress," I tell them, twirling to show off my killer look to its best advantage. "I mean, come on, these boots are amazing."

"'Tis true," Bella agrees, tipping her head further back upside down to get a better look. "Your legs look smoking hot in that mini-dress, boots combo."

"Exactly." I take the offered glass of wine from Amy and plonk myself on the couch next to Bella's feet. "And then she told me how few eggs I'll have left if I wait too long to have babies."

My friend's faces mirror back my horror as I remember her exact words: "Every month you don't fall pregnant is another month closer to being barren." *Yep, she actually used the word 'barren'.*

"Well, forget him. Forget *them*," Amy says, opening her desk drawer. "We can just move on to the letter B. I've got a good feeling about the letter B."

I roll my eyes. And snatch Bella's cocktail from her hand, taking a big slurp. "Can we not?"

Amy looks at me and places the folder back in the drawer, closing it with an emphatic thump.

"You're right. There's absolutely no need to move on with this dating plan. You are a strong, independent woman who can be just as happy alone as in a couple."

Bella and Lilly give this a drunken cheer and I can't help the smile that creeps onto my face. I love these women and their ridiculous antics.

"Thank you!" I stand up and give an unsteady bow. *Must slow down on the cocktails.* "I'm glad we're all on the same page."

"It's true," Bella says, sitting up, the wonky bun on the top of her head wobbling a bit. She needs a haircut. "You've got a successful career, which you love."

"I do."

"And the cutest apartment which you own all by yourself."

"Well, the bank owns most of it," I clarify.

"Meh," Bella charges on. "You have a pleasant relationship with your mum…"

I give them a so-so hand gesture, because this isn't entirely true.

"And you have us!" She finishes her monologue with a sweeping motion while Lilly and Amy nod along like bobble-head dolls.

"You don't need a man," Amy adds. "You are perfectly whole, just as you are."

It's true. Every word they've said to pump me up is accurate, and for the most part, I'm happy on my own. It's just those moments, the ones you want to celebrate the wins or the ones where you want your hand held, where having a partner would be…nice.

"And yet…" I trail off, not wanting to burst our girl power bubble. "I want what you guys have…"

My three married friends look at each other and then back at me with matching facial expressions. They understand exactly what I'm saying because the three of them hadn't been looking for love but were lucky enough to find it, anyway.

"So…back to the folder?" Lilly asks, her blue eyes shining with excitement. And intoxication.

My mind flashes to Tom and Mrs Walker. *Is the folder the best way forward?*

"OK, let's do it."

The three of them scramble to get the folder out of its resting place, flipping the pages with gusto to find which unsuspecting man is going to be next on my list.

"Bookkeeper?"

Pass, that's too close to an accountant.

"Baker?"

No, too many early mornings.

"Beekeeper?"

Is that really a job?

I watch on, amused, as they wade through the options of men and their respective professions, hoping that they land on someone better than Tom, the accountant.

PING.

My phone vibrates in my pocket. A message from Jake! I haven't heard from him since he encouraged me to go out on my date tonight and was wondering if I'd ever hear from him again.

JAKE: How'd your date go with the accountant?

(Hmmm, so he's still interested in hearing about my dating life? I don't hate it).

AMELIA: It didn't go.

AMELIA: He was a dud.

The three dots appear and disappear and I hold my breath, waiting for his response.

JAKE: I'm glad.

A squeal bubbles out of me involuntarily, distracting my friends from the task at hand. *He's glad??*

"What's happening?" Bella asks.

I hide my phone behind my back. "Nothing, just excited about who you're going to choose for my next date."

"That's the spirit!" Lilly raises her glass to toast me. "We're going to find a winner in here, for sure."

Once their attention is focused back on the folder, I pull my phone out, my hands sweaty and slippery on the smooth surface. What does he mean, he's *glad?*

JAKE: Millie? Are you still there?

JAKE: Was that rude?

JAKE: Should I want your date with the accountant to go well?

I re-read the three messages from Jake that had been sent in quick succession. Hating that text messages are so cryptic. There needs to be a way to infer tone from these simple sentences.

AMELIA: You're fine. The date was not.

JAKE: Want to talk about it?

AMELIA: NO!!!

JAKE: C'mon...

AMELIA: OK, I'll give you a four-word synopsis and then we'll never speak of this again.

JAKE: Deal.

AMELIA: He. Brought. His. Mum.

JAKE: ...

JAKE: ...

JAKE: ...

I can almost hear the shock and laughter in his three dots, appearing and disappearing with glee.

JAKE: He did not.

AMELIA: I can hear you laughing.

JAKE: What a waste. He saw you, right? Like he saw how gorgeous you are and still brought his mum along?

The butterflies in my stomach take off in a frenzy as I re-read this message from Jake. *He thinks I'm gorgeous?*

AMELIA: Well, it's over now.

JAKE: Good riddance...

I pause, unsure of how to proceed.

AMELIA: I guess now I have a date with the letter B to look forward to...

I wait for a response to this.

Nothing.

After three minutes—I time it by counting the seconds in my head—I'm resigned that he's probably tired of my nonsense conversation and put my phone under the couch cushion, away from the temptation to check it every thirty seconds.

"Millie!" I glance up at my friends who are all watching me, grins beaming from their faces. "We found him."

I groan, internally so as not to dampen their excitement.

Amy holds up the folder, waving to the page in front of her.

"We found the perfect guy for you."

They pass the folder over to me and I scan the information laid out on the page in front of me, which now includes photos and a small bio. They've really ramped up the calibre of their present-ation of prospective mates for me since the last time we'd looked it over.

"You guys are sure about this?"

They'd chosen a friend of a friend who works with Lucas, and who doesn't seem like a complete loser. On paper.

My three best friends nod in unison and I take a deep breath.

"Then it looks like I'll be going out with a biomedical scient-ist!"

Whatever that is.

CHAPTER 8

Amelia

"IT WAS SO HORRIBLE. HE made Tom the accountant seem like a prince!"

Bella chuckles from her position on the couch next to me, her gaze glued to my face, all her attention set on hearing my tale of woe.

"He can't have been as bad as the Mumma's boy?!"

I flashback to the night before, my big date with Julian the biomedical scientist and inwardly shudder. The evening with him had started off badly and only gotten worse.

"He took me to a lecture on science stuff," I say, narrowing my eyes at her to stop her from laughing.

"Science-stuff? Is that the technical term?"

I poke her with my foot which is resting at her waist. The two of us are stretched out head to toe on my couch, settling in for a sleepover. Luckily for me, Bella's husband Daniel is working the night shift in his job as a firefighter tonight, so I get to keep her all to myself.

"I don't know what the technical terms are. It was all gibberish to me!"

"Back up and tell me everything that happened."

Keeping my eyes closed, so I can relive every painful moment, I detail the events of my date with 'letter B' Julian. It had gotten off to a rocky start when he'd turned up twenty minutes late—just as I'd been planning on leaving, sure that I'd been stood up. He'd rushed into the coffee shop near where he works (not sure how he was late when we'd arranged to meet somewhere convenient only to him) and hadn't even apologised. Then he'd given me a long look, taking in my ripped jeans paired with my favourite silver sparkly top to match my favourite silver sparkly heels and had deemed my outfit 'inappropriate' for the evening ahead.

"He did not say that!" Bella squeals, her cheeks flushing with indignation.

"He did."

And it wasn't the worst thing he'd said to me that night. After that charming introduction, he'd asked if I could get my coffee to go because we were going to be late.

"For what?" Bella interjects.

"For the science stuff."

"Why didn't you just leave, right after he'd insulted your sexy date outfit?"

I shrug. At the time, I'd been desperate for date number two to go better than date number one and I'd lost all perspective. Plus, he was cute. In a nerdy, could-look-hot-in-a-lab-coat kind of way.

"So, you go to the lecture...?"

"Yes, getting nothing to eat beforehand," I emphasise. The two of us do not do well with skipping meals so I knew she'd appreciate this point. We are self-confessed 'hangry monsters'.

"Uh oh."

Uh oh, indeed. The lecture theatre had been only half full when we'd arrived, with many suitable seats up the back, where the cool kids hang. But was that where Julian seated us? Noooo. We were right up the front, in prime position.

"He did not!" Bella is suitably mortified, knowing exactly what happens to people who dare to sit up the front.

"He did."

And it only got worse from there. The lecture itself was all kinds of boring, incorporating the use of many words ending i -ases and -sis, but that wasn't even the worst part. That came when my date stood up at the end of the presentation and criticised everything that had just been presented.

"And it wasn't in a 'here's some feedback, maybe you can think of doing this next time' kind of way. It was in a rude, belligerent and arrogant kind of way. He did it to make himself feel big and the presenter feel very small."

"I hate those kinds of people." Bella's blue eyes are spitting fire. "What a jerk."

"I know, right? And he'd had the audacity, after all of that"—I swirl my hand in the air to encompass the entire mess of the date—"to think that he was entitled to a good-night kiss."

"Shut. Up."

A burst of giggles springs out of me at her dramatics. I love that she's on this emotional rollercoaster right along with me.

"I will not shut up," I grin. "But it's fine. I speared him with my most icy look. You know the one?"

She shudders in response. She knows it well.

"And then said: lose my number. And I flounced away."

Bella claps at this and I rise onto my elbows to give a half-bow. My performance in ending this date was worthy of the applause.

"Why do men suck?" she asks, flopping back down onto the couch to stare up at the ceiling.

"Not all men suck. Your husband, for example. He's pretty amazing."

She lets out a satisfied sound. "It's true, but remember how much of a jerk he was when I met him? They never make it easy."

When Bella had moved from her hometown of Florence to join her brother here in Melbourne, she'd been stuck living with Lucas's very grumpy (and very sexy) roommate. And he had been a bit of a jerk to Bella at the start, but we all know now that he'd just been keeping her at a distance to mask the very real, powerful feelings he'd already been developing for my gorgeous best friend.

"I think we can safely say that you found a good man. One of the few left out there in the world, apparently."

Bella's nose scrunches and she squeezes my hand in solidarity. "You know what will make you feel better?"

I scramble to think of something other than her company that will lift my spirits. "What?"

"Lilly's cupcakes!"

She catapults herself off the couch and skips to the kitchen. "Lilly dropped some round to my place earlier, obviously to assuage the guilt she's still feeling about Tom…and now Julian."

"Julian wasn't her fault," I call from where I remain on the couch, happy to have cupcakes delivered to my lap. "That was all Amy and Lucas."

"What were they thinking?" Bella mutters under her breath and quietly, I agree. Maybe Julian is one of those men, the good-on-paper men. Ticks all the boxes, but in reality, is a complete dud.

PING.

I bolt up from my lounging position at the text message notification, set to ring at maximum volume. Refusing to examine why I'm so keen to not miss a message, I open my app.

JAKE: You haven't finished telling me about your date.

I grin. After leaving me hanging the night of my 'A' date, Jake had finally messaged back, eager to hear all about the dating mishaps with the letter 'B'.

AMELIA: I told you it was bad.

JAKE: But how bad is bad?

AMELIA: There was science involved.

JAKE: ...

AMELIA: He took me to a lecture...

JAKE: About?

AMELIA: I'm remembering photosynthesis and maybe homeostasis...

JAKE: From my memory of my year eight biology class, those two don't really fit together.

This makes me smile. The nerd in Jake goes beyond his law degree.

AMELIA: Well, whatever it was, I didn't want it anywhere near my date night.

JAKE: Fair.

"Who's putting that smile on your face?"
I drop my phone like a hot potato and put my hands on my flaming cheeks. *Busted.*

"No one," I lie, going for casual and ending up with squeaky.

"Ohhh, you are messaging with a 'someone' for sure. Is it contestant number three? 'Letter C' guy?"

After the debacle of date night with science guy, you'd think we'd all have given up on this dating mission, but instead, each failure seemed only to make my friends even more determined to find me someone...decent.

"No, but I am meeting him tomorrow."

'Letter C' guy is actually someone Daniel knows; a carpenter, and I'm meeting him tomorrow afternoon. A daytime date, hopefully to take the pressure off.

"So, spill. Who's got your face looking like that?" She motions to my face and I wonder what it is she's reading there. I'm messaging with Jake; it's not like he's a contender to be my Mr Right. *Right?*

"I've been messaging with Jake…" I admit, waving my hands in front of me to cool down my cheeks. "That's all."

Her mouth drops open, a bit of cupcake falling out. "Jake? Robby's brother, who is like the hottest man alive?"

"Apart from your hunky firefighter husband?" I ask dryly.

"Of course, of course," she says, making a 'pfft' gesture with her hands. "But Jake, he's like a hot, nerdy guy. Those glasses…" She trails off with a faraway look and I join her in reminiscing the pleasure those glasses give to the wider female population.

"Either way," I say, snapping us both out of our collective daydreaming, "he's just been keeping in touch since we bumped into him at Love, Lilly's. It seems like he's pretty invested in seeing how our dating plan works out."

She smirks at this. "Invested to see it fail."

I gape at her. "What does that mean?"

"Come on, Millie. You can't have missed how that man looked at you. I was only in the presence of the two of you for a short time and even I could see it. He watches you like you've been put on this earth specifically for him."

Her words cause all sorts of butterflies, moths, insects and the like to take flight in my belly. If only it were true.

"You're seeing things," I argue with her. "You think I'm amazing, so you think everyone else sees me that way."

"That's true." She hands me a cupcake with a grin. "But it doesn't mean I'm making it up. I think hunky Superman has a thing for you."

"He's Robby's brother," I burst out. "His *brother*." I repeat for good measure.

Bella looks unperturbed by this. "So? Robby was the worst. And he dumped you. And he has a girlfriend. In my mind, you're free to do whatever you want. Including Jake. Especially Jake."

Her words echo Andrea's so closely I wonder if they're colluding against me. *Can't they see it would be wrong to go from one brother to the next?*

"Picking Jake after being with Robby isn't wrong," she tells me, reading my mind apparently. "It would just be a way of righting a wrong. Maybe you were with the wrong brother from the start?" I bite into my vanilla cupcake with buttercream frosting with gusto, hoping to end this conversation. Because as much as I wonder, in my quiet times, whether it should have been Jake all along, I can't help the guilt I feel about Robby. Even though he'd treated me poorly for the entire relationship and I'm pretty sure he cheated on me (several times) he doesn't deserve to have me jump to his big brother. *Does he?*

"It doesn't matter." I shove the rest of my cupcake into my mouth and chew vigorously. "I'm going out with Hank the carpenter. And I've got a good feeling that maybe third time's the charm."

Bella wipes the icing from her lips while giving me a speculative look. "OK, I'm letting you get away with avoiding the topic. This time." She shoots me a glare. "Now tell me, where are you and the good carpenter going tomorrow? Somewhere more exciting than the lecture hall at Melbourne Uni, I hope."

I scroll through my messages, re-reading the one Hank had sent earlier today.

"We're meeting at an escape room. That sounds like fun, yes?"

She gives what can only be read as a doubtful look, and I secretly agree.

An escape room doesn't sound like fun at all

Always trust your instincts.

This thought is bouncing through my brain ten minutes after the door to the escape room locked behind me and Hank. Forcing us to work together to find our way out.

So far, this date has been no better than the first two. Hank the carpenter had turned up on time (one point for him) but had also turned up drunk (minus one hundred points for him). At first, it was hard to tell what exactly was off with him, but then the door closed and we were given our mission—to "help save the Prime Minister who'd been kidnapped"—and he started freaking out. Like this is all real.

"We have to save him," Hank yells in my face, the pupils in his blue eyes dilated almost completely, making them a scary shade of black. "The fate of the country rests with us."

I hold back my laughter because really, it's kind of funny that he thinks he's capable of saving anyone right now. I give him a solemn nod. There's zero point trying to convince him this is all make-believe, given how 'out of it' he is.

"You're right," I say, rubbing his arm to calm him down. "So, we need to be focussed."

Hank's very unfocussed eyes lock with mine and I see pure panic in there. *This is going to be a long afternoon.*

"I guess we should look at the ransom note the kidnappers left behind?" I say to get the ball rolling; the sooner we get out of here, the sooner I can get away from whatever Hank has going on.

"We're running out of time!"

My date looks like he's about to lose it and I scramble to figure a way out of this mess. As far as I can tell, we have two hours to get out of here—to 'save the Prime Minister'—and no one to step in to help us. We're on our own.

"Why don't you take a seat?" I guide Hank to the plush armchair in the corner of our room, gently pushing him into it. "Conserve your energy while I try to decipher the first clue."

He looks at me, his bloodshot eyes blinking frantically, and then before I can blink back, he's asleep.

Why is this happening to me?

"Hank?" I shake him. Hard. "Wake up!"

Nothing. My would-be partner in this escape plan is now passed out cold and it's up to me and me alone to get us out of here (and to save the Prime Minister, of course).

"You can do this," I give myself a little pep talk, reading the first clue. Which is a lot of numbers and a few symbols on a page. It's something I obviously need to de-code, but I have no idea where to start.

"Hank!" I try one more time to wake him, a snore the only response I get. "Grrr."

With no other ideas and also because I'm not hating having an excuse to call him, I dial the number of the smartest person I know (and it's not Julian the scientist!).

"Amelia?" Jake's shocked voice over the phone brings me a level of comfort I tuck away to examine at a later date.

"Jake," I reply, my voice breathless with the weight of emotion I'm feeling at just hearing his voice. "I need your help."

"Of course." His reply is immediate and sure. As reliable as he is. "What do you need?"

Chewing on my bottom lip, I contemplate what to tell him. "I'm on my date with Hank the carpenter." I stop when I hear a growl from his end. At least I think it's a growl. "Do you have a dog on your lap?"

"What?" he asks, confused. "No."

"Oh."

"So, you're calling me from your date. Do you need me to come get you? Are you OK?"

"I'm fine," I hasten to reassure him. The concern in his voice is like a weighted blanket for my growing anxiety. "It's just that I'm in this escape room with Hank."

"Pfft, Hank," he mutters and I smile.

"And, well, you see..."

"Spit it out, Amelia." He's grumpy now.

"He fell asleep."

Silence.

"Jake?"

"He fell asleep?"

"Um, yes?"

"Where on Earth are you finding these guys?" he groans. "How is he asleep?"

I'm as baffled as he is. "He may be drunk? And now I need help to get out of this room, or else I'll be stuck in here with sleeping beauty for the next two hours before anyone comes to rescue us."

"That is quite the situation," his dry voice makes me giggle. "What can I do to help?"

I turn the phone and press the button for video call, instantly relieved when I see his face fill my screen. His handsome face, *with* his glasses on.

"I need you to escape with me."

His green eyes pierce through my iPhone screen and I wish I could read his mind. He must think these dating shenanigans are ridiculous. Because…they are.

"O-K…" He draws out the two letters, making them into an entire sentence. "But only on the condition that you stop going out with these losers."

I turn the phone to where Hank is snoring in his green chair, a line of drool running out of his mouth.

"Deal."

"Then let's begin. What's our mission?"

I'm laughing while I outline our current 'situation'. The kidnapping of the Prime Minister and the first clue being in some sort of hieroglyphics.

"Show me," he demands after I've described the ransom note to him.

I angle the camera on my phone so he can best read the clue and am astonished when he solves it in under three minutes. *The man is a genius.*

"The next clue is under the bed," he declares while I stare at him in amazement.

"How do you know that?" I ask, kneeling down to look under the mattress.

"It was a simple code. Every number is a letter and the symbols are punctuation."

I look at the note again, mentally rearranging the numbers for letters. *Incredible.*

"I'd have been stuck on that one all afternoon," I mumble, putting the phone on the bed and pulling myself further under the mattress. "And the Prime Minister would never have been saved."

"Have you got the next clue?" Jake asks this as I emerge triumphant…and slightly dishevelled.

"Bingo!"

I show him the next clue and wait for him to solve it. And sure enough, he does, guiding me from one room to the next, finding a new clue in each location.

"Have you been here before?" I ask, suspicious after he'd successfully directed me to the last clue. The one that should get me out of here. Freedom at last.

"Nope," he answers. "But I love a good detective show. A good murder mystery. It turns out I've been training for this day for years now."

The playful tone in his voice has my stomach clenching. His playfulness has me melting.

"So, are you ready for this?" I keep my tone dead serious. "Are you ready to complete the mission and save our fearless leader?"

Jake's face lights with laughter and I only just refrain from taking a screenshot. To have for later. And forever.

"Let's do it."

Together we unjumbled the last clue and he watches as I enter the final code into the lock-pad next to the door. We both hold our breath as I press in the last two numbers, yelling with equal levels of excitement when the door turns green and opens.

"Congratulations," an automated robotic voice comes over a loudspeaker. I jump at the sound of it. "You've rescued the Prime Minister and your mission is now complete."

I keep a firm hold of the open door with one hand, scared it will accidentally shut and I'll have to start all over again. "Thank you, Jake. I literally could not have done this without you."

He grins back at me, flashing his dimple, making my knees tremble. "It was my pleasure. And look, it turns out we're a great team."

My smile slips from my face at these words. Not because they're not true. But because they are.

"What are you going to do about Sleepy McSleeperson over there?" Jake's voice is serious now, the mirth from a moment ago all but disappeared.

I glance to the room where Hank is *still* asleep and turn away.

"He's not my problem."

"Good for you." Jake's soft response gives me the courage to walk out of the room, letting the door close behind me. When Hank wakes up and finds himself alone, I hope he doesn't freak out too much.

OK, maybe he can freak out, just a little.

"Where to now?"

I turn the phone from video back to just audio, reluctantly giving up the pleasure of looking at Jake's face. "I'm heading home," I answer his question. "To sleep away the horror of yet another date gone wrong."

He's silent on the other end and once again I wish I knew what he was thinking.

"It wasn't the worst way to spend an afternoon…" he trails off, leaving an opening for me.

"No, spending the afternoon saving the leader of our nation definitely wasn't a terrible use of my time."

He laughs, a deep, rich sound I want to bathe in.

"Well, feel free to call should you ever find yourself on another such mission. Or if you just want to chat."

Again, he leaves an opening for me. One I should shut down, given his status as my ex-boyfriend's older brother.

"I like the sound of that," I tell him before hanging up. Because I like the sound of it altogether too much.

And it's becoming a problem.

A very big problem indeed.

CHAPTER 9

Jake

S HE'S ON ANOTHER DATE.

It's been a week since my virtual escape room date with Amelia and we've spoken every day. And as feared, it's been wonderful. Being around this woman, even if it's just over the phone, is as natural as breathing, and it's why I stayed far, far away from her when she was dating my brother.

"You alright, Jake?"

That's Steven. He's dragged me out of my house—literally came to my door and pulled me off the couch in the middle of the penultimate episode of *Alone*—claiming it's his duty as my best friend to ensure I don't end up as a sad, lonely guy. Not that I care about having that title. It's been well-earned and well-deserved. Especially considering the tiny but impactful bombshell Amelia dropped into our last call. That despite vowing to end this crusade to find her perfect match, she'd been convinced by her friends (damn them) to give Dr Dave a chance. She's out with him right now. Hence the need for me to be out of the house, drinking with my mates, despite it only being two weeks since my last enforced social engagement.

"I'm fine," I sigh, hoping that if I say it often enough, it will eventually be true.

"Good, because tonight we are getting you out of your self-imposed life as a monk. It's time for you to start dating again."

I snort. The word *again* implies that the dating ever began. And given it's been at least a year since I last looked at a woman in that way, I'm guessing I'm probably more than a little rusty in this department.

"Come on man, the Eeyore mood is killing our vibe." This is from Aaron, a friend from law school whom Steven had convinced to join us. An effort to make it more festive, perhaps.

"Shut up," I grunt at him, not in the mood for any crap. "I'm here under duress and refuse to be happy about it."

My friends both grin at me. "A few more drinks and you'll be fine."

Aaron disappears towards the bar, intent on finding the magic cure for my anhedonia. I want to tell him that his efforts will be in vain, that with Amelia out there on another date, with a doctor this time, there will be no cheering me up.

"Snap out of this," Steven slaps me on the back. "She's not worth it."

My blood bubbles at this. "You don't know what you're talking about." I grit this out between my clenched teeth, wondering if this will be the time. The first time I punch my best friend in over twenty-five years of friendship.

"I just mean," he backtracks, his hands up in surrender, "that she's clearly looking for something and she's not seeing it in you."

The truth in his words hit me like a bullet train. Amelia, for all her friendly chats and flirty messages, is persisting with this quest to find Mr Right, while I'm sitting at home, waiting for the phone to ring. There's definitely something wrong with this picture.

"You're right," I say. "Why am I being like this?"

He gives me a look, sympathy plastered all over his face. "Because you really like her? And you think maybe she could like you back?"

We sit in silence, his words heavy between us.

"Why don't you just try to forget about her for one night?" he finally speaks up, continuing his mission to cheer me up, not knowing he's asking for the impossible. I haven't been able to forget about Amelia since I sat next to her at that bar all those months ago.

"Hey, isn't that Amelia?" Aaron says as he puts the three precariously balanced bottles of beer he's holding on the table between us and points to the door. "It's her, isn't it?"

I turn at such a speed that I'll later require a massage to fix my neck, and my eyes land on her. She's with her friend Bella and she looks…spectacular.

"That's her."

Amelia struts into the bar, wearing a dress made to torture all of mankind, a little black number that hugs her slight curves and stops mid-thigh, combined with sky-high heels that make her legs look miles long. Her hair is dead straight, parted in the middle and hanging down her back. The honey colour has been lightened, and the ends have a lavender haze. She's gorgeous and so out of my league.

"I thought you said she's on a date tonight?" Steven's voice sounds like it's coming from far away, only just cutting through the loud ringing noise that started in my head the minute Amelia entered the room.

"I thought she was," I mutter into my beer bottle, my mind whirring with possibilities. *What happened to Dr Dave?*

"Are you going to talk to her?"

I'd have to stand in line. I watch through the lens of the green-eyed monster as hordes of men surround Amelia and Bella as they approach the bar, each vying for the attention of the beautiful women.

"At least say hello," Aaron urges me.

My feet move in her direction without my brain giving them permission, and I go with it. By some stroke of luck, not only is Amelia not on a date with a doctor looking like *that*, but she's also here in this room with me. *It has to be a sign or something?*

"Hey."

I touch her elbow to get her attention and feel the customary buzz of electricity that happens whenever her skin makes contact with mine.

"Jake!"

That's excitement I'm hearing in her voice? Right?

"Hey."

Come on, man. Find some more words.

"What are you doing here?" she asks, going up on her tippy toes to speak into my ear.

I point to where Steven and Aaron are grinning at us. "They forced me out of the house."

She laughs, a light sound that I imagine pixie dust would sound like. "You sound so thrilled about it."

"I'm here under duress."

"I thought there were at least a few more weeks until you were due to leave your house."

A thrill courses through me. She's been paying attention and keeping track. I love this more than I should.

"Hey, Jake."

My gaze reluctantly leaves Amelia and I turn to see her friend looking at me, big question marks written all over her expression.

"Hi, Bella. What are you guys doing here?"

Her face drops. "Amelia called me…." She trails off, biting her lip, giving her friend a querying look.

"I called her because my date didn't show up tonight and I needed to be rescued. And then I needed a drink."

My hands clench into a fist. Amelia's cheeks are tinged in pink and her eyes are watering and I can feel the hurt rolling off her. *She was stood up? What is wrong with these men?*

"Here, Millie. The drink I promised you."

She takes the elaborate-looking cocktail from her friend, her pink tongue peeking out to lap at the cream on the top.

"Hmmm, so good."

My gut tightened and I lose what's left of my breath. She's so effortlessly sexy, it's a pure miracle that she's ever spent a minute single.

"So, what happened tonight?" I ask Bella. Amelia looks too happy slurping at her frothy drink. I don't want to disturb her.

"I'm not sure," Bella shrugs. "She called me about an hour after her date was supposed to start and said he hadn't turned up. What a jerk."

"I thought you said no more dates," I growl at Amelia, my anger at the unknown doctor boiling to the surface. Sure, he probably saves lives for a living, but at this moment I'm just about ready to end his.

"I did. And I was done," she says, taking the cherry from the bottom of her glass and sucking on it briefly. *God, she's killing me.* "But then Amy said she's got this perfect guy from the hospital who she's dying for me to meet. She begged me to go out with him. And now she's dead to me."

Bella takes her empty cocktail glass from her hand and replaces it with another one. A pink concoction this time.

"I'm sure he's a good guy. He's a doctor who's probably on call and something must have come up," Bella offers with a weak smile.

"Nope."

I say this so loudly that several people around us stop their conversation to give me a side glance. To be fair, I do sound pretty angry.

"No," I repeat, keeping my voice softer this time. "Do not excuse this behaviour. Amelia deserves more than this. She deserves better."

Amelia's already pink cheeks shine brighter and Bella's smile grows more knowing.

Gulp.

"You're right, Jake. Amelia deserves the best. Dr Dave is a jerk, and he's best forgotten."

The two women cheers, vigorously and somewhat drunkenly. *Maybe I need to get them some water?*

"I'm done with men," Amelia yells, garnering protests from the men behind her. Like they ever had a chance with her. "I'm going to get a cat. Maybe two cats!"

Bella's face visibly pales. "Let's not go crazy, Millie. Remember all the plants you killed? Cats need even more care."

Her friend pouts back at her and I refrain from reaching out and tucking her under my arm, while promising to buy her all the cats.

"Well, I need something. Clearly, men aren't for me..." she trails off, her unfocused eyes shadowed with sadness.

"You don't need to decide right now." I stroke her arm, feeling goose-pimples bloom on her skin under my hand. "Maybe you just need to stop with the dating plan. Let a relationship happen naturally?"

She taps her finger on her bottom lip, thinking. "Nah, I'm done."

She slumps into the barstool next to her and Bella gives her a hug. "Let's wait until we have clearer heads in the morning before deciding."

Amelia gives a stubborn shake of her head. "Bella, I'll never have what you have with Daniel. There's something wrong with me...I mean, even my dad didn't love me enough to stay."

I freeze, my heart pounding at this sad confession.

"Oh honey," Bella's face is filled with pain as she looks at me over her friend's shoulder. "That's not true."

A trail of tears makes their way down Amelia's cheeks and I flounder, my own eyes watering as I watch her. *When was the last time I cried?* I ponder this, feeling helpless in the face of her hurt.

"I'm tired."

Her voice is so sad, I act without thinking. Moving Bella out of the way, I pull Amelia to me. "Amelia, you listen to me." I whisper the words directly into her ear, needing her to hear me. "You do not need a man to tell you how amazing you are, but I'm here now and I want you to know it. I want you to feel it from me. You are incredible. You are wonderful. You are enough."

She gapes up at me and I know I've probably said too much. But stuff it, I'm not guarding my heart at the expense of hers. If saying these words to Amelia right now, in this moment, exposes me and my own hidden feelings, then I can live with that. As long as it takes away some of her pain.

"Thank you, Jake," she breathes into my ear and I pull her closer to me. Holding her to my chest, breathing her in, wishing I could have more than just this moment with her.

"I mean it."

She squeezes me tight in response and rests her head on my shoulder.

"Maybe we should get her home?"

Bella's voice startles me. I'd forgotten she was there. I'd forgotten anyone else existed.

"Yes," I agree. "Can I take you both home?"

She nods. "I think she'd like that."

Amelia's head remains on my shoulder and I gently lift it up, using a finger to raise her lovely face to mine. "I'm going to say goodbye to my friends and then I'll take you home. Is that alright?"

"Yes," she hiccups. "I'd like that."

I hand her over to where Bella is hovering, looking worried. This night had definitely taken a turn for the worse, exposing a lot of unspoken pain that's been bubbling in her friend.

"I'll be right back." I jog to where my friends are finishing another round of beer, matching bemused looks on their faces.

"What's up?" Steven asks, tilting his head to the bar where I'd just come from.

"I'm taking them home." I don't go into any details. "They've had enough of being here. And so have I."

They grin at me. "Aren't you happy we dragged you here tonight?"

I look back to where Amelia is leaning against her friend, the two of them with their heads pressed together, a united front of sadness.

"I'm forever grateful." I thump them both on the back to say goodbye. I'm so glad I was here to be with Amelia tonight. It feels like she really needs me.

"Call me!" Steven yells after me with a cheeky smile. It's like having a thirteen-year-old girlfriend with him sometimes.

I wave him off and lengthen my stride to get back to Amelia. She needs to be home, somewhere warm and safe. Somewhere she can lick her wounds, so that she can come back stronger, so that she can understand just how incredible she truly is.

"Ready to go?"

Amelia looks at me, her brown eyes sad but also filled with trust, holding me captive, like they always have.

"Take me home, Jake."

The words I've always wanted to hear. Only not in quite these circumstances.

"Do you want to stay at my place tonight?" Bella asks her friend once we're buckled in my car, ready to get on our way. "We can have a sleepover."

Amelia shakes her head where it's resting against the window of the passenger seat. "I just want to go home. I want to be alone. Is that OK?"

Bella and I exchange a look. *Do we want her to be alone tonight?*

"If that's what you want? Are you sure you'll be OK?"

She responds with a limp nod, closing her eyes. A picture of weariness.

"Right," Bella decides. "Well, Jake, it makes sense for you to drop me off first. Is that OK?"

"Of course, just point me in the right direction."

She gives me her address and we fall into silence, the two of us throwing worried glances in Amelia's direction.

"You'll make sure she gets up to her apartment safely?" Bella asks when we're stopped in front of the house she shares with her husband. Her face is creased with concern and I hasten to reassure her. She needs to know I'd never let anything happen to Amelia.

"Of course. She's safe with me."

Bella flashes me a smile, a grateful smile that makes me feel ten feet tall. "Thank you. Make sure you pop into the café tomorrow. You've earned yourself a brownie on the house."

My mouth instantly fills with saliva at the thought of this. The Love, Lilly brownie is legendary around Melbourne and I'm already looking forward to biting into my promised free one.

"Done."

Bella reaches into the front seat to kiss her friend on the cheek, rousing her briefly from her slumber. "Millie, I'm leaving you with Jake now. Is that OK?"

Amelia's lips tip up, her eyes stay closed. "Of course. Jake's the best."

My chest puffs up and Bella lets out an amused-sounding snort.

"Great. I'll call you tomorrow to check up on you. Drink lots of water before bed. Clearly those two cocktails were a lethal combination."

Amelia waves her hand in the direction of Bella's voice. "Bye Bella! Thanks for rescuing me."

Bella gives her one last kiss on the cheek before doing the same to me. "I like you," she whispers into my ear, shocking me, "so much better than your brother."

And with that bombshell, she opens the car door, skipping down the front path and into the house. Where her husband is no doubt waiting with open arms. I've only seen them interact when Daniel has come in to visit his wife at the cafe, but the two are the very epitome of two people deeply in love with each other.

Watching them together makes me ache for something I didn't know I wanted.

"Home time?" Amelia's sleepy voice pulls me from my thoughts.

"Yes, let's get you home."

I put some music on to fill what is suddenly a different sort of silence. With Bella out of the car, the buffer she afforded me between me and my big feelings for the woman sitting in my passenger seat is now gone.

"You like Taylor Swift?" I turn to see Amelia now awake, watching me with her brown eyes wide in her pale face.

"Eh." I make a so-so gesture with my hand as we sit at a red light. "But I know you do."

It is one of the many things I know about Amelia that I probably shouldn't.

"I love her," she admits, her tone filled with reverence. "She writes songs like she's been reading my diary."

"You keep a diary?" There's a smile in my voice as I think about this.

"Shhh." She turns up the music and leans her head back, her eyes closing again as she mouths the words to 'All Too Well'. I can't believe I know the name of this song.

I listen intently as she sings along, identifying completely with the idea of being OK, but not fine at all, and there's a twinge in my chest as I hear the truth in the words she's singing. What sort of pain is Amelia hiding behind her bright smile and her quick wit? It feels like there's a lot there to unpack.

"This is the best song she's ever written," she says when the ten-minute Taylor's version ends. We've been sitting in the car outside her apartment waiting for it to finish, both wrapped in the haunting melody of what I can now hear is a deeply sad song. But there's something so strong and confident in the way she sings the lyrics. I wonder if that's why Amelia connects with it so much. She's been through so much and has come out stronger than she's realised.

"I like it." My simple praise for her favourite song earns me a smile and I gesture out her window with my head. "Ready to go up?"

"I guess." She's back to sounding sad and I want to make it better but have nothing to offer her. Except a shoulder to cry on.

"I'll walk you up."

She doesn't argue, letting herself out of car and waiting for me to walk around to reach her. I pick up her hand and guide her to her front door, matching the meandering pace she's setting, happy to draw out our time together.

"Thanks for driving me home tonight."

I look down at her slightly dishevelled state and squeeze her hand. "Any time." I mean this more than she will ever know.

"And for what you said earlier at the bar?"

We're stopped outside her apartment, merely inches apart. She's looking up at me with a vulnerable expression, thanking me for just telling her the truth. That she's the most amazing woman I've ever known.

"Any time," I repeat, watching the smile grow on her face.

"Seriously." Her expression is earnest now. "I know I shouldn't let these disastrous dates get to me, but it's all been a bit too much. You know?"

I do know. Mainly because I know she shouldn't be going out with these clowns at all.

"You deserve better." I say this again because I really, *really* need her to believe it. If she can't be with me, she should be with someone better than Dr Dave (the jerk!)

"I know," she says, but her voice is small and unconvincing. "Anyway, thanks again."

She looks between me and the door and bites her bottom lip. Looking uncertain.

I lean all the way over—she's still tiny even in those sexy heels—and let my lips brush across her cheek, tracing the constellation of freckles that intrigue me so much. I do it once, twice, three times. It's the first and last time my lips will ever touch her skin and I take a moment to savour it. To drink it in. To drink her in.

"Good night, Millie." My voice is gruff and I make myself take a step away from her, my fingernails biting into my palms to stop from reaching for her.

"Good night, Jake." Her eyes search mine and I close my own to hide what I'm feeling. "I'll see you soon?"

I leave her question hanging as I back away, needing some space from her velvety chocolate eyes, her plump pink lips, her sweet coconut smell. I've reached my Amelia overload limit for the day and it's time to get out.

Her door closes behind me and I take it as my signal to sprint down the stairs, away from this woman who should have been mine but was with my brother instead. And once I'm in the safety of my car, I put Taylor Swift on Spotify and sing out loud all the way home. Hearing the pain in her lyrics, which now so completely mimics my own...all too well.

CHAPTER 10

Amelia

THERE'S A TINY PERSON IN my brain. Hitting me with a small, but very real hammer.

What on earth were in those cocktails last night?

I'm in bed, my eyes refusing to open, replaying the events from last night. Starting with the long, embarrassing wait to be stood up at the fancy restaurant and ending with Jake's lips on my cheek.

Why did that feel better than any proper kiss in recent memory?

"Amelia, your alcohol-riddled brain is clearly making you remember it wrong."

Even saying this out loud isn't working. It had been only a few seconds maximum, but my cheek feels like it's been forever changed. Jake's lips have ruined my face forever.

PING!

PING!

PING!

PING!

The frantic notifications from my phone send arrows shooting through my frontal cortex (*that's in my brain, right?*) and I blindly reach towards my bedside table where I know I'd plugged my phone in last night. The one and only responsible thing I'd done last night.

Peeling an eye open—*why must the sun be so bright?*—I read the first message. It's from Dr Dave. The Jerk.

DAVE: Amelia, I'm so sorry about last night. We had an emergency come in at the hospital and I only just got out of surgery. Can I make it up to you?

I see this message was sent at 7.33 a.m. *He'd been working all night? Saving a life, no doubt. Maybe he's not quite the jerk we'd labelled him.*

I swipe the message away, leaving thoughts of Dr Dave for later, and read the next one.

AMY: Bella told me what happened. I'm SO SORRY! Wait till I get my hands on Dave...

I sigh. *Poor Dave. The wrath of Amy is quite the sight to behold.*

BELLA: BellaAre you OK? Call me! Come to the café for some hangover-curing treats.

This is why she's my best friend. Already in solution mode for the damage those cocktails had caused.

I send her a quick thumbs up, knowing she'll be worried about me until I respond and then read the last message, my heart racing as I do.

JAKE: Play me! <LINK>

My heart sings as I press on the link he's sent with the message, a grin splitting my face in two as the first notes of 'New Romantics' blare out of my phone. Jake can't have known, but this song is a favourite of mine.

The words pour out of my body, my pounding headache all but forgotten as I channel the power of Taylor Swift and get my sorry butt out of bed. Bad dates be gone. I'm ready to face the day. Just like Jake had known I would.

"So, we're done with the dating plan?"

My friends give me matching sorrowful looks, and I harden my heart against every one of them. It's all their fault that I'd been suckered into four dates from hell in the span of less than a month. I think it's officially time to retire them as my matchmaking team.

"What about the month of horrors that I've just described to you makes you think I want to continue with this debacle?" We're sitting in Amy's living room—Amy who's been apologising profusely to me via calls, texts and carrier pigeons (*OK, that last one may be a stretch*)—under the guise of discussing the latest book club book. We're supposed to be analysing the wonders of Emily Henry's latest masterpiece, which I devoured and adored, but instead are focussed on my dismal love life. *Again.*

"But we only got up to the letter D." This protest comes from Madi, who I had thought would be the last person to be on board with a matchmaking scheme, given her eternally single status, but who instead seems to want to see this whole thing through. Right down to the letter Z. *I wonder if she has a zookeeper friend that she's dying to set me up with?*

"That's more than enough terrible dates for me to know that it's quitting time."

"To be fair, you didn't *actually* have a date with Dr. Dave."

I throw a pillow at Lilly to get her to shut up. What about being stood up by a man does she not understand? I'm not exactly keen to give him another shot.

"OK, if you won't go for any of the guys we set you up with, what about Jake?" Bella asks, a sly grin creeping across her face. *What's she playing at?*

"Oooh, yes. Date Jake!" Lilly's face is shining with excitement at this idea and I throw another pillow at her. For good luck. And to shut her up.

"Who's Jake?" Sammi asks, her eyes pinging between me, Bella and Lilly.

"Jake is Robby's delectably handsome, wiser and infinitely nicer older brother."

When did Bella become Jake's biggest fan?

"Robby?" Sammi looks confused. "Your ex-boyfriend Robby?"

"Yes," I say, shooting Bella a meaningful look. "He's my ex's brother. So not an option for me." Even though I desperately want him to be.

Shut up, inner voice.

"Why not?" Amy asks. Now it's her turn to look confused. "Robby dumped you. Unceremoniously, if I remember."

"Thanks for the reminder." I humph in her direction.

"So, he left you. Ghosted you for the last six months. Why can't you go out with his brother?"

The five of them look at me expectantly, and I shake my head. Surely, they know the rules of dating, the rules of *society*. You can't just go out with an ex-boyfriend's brother. It would be like cheating in the future. Or something.

"And Robby has a new girlfriend," Bella adds to the case in favour of my dating Jake. "And he was and is a douche. And Jake is so yummy. I don't see the problem."

"You guys don't think it's wrong? That it would seem like I wanted Jake while I was with Robby?" This is a secret fear of mine, that it would look like I was unfaithful to Robby by being emotionally attracted to his brother while we were together.

"Is that true? Did you have feelings for Jake while you were with Robby?" Amy asks the sensible question and silence follows as I gather my thoughts.

"I met Jake first," I admit, watching their eyes grow wide at this new piece of information. Well, all of them except Bella, who'd known about my first encounter with Jake from almost the minute after it happened. I'd called her from the bathroom stall that very evening. "I'd been waiting to meet Robby on a date. You know, that Love Is Blind dating app I used?"

They all nod. They lean forward, hanging on my every word.

"Jake came up to me at the bar and there was an instant spark. I mean, the man looks like Clark Kent, but hotter."

"Amen to that," Lilly agrees, cheers-ing her wine glass in my direction.

"But then Robby came over and we realised he was my LIB perfect match. So, I spent the evening with him. And really, he was my type. A musician, a bit of a rebel, a man who moved to the beat of his own drum. He seemed like the guy I should be with."

"You wanted Robby?" Bella asks, only a hint of doubt in her voice. Because, upon reflection, who would choose Robby over Jake?

"I did. Jake appeared to be everything I didn't want in a man. He was career focussed, married to his job and I put all thoughts of him and that initial meeting behind me. I went all in on Robby. You guys remember how mad I was about him."

They give me matching, frowny nods.

"You were certainly infatuated with him," Amy says after another pause. *Infatuated. An interesting choice of word.* "But I always wondered if it was more about the chase with Robby. He was never fully in with you, you know? So, you never felt safe. You were the one always trying to get him to commit."

That isn't how it was. Was it?

"That's how you guys saw my relationship? Like I was the desperate one chasing after a guy who wasn't into me?" My stomach churns at this. *How pathetic am I?*

"No!" Bella comes to sit next to me, rubbing my back in a soothing motion. "That's not it. It's just that with Robby, and really all your relationships, you are the giver. The one putting in the effort. You're in 100 per cent and the men, they seem to…not be in it as much."

"Is that how you all see my relationships?"

Their silence screams their answers to me.

Huh. I knew I had a messy dating history and that my parental example hadn't set me up for a healthy view on relationships, but had I really had such an obvious pattern of dating men who don't care for me as much as I care for them? Have I been unconsciously picking unsuitable men and therefore setting myself up to repeat my relationship with my father over and over again?

"Well, that sucks." My bottom lip trembles and I take a sip from my wine glass to cover it up. Not that I want to be drinking, still nursing last night's hangover, but it gives me something to focus on other than my emotional baggage being strewn all over the living room floor.

"You're not the only one with terrible dating habits," Madi says, a frown worrying at her brow. "I only attract men who want to settle down and get married."

"What's wrong with that?" I ask, perplexed.

"I don't have time for any of that. What's wrong with just a casual date, two people enjoying a meal together? Why does it have to go somewhere?"

"Maybe you and I should swap? I'll date your guys and you can date my losers?"

We laugh at this, but mine sounds as hollow as I feel. I'd known my dating history hadn't been great—a lot of no-hopers in that bunch—but I hadn't realised how emotionally unavailable all the men I'd chosen to date were. *There's definitely a lot I need to unpack here. Time for a few therapy sessions, perhaps.*

"So, that's a no for dating Jake?" Bella pipes up, bringing us back to the original point of this conversation. Jake. Right on cue, my cheek tingles at the memory of his lips and I squash it all down. *He's not an option for me. He can't be. I can't be that person.*

I've seen the devastation that's left behind when a person cheats, and I don't want any part in it. Even if it's only th*e perception* of cheating. In the past.

"I can't do it." Both my words and my voice sound as sorrowful as I feel, and my friends take pity on me, not pushing the point. Too much.

"I still think you can and maybe one day you'll figure out why you're actually pushing him away," Bella says, holding up a hand to stop my protest. "But if you insist on being a martyr about this, I have one more guy for you to meet, he—"

"—Nooooo—" I elongate the word to really emphasise how much I don't want her to finish this sentence.

"—He's an electrician," she continues like I hadn't just said the world's longest no. "And I had him lined up for the next date, knowing Dr Dave would be a dud."

"Hey!" Amy jumps in.

"I was right," Bella tells her sister-in-law with a smug smile. "But this guy I've vetted and he's perfect for you. Tall, blonde, handsome. He comes from a family with four sisters, so he knows how to be around women and hopefully treat them with respect. And he's funny. Have you ever dated a funny guy?"

Turns out I've never dated a decent guy, so funny hasn't really been on my radar. "Umm, no?"

"What have you got to lose by dating one more guy?"

"My dignity, my sanity, my will to live." I tick the reasons off, counting on my fingers as I go. "I said no more dating plan."

"Just one more," she cajoles while the other ladies send me pleading looks. Clearly, my dating life is the only entertainment these women have in their lives.

"Ugh, Bella. I really don't want to." I dig my heels in, memories of the drunken Escape Room guy flashing through my mind. "None of this is worth it."

"But you want to find someone, Millie. That's what started all of this." She has me there. I'm tired of being alone. Of being the seventh wheel in a group of coupled-up people. Of navigating my way through the world by myself.

My resolve weakens. Would it be terrible to agree to just one more date?

"Alright, I'm in. I'm giving you one more chance."

The five of them look at each other, their faces alight with joy. "You won't regret this, Millie. This guy will be perfect for you." *Famous last words.*

I have five days to regret my decision to go out with Mike, the electrician. Five days where I visit the Love, Lilly café daily in search of a soul-soothing brownie and nothing more. Definitely not in search of a certain man with green eyes that flash behind mine whenever I close them.

"You've been here a lot this week," the ever-observant Bella says as she sits across from me, a heart-shaped chocolate chip cookie in her hand.

I shrug. It's not like she's wrong. "I've been needing Lilly's treats more than usual."

She watches me closely, her brow furrowed. "Are you OK?"

I want to reassure her with lies, but I don't. It's Bella, and she knows me too well. "I've been thinking a lot about what you guys said. You know? About only being with emotionally unavailable men?"

"That's not uncommon, Millie. Lots of people end up in that sort of pattern. I think it's a protective mechanism, so you don't get hurt."

"But I do get hurt," I protest into my brownie. "I choose the wrong men to guard my heart, but still end up getting it broken when they inevitably leave me."

She looks at me closely, giving me the best friend stare. "I don't want to take away from any of the hurt you feel when your relationships blow up—"

"Gee, thanks."

"—But," she holds up her hand. "But I think if you'd been with someone you'd really wanted, really loved and they left you the way Robby did, you'd feel differently."

I frown. "What do you mean?"

"Don't get mad," she starts and immediately my hackles rise. "But I think you chose these men because you know they will inevitably let you down and you won't ever have to be in an actual relationship. You won't ever have the fear of really getting hurt."

"Ouch." I rub my temples, my head and heart hurting at her words. "Is that what you really think?"

"I'm not a therapist, Millie." She takes my hand and squeezes it. "It's just something I've observed. Maybe something for you to think about?"

My tear ducts stand at attention as I look at the sympathy on Bella's face. *Have I really been choosing these Mr Wrongs as a way not to get my heart truly broken? Is that why I can't seem to let myself give in to the thought of a certain someone? Because deep down I'm scared to be in something real?*

"I have some stuff to sort through," I mumble, my shoulders slumping under the weight of it all. "Maybe I'm more messed up than I thought?"

"We're all messed up in some way," she says with a watery smile of her own. "Remember how long Daniel kept me at arm's length because he feared getting hurt? Everyone has baggage by the time they get to our age."

It was true; Bella's husband had been terrified to let her close to him, guarding his heart that had been broken after the death of his mum. It had taken a lot of time and patience before Bella finally got him to open up.

"You just need to find someone worth taking the chance on. And when you meet that someone, you need to be brave enough to let that person in."

Her last words are drowned out by the tinkle of the bell sounding, announcing a new customer.

"Jake!"

My head darts up and I'm instantly entranced by his green eyes, already zeroed in on mine.

"Ladies." His deep voice, like always, is a balm for my jangled nerves. "It's good to see you."

I attempt to respond but my tongue has forgotten how to work, so I send him a smile instead, hoping I don't look a deranged as I feel.

"You sit here with Millie while I get you your usual." Bella skips off behind the counter, leaving the two of us to stare at each other. In silence because, all of a sudden, I have so much I want to say to him and I don't know where to start.

"Are you OK?"

His voice, his damn voice is so soothing, I want to lie in bed and have him talk me to sleep.

I nod. Still no words.

"Are you sure?" His eyebrows are drawn into a point between his eyes. He looks really concerned.

Time to get it together, Amelia.

"Eh, it's been a long week."

"Want to talk about it?"

I do. I do so much want to talk about it with him that it scares me.

"I'm all talked out." I motion to where Bella is flitting about, making his coffee. "But thanks."

My phone chirps, the alarm I set to remind me to go to work. It's been that sort of week, where simple things like getting to my job may slip through the cracks.

"I've got to go." I'm reluctant to leave him, annoyed that we've only had a minuscule amount of time together. Most of it with me being mute. "I have to get to work."

He stands at the same time as me. "I'll walk you out."

I want to protest, to tell him I can walk myself out without help, but then I also want more time with him. So…

"OK."

"I'll be right back, Bella," he tells my friend as we walk to the door, her responding smile and wink not subtle at all.

"Take your time," she yells after us, delight coating her voice.

Jake opens the door and motions me to walk in front of him, falling into step beside me as we walk down the block to where I'd parked my car.

"Do you have any plans for the weekend?" He sounds nervous, and I glance up to see him watching me closely.

I hesitate, not wanting to tell him about my date with the electrician. "Sort of."

He frowns and I look away from him, keeping my gaze forward. Not a bad idea on this busy Richmond sidewalk, where one has to dodge both pedestrians and cyclists at any moment.

"Sort of?"

"I have another date," I blurt out.

We stop in front of my car, a red Mini Cooper I love more than almost anything in the world, and I wait for his response.
"Another date?" He sounds shocked.
And maybe, annoyed?

"Bella is convinced this guy is 'the one'." I roll my eyes, still regretting agreeing to this one.

Jake takes a step closer to me, forcing me to take a step back, my body now pressed against the side of my car.

"You're still looking for the one?" He puts emphasis on 'looking', like he's stuck on that word.

"I don't know," I tell him honestly. "I'm a bit of a mess."

He leans in even closer, his body now touching mine, and I hold my breath. *What's happening?*

"I happen to like mess." His words, in that husky tone, send a jolt through me and I can do nothing but gape up at him.

"W-hat?"

"Amelia," he starts, then stops, staring up at the sky, his jaw clenching. "I think maybe you've been looking in the wrong places."

This echoes what Bella had just said, and I tilt my head back to get a better look at him, my heart racing with anxiety and...anticipation?

I gulp in a painful breath. "Jake?"

He leans forward and in slow motion, his face inches closer to mine.

"Have fun on your date." He whispers this, his lip tickling my lips as he does. Then he straightens up, runs his hand through his hair at the same time as he runs his eyes over me, and with a deep breath, he turns and walks away.

Did he just almost kiss me? My body sags against my car door, the metal frame absorbing my body weight as my knees buckle over what had almost just happened.

He definitely almost kissed me.

With shaky hands, I get into my car and drag in some much-needed air. My mind is a pickled mess and I need to sort through it all to figure out what I really want. Who I really want. I can't keep tumbling around in this vortex of 'what ifs'.

My heart is screaming at me that Jake is the one I want, but my head is firmly taking control, warning me that getting too close to this man is a recipe for getting hurt. And as is always the way, my head wins the battle and convinces me that dating the electrician is the way to go.

And I let it win. This time.

CHAPTER 11

Amelia

"So, he was…nice?" Andrea says the word 'nice' in the same way she'd say the word 'evil'. Like it's a bad thing.

"There's nothing wrong with nice," I defend Mike the electrician, half-heartedly though, because I'm not invested enough in him to care what my boss and mentor thinks of him.

"You're young and beautiful. You're in the prime of your life. Please don't settle for *nice*."

We're sitting in the salon, taking advantage of the Saturday afternoon lull between appointments, discussing my date from the night before, which, as mentioned, had been…fine.

"He turned up, he was on time, he wasn't drunk and he didn't bring his mum. I'd say the night was a success."

Her mouth twists in disgust. "You need higher standards."

"When you've been on as many bad dates as I have, just common decency is a win."

She pats my leg. "You've had some pretty bad luck. Your friends are terrible matchmakers."

"Try telling them that," I grumble into my much-needed cup of tea. "They won't let up; they're convinced they have the perfect guy for me." Big quotation marks around the word 'perfect'.

"So, was there chemistry? Any steamy kisses that can make up for his...niceness?" She begins sweeping the salon floor to prepare for her next customer, and I follow suit. My last appointment had cancelled, which means I'm technically done for the day and once my station is sorted, I'm hoping to leave early. A night in on the couch with my friends from Stars Hollow is calling my name.

"There were no kisses, steamy or otherwise." I fan my face, which is heating at the thought of the almost kiss that has been floating in my mind for the last twenty-four hours. "He may have been decent, handsome even, but there wasn't a single part of me that wanted his lips on mine."

Andrea purses her lips. "You can't force chemistry. It's there or it isn't." The salon door opens. "Speaking of chemistry..."

My head jolts towards our latest customer, and I'm floored by who is standing there. It's the man who's been consuming all my thoughts, appearing like I'd conjured him up out of my sheer will alone.

"Jake!" Andrea rushes to greet him like he's a long-lost friend.

"Oh, hi." Jake looks startled. "You're Andrea, right?"

My friend beams at him while my heart bangs about in my chest. *Why is such a simple thing, like remembering the name of someone important to me, so impactful?*

"Are you here for Amelia?" Andrea asks this with a bucket-load of innuendo in her voice.

I groan. "Drea!"

He looks between us, bemused. "Um, I came for a haircut?" His voice rises at the end, like it's a question. Like he's not exactly sure why he's here at all.

"Wonderful. Millie's appointment has cancelled, and she has time now." They both turn to look at me. I remain frozen in place. "Don't you?"

My mind whirls with the implications of this. A haircut will mean touching him. Touching his beautiful, lush head of hair. Standing close to him. Breathing him in. I'm not strong enough, not with the almost kiss of yesterday lingering between us. "Ummm." *Brilliant response, Amelia.*

"I should've made an appointment." Jake's voice sounds apologetic and disappointed, and this makes up my mind.

"No, it's fine," I say, earning a flash of his dimple. "I have time."

"Wonderful." Andrea claps and I shoot her what I hope is a warning glance. *Calm down*, I tell her telepathically. *It's just a haircut.*

I motion Jake into my chair and then turn away to wash my hands. And re-group. I can do this. It's what I do all day, every day. It's just hair.

Thick, dark, luscious hair, the devil in my ear whispers. Sounding an awful lot like Andrea.

"So, what are you wanting done today?" I stand behind Jake, focusing on the back of his head to avoid looking at his green eyes in the mirror.

"A trim?" Again, it seems like he hadn't given any thought to this haircut, like he'd just ended up here as an afterthought.

Tilting his head from side to side to get a better idea of how much I can take off, I secretly love the unfettered access I now have to just look at him.

"I can cut a bit off from the top yand then neaten up the sides?" I offer this because really, he doesn't need a haircut. His hair is as perfect as the rest of him.

"Sounds good." He catches my gaze in the mirror and I'm captivated. Unable to breathe while he's looking at me like that.

"You usually start with washing the hair," Andrea sing-songs from the other side of the salon, her face alive with mischief.

I clear my throat, my cheeks flaming red in my reflection. "Right, yes. Come with me."

He follows close behind me, so close I forget how to walk. *It's one foot in front of the other, right?*

"Are you OK?" Jake asks as he take a seat in one of our famous massage chairs.

Am I OK? I had been OK until he'd brushed his lips oh-so-close to mine. And since then, my world has been slightly off-kilter.

"Fine, just a bit tired."

He sits down, taking off his glasses (*those glasses!*) and tucking them into his top pocket before leaning back in the chair and closing his eyes.

"Tired?" he asks as I turn the water on, checking the temperature before turning the hose on the top of his head. "Late night?"

He opens one eye briefly, piercing me with a look that is as loaded as his question.

"Hmmm, not too late." I know what he's asking without asking, and part of me wants to make him wait. To make him suffer as payback for the almost kiss.

"So, your date went well?" he asks finally, through clenched teeth.

I don't answer, instead getting to work washing his hair, allowing myself the indulgence to run my fingers through its thickness, massaging his scalp as I go.

"Oh my God," he moans, a sound that I feel all the way through my body. "That feels amazing."

My fingers tingle and a shiver takes over my body. I shouldn't be enjoying this as much as I am. It's just hair-washing. *Why does it feel like more?*

"Don't stop," he sighs as I turn the water off, making me want to turn it back on again.

"The washing portion of the haircut is done," I tell him, my laugh breathless and strained.

He opens his eyes, staring straight into mine. "Shame."

With wobbly legs, I guide him back to his seat, turning away to gather my supplies and my wits.

"So, just a little off the top?" My voice is as wobbly as my legs.

"Sounds good." Jake's voice is also unsteady.

Right, what now?

"Scissors," Andrea whispers to me, smiling kindly.

"Yes." Flustered, I pick up the scissors and running my fingers through his hair again, I show him how much I'm going to cut off.

"OK?"

His eyes, greener without the lenses of his sexy glasses, lock with mine in the mirror. "OK."

I wrench my gaze away from his, focussing on the job at hand. The sooner I finish, the sooner he'll be gone and I can pull myself together. I've been in Jake's presence many times before and never felt like this, like I'm a magnet and he's a giant piece of metal, drawing me in and holding me there.

"Just tilt your head forward." I get to work on the back of his head, straightening his hairline at the base of his skull, blowing a few stray hairs out of the way to get it perfect.

"You're killing me, Millie." His voice is low and strained.

I stop what I'm doing, looking in the mirror to see his jaw clenched tight, his lips in a straight line.

"Should I stop?" I say this as I run my fingers through the strands at the top of his head to shake out any loose ends, earning another strangled groan from the man in front of me.

"Don't ever stop," he replies, so softly I think I may have imagined it.

I shake out my hands to stop them trembling—that really doesn't help when working with scissors—and spin his chair around to work on the front of his hair. Standing between his legs, I get down low to check that what I've cut is even on both sides.

"What are you doing?" His lips are close to mine and I can't find the will to move away.

"Checking that it's perfect," I whisper back, my eyes on his hair, refusing to look anywhere else.

"Hmmm," he mumbles back, his hands now on my hips, pulling me closer into him.

"Jake," I say as a warning, but it comes out like a plea.

"Amelia." His hands squeeze my hips and my eyes follow suit, closing tightly, trying to gain some composure.

We stand in this state of suspended animation, faces almost touching, his hands on me, and wait. For something to happen. For someone to make the next move.

Andrea, it turns out, is that someone. The blasting of the hairdryer, two seats over, snaps us both back to reality. I straighten up while Jake's hands slip away, clenching as they go.
"I'll just put some product in, and you'll be good to go." Avoiding looking at him, I stumble over to the display cabinet and grab the first thing I see. *Pomade? That'll do.*

Running it through his hair as quickly as possible, touching as little of him as I can, I blast the hair dryer—on the cold setting— over his head, surreptitiously running the cool air over my body as well, before declaring my job done.
Finally. Thankfully.

"All done."

He puts his glasses back on and inspects my work. "Best haircut I've ever had." He smiles at me in the mirror and I can't help but smile back.

"Thank you."

I remove the towel from around his neck, swiping off a few remaining strands and earning a shudder from him in response.

"Can you book me in for another cut?" he asks as he hands over his credit card. "Next week?"

I laugh at his hopeful expression. "Let's give your hair a chance to grow before we cut it again."

His face drops, looking crestfallen and oh-so-charming. "OK, the week after then."

I pencil him in for the same time next month, much to his chagrin, and then push him towards the front door.

"It's time for us to close up now, Jake," I tell him, trying to keep my tone firm but struggling. He looks so reluctant to leave.

"Oh, OK." He looks around at the now-empty salon. "I guess I'll see you soon?" He lingers by the door, his gaze intent on me.

"Yes. Soon," I agree, though I can't think of a reason I'd be seeing him soon. Other than that I really want to.

"Bye, Andrea," he says to my friend, who's been watching this all unfold with a grin.

"It's nice seeing you, Jake. Don't be a stranger."

He gives a small salute, lingering in front of me like he wants to say something. But then doesn't.

"Bye, Millie."

I close the door behind him, waiting for him to be out of sight before leaning against it with a sigh. *That was...something.*

"I think I need a cigarette."

My head snaps up to look at Andrea, whose grin has grown to cartoonish proportions.

"What?" She doesn't smoke.

"Watching the two of you." She fans her hand dramatically. "That was hot. H. O. T. Hot."

I throw a towel at her. "Shut up!"

"Honey," she says, her voice serious now. "If you want chemistry…" She points at the door. "Well, *that* was combustible."

I don't reply, because I can't argue with her. What just happened with Jake was the steamiest thing to happen to me in a long time. Perhaps, ever. And we didn't even kiss.

"Drea," I whine. "What am I going to do?"

She hugs me. "Your heart knows what it wants, Millie. You just need to be brave enough to listen to it."

And with that wonderful piece of useful but scary advice, she turns on the music and starts the final clean-down of the day. Leaving me in a puddle of indecision. And mess.

She's right. My heart knows what it wants, it's just the rest of me that is too terrified to reach out and take it. Too damaged by my past to believe I could ever have something real with someone as special as Jake.

So, I'm stuck.

I have no idea where to go from here.

To a gala dinner. Apparently, that's where I'm going from here.

This is according to Bella, who is forcing me to get all dressed up and attend a fancy charity ball when all I want to do is curl *into* a ball and shut out the world.

It's been a week since the sexiest haircut of all time, a term coined by Andrea and now adopted by my friends, and apart from a few casual text messages and funny memes from Jake, it has been wholly uneventful. No random run-ins at the café or salon. No flirty banter or inquiries about my dating experience. No anything, really. And it's maddening.

"What does he want from me?" I ask Callie the Cactus, hoping for some sort of clarity. Some way to move forward.

When she gives me nothing, because fair, she's a plant, I pick up my phone to text Bella that I'm not going tonight. I've had enough peopling for the week; I need to recharge my battery. Munching on a handful of Tiny Teddies, I'm typing a long, very detailed explanation of why I won't be attending the fancy gala ball, even though it's for charity and probably a good place to meet a man (her words, not mine) when my phone rings.

It's my mum.

"Hi Mum." I keep the groan out of my voice, but really, I don't have the energy for this conversation right now.

"Amelia," she says, sounding ready to launch into a whine or a rant, "you haven't been over to visit in a while."

So, she's settled on a guilt trip this time instead.

"Sorry, Mum." I put the right amount of contrition in my voice, hoping this will stem the tide of her displeasure. "I've been really busy."

"I know you have a full life without needing me in it." I wince at the mum-guilt she's dripping all over me. "But you know this time of year is difficult for me."

Every year, like clockwork, as soon as the Christmas decorations go up in shopping centres and on street lamps, my mum's mood descends with it. Any celebration that reminds her of what she once had, what my dad now has with someone else, another family, sends her spiralling downhill into depression. Most years, she drags me along with her. *Maybe it's time to change this pattern?*

"Sorry," I repeat, not having anything more to add. I am sorry to have neglected her, but sometimes being around her energy takes me weeks to get over. And I don't have it in me to wade through that at the moment.

"Have you heard from him?" There's no mistaking who she's talking about. Her voice changes whenever she speaks about my dad, taking on a bitter quality before the sadness reclaims her. She never got over him leaving her the way he did. I'm not sure she even tried.

"No, Mum," I tell her huffily. I have no relationship with my dad and she knows it. Apart from the obligatory birthday card he sends every year, I haven't had any meaningful contact with him since he left us eleven years ago.

"I heard his wife is pregnant again." Mum never gives his wife the courtesy of calling her by her name. She'll forever be the 'other woman'.

"That's nice." I keep all emotion out of my voice, walking a fine line here with my mum. If I sound happy for him, she'll blow up. If I sound overly upset, she'll take it personally. It's hard work, these conversations.

"He never had time for his family when you were growing up. Now he's happily popping out baby after baby." What she's saying is true—she did the bulk of the child-raising with me—but the bitterness in her voice reinforces the feeling that I was a burden to her. To them both. Especially now that my dad seems to be a doting father to the two, almost three, step-sisters I've never met.

"Maybe he's changed?"

"That man will never change. I just feel sorry for that woman. What he did to me—to us—he'll do to her too." My mum continues ranting, and I attempt to tune her out. It's best to just let her say what she needs to say, but as her anger and her hatred wash over me through the phone, I can clearly see now how much of this attitude towards men and relationships has seeped into me and my ability to be in a healthy one. The sentences "married to his job," "men are never faithful" and "all men are the same, they'll hurt you in the end," echo through my brain, and I realise they've always been there, bouncing around while I've been navigating my way through the dating scene.

And like a lightbulb going off in my head, I see that this is why I've been doggedly picking the wrong men for so long. Because it's been ingrained in me that all relationships are doomed to fail because all men are doomed to fail us. The blinding clarity of this as the underlying cause of all my relationship angst leaves me breathless.

"Anyway," My mum is wrapping up while my mind spins with revelations. "Make sure you come and see me soon."

"Sure thing, Mum. I'll come by next week."

She makes kissing sounds and hangs up and I stare at the screen, at the half-typed message to Bella. My hands shake as I delete my excuses, now determined to not shut myself away from having a night out with friends. I need to *not* become my mother, to *not* become a person who lets their past define them.

"Callie, I'm off to get ready for the ball." And like Cinderella before me, I'm hoping this may be the night that I meet my Prince Charming. Conveniently forgetting that I've already met him, and he comes with the most delightful, black-rimmed glasses.

"You look sensational."

Bella's gushing praise warms my insides.

Once I'd decided to embrace my night out at the ball, I'd taken a great deal of care getting ready. My hair (now mostly blonde) had been curled into loose waves and then swept up into an elegant-looking braided bun, making sure the purple ends were tucked away to keep the look classy. My silver dress has a deep v in the front and a high slit, the fabric clingy to my body, making the most of my slight curves and my feet are adorned with the most stunning pair of shoes I own. The strap across my toes is clear, so it looks like I'm barefooted, and the heels are covered in sparkly diamantes. In this outfit, I'm the most glamorous version of myself.

"Thanks, Bella. You look beautiful, as always."

My friend grins and spins around to show me the low back of her champagne-coloured gown. With her Mediterranean olive skin tone and her dark hair swept to one side, she looks like a goddess. A fact that isn't lost on her husband, who has been glued to her side the entire time we've been here.

"I was sure you were going to cancel coming tonight," she says, taking a sip of her pink champagne. "In fact, I checked my phone every five minutes, expecting a message from you with some lame excuse for why you wouldn't be here."

My cheeks heat at her very accurate read of my character, knowing that I'd been a few seconds away from doing exactly that. "My mum called."

Her mouth twists down into a frown. Bella knows better than anyone the difficult relationship I have with my mother. "And?"

I huff out a sigh. "And I decided I don't want to be like her." I continue on when I see her puzzled expression. "She's so angry, you know? So bitter, so determined to never trust a man again. I don't want to end up like that."

"Oh honey, you won't." Bella runs her hand down my arm while Daniel nods along. "You haven't shut yourself away from relationships. In fact, you're the opposite. You give everyone a chance."

"Yes, usually the wrong 'everyone'. And that's the problem. I've been choosing men that would inevitably fail me. And I need to stop."

"You won't hear an argument from me," she chuckles. "You've chosen some real stinkers in the past."

"And it's time to break the pattern!"

Her face lights up like a Christmas tree. "Does that mean…?"

I put my hand up to stop her, dimming her light. "No more dating plan."

"Hmmph." She lets out a disgruntled sound that has Daniel tucking her under his chin and kissing her on the nose.
Ugh. They're so darn cute.

"How about just one more?" Daniel asks, shocking us all. Since when did he let himself get dragged into our shenanigans?

"What are you talking about?" Bella asks her husband, looking up at him with curiosity.

"My mate Joe is here tonight and I know he'd love to meet Amelia."

"Joe?" Bella squeals at the top of her lungs, causing heads to turn to see who was making such a racket. "Joe?" she repeats in a softer voice.

"Hang on," I butt in. "I don't want another set-up."

"But Joe is perfect! I can't believe I didn't think of him before." Bella's words are racing together, making her sound like a chattering monkey in her excitement.

"It's because you were doing the whole ABC thing," Daniel reminds her in a dry voice. "And he's a firefighter."

Bella turns to me and my stomach drops at the look on her face. It's like all her stars have aligned and every one of our problems has been solved. Right here and now. At this gala dinner.

"That's right, he *is* a firefighter. And we just so happen to be up to the letter...F!"

I guzzle down the rest of the champagne in my glass and grab another one from a tray that's floating by me. "I told you, Bella. No more dating plan."

"But that's the beauty of this. It's not in the plan, it's just...meant to be."

I scoff at her dreamy expression and shake my head. "Not going to happen."

"But..."

"No, Bella. No more set ups."

"What if it's not a set up?" Daniel asks. "What if you are both just at the same place at the same time? And he just was walking up right as we speak?"

The two of them have their attention glued to something behind me, and I search frantically for a way to get out of this. I simply cannot deal with another random set up that is bound to go horribly wrong.

"Daniel."

I turn slightly at the gruff voice from directly behind me...to find a very attractive man in a tuxedo, smiling brightly at the three of us.

"Joe!" Daniel thumps his friend on the back. A manly greeting. "Good to see you. You remember my wife, Bella? And this is her friend, Amelia."

Joe smiles at Bella before turning his dark brown eyes on me. Objectively speaking, this Joe character is hot. Like stupid hot. A man-mountain, stacked with muscles and wavey hair and a charming grin. And it's making me feel...nothing.

"Hi." I give him a small wave, earning a wide grin in response.

"Nice to meet you."

From the corner of my eye, I see Bella nudging Daniel away and I vow to kill her at the next available opportunity. She's so determined to play matchmaker; she's forgotten her role as best friend. As in, don't leave me to deal with another strange man who will inevitably end up a dud, best friend.

"I've heard a lot about you," Joe tells me, swirling the ice around in the glass he's holding.

That can't be good.

"You have?"

"Daniel has mentioned you a few times. I'd been hoping to meet you one day."

The bashful look on his face has me melting, just a little, and I stop looking for a way out of this conversation. "What's he be saying?" I'm suspicious.

"Only good things," he hastens to reassure me. "And just that he thought we should meet one day..." He trails off, rubbing his hand on the back of his neck.

"Well, that's nice." I'm stumped what to say next. This gorgeous man is looking at me like I'm a slice of bread and he's been starving, and yet I'm struggling to find any enthusiasm for this conversation.

"Amelia? Is that you?"

Hoorah, someone to get me out of this!

I turn swiftly to see which one of my friends is calling my name and is ultimately going to be my new favourite friend when I see it. *Him.* The owner of the voice.

"Mike?" It's Mike the electrician. Otherwise known as the perfectly nice man I'd gone on a perfectly fine date with a week ago and then never called back.

"It *is* you!" He beams, like he's struck gold and I can do nothing except flounder.

"Uh, hi?"

"I didn't know you'd be here." He kisses me on the cheek, taking my hand and squeezing it in his.

Now I'm wishing I wasn't here.

"Um, yes. I'm here with Bella and Daniel…and…" I turn back to where Joe is watching this all unfold. "And this is Joe."

Joe and Mike nod at each other, and their chests puff in unison as they size each other up.

What to do now?

"How do you two know each other?" Mike asks Joe as my temples throb. There are too many men to keep track of here.

"We just met. You two?" Joe asks, indicating between us.

"We went out."

"Huh."

"Yes," I add uselessly. "That's right."

Silence descends over our awkward threesome. *Where the hell is Bella when I need her?*

"Amelia, is that you?"

Now what?

My stomach now down in my fancy shoes; I turn to see who is calling my name.

NO!

"Jake. Hi."

How is this my life?

CHAPTER 12

Jake

I HADN'T WANTED TO COME tonight. In fact, I'd told Steven no several times over the course of the week and each time he'd vetoed my objections.

"You're becoming too much of a hermit. It's not good for you."

"I've got a lot on my mind," I'd responded.

"You only got one thing on your mind. One tiny woman who is consuming all of your thoughts and, as your best friend, I've got to get you help."

"In the form of a ball?" I'd asked dryly.

"Exactly."

And it had gone back and forth like this for five full days. Five days where I'd been determined to not get dressed up in this uncomfortable suit and bowtie and instead indulge in the latest series of *Alone: The Australian Wilderness*. But he'd pushed and prodded, reminding me I need to get out and meet people. That *Amelia* is out and meeting people. And that I can't sit around and wait for her to be ready for me.

So here I am, in an effort to get over the woman who'd captured my heart, standing in front of her. While she stands in front of not one, but two men. Both vying for her attention.

This is not happening.

And she looks incredible. Like a vision in her glittery dress, sparkling bright, drawing all the light in the room onto her. Her shiny hair is swept up and away from her face, exposing her long, creamy neck, and between the deep V of her gown and the high split, my eyes can't decide where to land. Except that they can. On her big, brown, velvety eyes, which are currently looking at me with regret. Or remorse? Or something other than the adoration I know is in mine when I look at her.

Bugger this.

I make myself turn away without responding to her weak greeting, leaving her to her flock of admirers, now determined to find alcohol. And lots of it.

"Is that Amelia?" Steven asks as he plants himself next to me at the bar, where I will remain for the foreseeable future. "What's she doing here?"

I shrug. Torturing me, is my guess. "Don't know."

"Is all of Melbourne here tonight?"

We look around, taking in the swarms of people surrounding us. "Feels like it."

"Still, that's some bad luck. You come out to get away from your thoughts of her, and here she is. The irony."

I glare at him. "Yes, and because I live for irony, I'm thrilled to be caught up in it."

"Calm down, grumpy. I'm just pointing out the obvious."

I pinch the skin between my eyes. "Well, don't. I can see her perfectly well without you pointing it out. I can see her and the men she's with. Men. Plural."

He squints in their direction. "Can we have another two of these? And keep them coming," he says to the bartender, indicating to the whiskey in my hand.

The bartender nods, giving me a sympathetic glance. My misery is on full display tonight.

When his drink arrives, Steven takes a sip and hums in appreciation. I don't blame him; it *is* good whiskey.

After a long silence in which we fully concentrate on appreciating our brews, Steven returns to the topic at hand. "So, what are you going to do about it?"

"Nothing." I stare into my half-finished glass and contemplate having one more before going home. "She's never not with someone else. First my brother"—a sour taste fills my mouth—"then the dating plan, now those two buffoons. She's not available. For me."

He pats my shoulder and wisely chooses not to respond. Because what is there to say? I met Amelia before Robby, before the ABC of men, before those two men standing over there with her now even knew of her existence—and yet despite what I feel when I'm with her, what I feel when I think about her, I just don't think she feels the same. If she did, we'd be here tonight together. And we're not.

"To be fair," Steven speaks up, deciding he's held his tongue long enough, "you've never come out and told her how you feel. You've never even asked her out."

My body rumbles and I clench my fist. "When was I supposed to do that? Before or after she had a relationship with Robby? Or while she was on the date with the biomedical physicist, whatever that is. Even last week, after I almost kissed her, after we had a *moment*, she still went on a date with an electrician. Just because her friends asked her to. Is that the actions of a woman who wants me to ask her out?"

He shakes his head sadly, finishing the rest of his whiskey in one gulp.

"I have to face it, this thing between us, it's all in my head."

"Well, don't look now, but the woman who you believe feels nothing for you is making her way over to see you. And that's not 'nothing' I see written on her face."

The hairs on the back of my neck stand to attention as I feel her before I see her. Steven drifts away and with my stomach in knots, I steel myself to turn around and face her, hoping for a blank expression on my face.

"Hey Jake." Her husky voice has my blank face twitching. Not off to a good start.

"Amelia."

"Did you not see me earlier? I said hello?" Her lower lip, so full and painted a soft pink, trembles and my heart sinks. I've made her sad, and I never want to do it again.

"You seemed busy." I give her a half-smile to lighten the mood. "I didn't want to interrupt."

She grimaces. "I would've welcomed an interruption...from you." Her emphasis on the word *you* propels me closer to her. Against my will.

"Were those guys bothering you?"

"Not in the traditional sense of the word." She shrugs, turning to order herself a glass of champagne. "It was just royally bad timing," she elaborates once she's been served.

"Tell me." I want to know in equal amounts as I don't want to know.

"The tall one, the one that looks like a mountain?"

I laugh at her description. It's spot on. The man had to be carved out of stone. There's no other way to explain it.

"Well," she continues, "he's a friend of Daniel's, who was here tonight and is apparently 'perfect' for me."

I flinch at that word, being used again to describe a man for Amelia. A man who isn't me.

"And the other guy?"

"He's the electrician. The one I went out with last week and never returned his calls."

My breath whooshes out at this titbit of information. The date from last week, the one before the best haircut I'd ever had, was the same man who she didn't call back. Suddenly, I'm loving this conversation.

"And they're both here tonight?"

Her look mirrors my own. Total shock mixed with the horror of it all. "I know, right? What are the chances?"

I indicate for her to look around. "Pretty high, considering most of Melbourne has turned up tonight."

She twirls on her heels, doing a full 360-degree turn before facing me. "Apparently, we run with a pretty popular crowd." Her nose scrunches up in that adorable way as she beams up at me.

"Not me." I smile back at her, tucking a stray piece of her hair behind her ear, stroking the soft skin of her jaw as I go. She shivers and I notice. "Steven dragged me here. He's the popular one."

She laughs again, her sexy, gets-under-my-skin laugh. "If it weren't for Steven, I'd probably never see you."

"You want to see me?" My voice is flirty and I move a step closer to her, all thoughts of moving on and forgetting her clearing out of my head.

She tilts her head, examining me. "Where are your glasses?

Her question throws me and I touch my face, confused for a millisecond. "My glasses?"

"I hardly ever see you out without them," she frowns, looking annoyed.

"I'm wearing contacts. Thought it would look better with the suit."

Her shoulders shrug and her earrings jangle as she shakes her head. Vehemently. "I like your glasses."
That's it, I'm super-gluing them to my face! Anything to keep that look on hers!

"O-K." I draw the word out, my heart thumping in my chest. "Glasses it is."

"Good," she replies. It's sorted. "Now what?"

I wrench my gaze away from her, specifically from that smattering of freckles, so nicely on display across her small nose. "Do you want to dance?"

"Dance?" she mutters the word under her breath, deliberating. "With you?"

I chuckle. "No, with the man mountain and his friend the electrician."

She thumps me on the arm.

"Yes, with me." I'm back to serious now. I *really* want to dance with her.

"OK." Her front teeth bite into her bottom lip. I pick up her hand, guiding her to the dance floor, which is overflowing with couples swaying in time to the crooners on stage.

"I didn't know this ball was going to be this extravagant," she says as we edge our way into the middle of the dancefloor. "I was expecting a DJ, but not this." She points to the three Italian men singing in perfect harmony, accompanied by a full jazz band.

I pull her close to me, my hands settling on her hips like they were always meant to be there. Her arms loop around my neck and I can't help it; I pull her even closer until there's a mere millimetre of space between us. She looks up at me, her heels raising her to my collarbone, the perfect height for me to gaze at her beautiful face up close.

"I love this song," she whispers.

Quieting the ringing in my head, the sound that plays on a loop whenever she's nearby, I listen. "I don't think I know it."

She hums softly under her breath. "It's an old 80s power ballad. My mum and dad loved to listen to these sorts of songs and belt them out at the top of their lungs." She stops, a strange expression crossing her face.

"What is it?" I pull her even closer until we are chest to chest.

"It's just that I have so few memories of my parents together and happy. This one hit me hard." Her hand moves away from my shoulder and rubs the spot above her heart.

"Want to talk about it?"

She shakes her head. "There's not much to talk about. You know my dad used to work a lot. He was away all the time when I was growing up. Until one day, he just didn't come home. That's why this memory is so unsettling; I've only ever remembered the bad times, when there were clearly some good mixed in there."

"That's human nature," I reassure her. "To remember things through a particular lens."

She peers up at me through her long lashes. "Do you do that?"

I think about it. *Do I?* "I guess my life growing up is coloured by the arrival of Robby. I don't really remember a time when I didn't feel responsible for him. When I was the one free to be the little kid, you know?"

"I can see that. Robby would have taken up all the space. He still does."

I laugh, a bitter sound. "My parents had given up having any more kids after trying for years. And then he 'blessed' us with his arrival." *Big* quotation marks around the word blessed. My hands return to her waist like a magnet and I continue. "They were thrilled to have another baby, and even though I was seven and still a kid, I was forced to grow up pretty quickly. To allow them the luxury of babying him without me in the way."

"That's tough." She squeezes my shoulders in sympathy.

"I'd never really thought of it that way, but yeah. It sucked. What's worse is that I'm still that way with Robby. I'm still picking up his pieces."

Amelia freezes under my hands and I shake her. "Do not even go there. I'm not talking about you. You are the best thing that Robby ever brought into my life."

Her smile is wide and blinding, and I don't care that I may have said too much. Because it's true: every single mess Robby has made that I've had to clean up is worth the time I now get to spend with her.

"Have you heard from him? How's the band going?" She laughs as she asks this.

"He's gone so quiet that my mum's been calling me in a panic, worried about her baby boy. You remember how overprotective she is of him."

She nods. "Oh, I remember. I don't think she ever thought I was good enough for Robby."

I grunt, feeling this like a blow. How ridiculous; Robby wasn't worthy of breathing the same air as Amelia. "Don't take it personally. Mum wants him to find a woman who will look after him the way we all have."

"I could've done that," she argues.

"But why would you want to?"

She nibbles on her lip, blowing out a deep breath. "I can't even keep a plant alive. I'm not sure I would've been able to keep Robby alive long-term."

"Nor should you have to. A partnership goes both ways. I'm pretty sure Robby wasn't bringing anything to the table."

Amelia remains silent, perhaps not wanting to badmouth my brother to me, but her expression reveals all of her inner thoughts. She agrees with everything I've said.

"Either way, I don't think I'm that type of woman. You know, the nurturing kind?"

I gape at her. *Is she crazy?* "Um, Amelia, what gave you that impression?"

Her head tilts, and she stares up at me. Unspeaking.

"I watched you take care of Robby, when he never returned the favour. I watch you look after your friends. I watch you be kind to all these men you're dating." The word men, plural, is wrenched out of me. "You don't see it, but you are nurturing and caring and considerate. And you'd make a wonderful partner, to someone who deserves you."

She gazes at me, still not saying anything, and sweat drips down my back. Lucky I'm wearing a dark suit or else we'd be in a sweat-patch situation pretty soon.

"You really think so?" she finally asks, softly. "That's how you see me?"

I snort. I can't help it. "That's how everyone but you see you."

Her brown eyes take on a liquid quality and I wonder if I've upset her. By once again saying too much. *Maybe you should keep your big mouth shut, Jake!*

"Thank you." She whispers these two words, a wealth of sincerity behind them. "I mean it, thank you."

We sway together, pressed close, and I give in. My cheek rests on top of her silky hair and I feel it: that this is where I'm supposed to be. And that it's time to do something about it.

"Do you want to get another drink?" I ask as the music stops and I have to pull away from her. Reluctantly.

She looks over my shoulder and panic dances across her face.

"Uh oh."

I turn to see what she's looking at, and there, standing a few metres away from us, are the man mountain and the electrician. Still together, eagerly scouring the room. I only need one guess to figure out what—who—they're looking for.

"Hide me!" Amelia jumps behind me, her small frame completely hidden as she tucks herself close to my back.

"Gladly," I mutter, secretly thrilled that not only is she choosing to hide from these two men but that she's involving me in the shenanigans.

"How do you want to play this?" I ask over my shoulder through clenched teeth, like we're together on a secret mission again.

She flashes me a smile, clearly thinking back to the escape room as well.

"Is there any way we can back away, slowly, out of the room? With you keeping me out of their sight?"

The whole thing is absurd, but I'm not hating the way she's pressing her body against mine.

"Let's take small steps backwards. The exit is just over there." I tilt my head towards the front door and I feel her nod against me.

"You keep watch."

"Yes, mam."

She giggles. I love it.

"Ready?"

I put my arm around her, securing her close to me, and in unison, we take slow measured steps towards the exit. Not looking ridiculous at all.

"How did I let you get me in this situation?" I ask, smiling at the people watching us with bemused expressions on their faces.

"It's all Bella's fault," she grumbles, now putting her arm around my front and holding on. Wonderful.

"Remind me to thank her later," I mutter, revelling in the feel of *her* holding on to *me*.

"What?"

"Nothing. Are we almost there yet?"

So far, we'd drawn the attention of about half the people in the room, but luckily not that of the two men she's running away from.

"Just a couple more steps."

I feel the cooler night air on my back and know we are close to mission success. A shame really; I could've done with a few more minutes of Amelia this close to me. Of Amelia needing me, if only to help her run away from her other potential suitors.

"We did it!" She lets go only to step in front of me, looping her arms around my neck and hugging me, from the front this time. "Thank you!"

Her voice, that husky voice, is higher with happiness and relief, and I squeeze her back. Breathing her in.

"You're welcome."

We smile at each other.

"Now what?" I echo her earlier words back to her when the silence has stretched on a smidge too long and I worry she may leave me too.

She looks up at the entrance of the Brighton Beach Club, where this fancy shin-dig is being held, and then out at the stretch of coastline in front of us, the ocean glimmering like a beacon in the full-moon light. A more romantic setting I've yet to see.

"Well, I don't want to go back in there." She points behind her with her thumb. "Do you want to go for a walk on the beach?"

More than you'll ever know.

"Sounds good." I keep my voice even, reaching out to take her hand. She lets me and together we walk down the ten steps that lead to the sand.

"Hang on," she drops my hand—*grrr!*—bending over to take off her shoes. "There, that's better."

With her shoes in one hand, she picks up mine again—*yes!*—and leads me down to the deserted beach. And I follow her, because that's a given in my life.

Wherever Amelia is, that's where I want to be.

CHAPTER 13

Amelia

HE HOLDS MY HAND LIKE it's the most natural thing in the world. And I'm concluding that it feels this way because it is. Being with Jake is as easy as breathing; easier, sometimes.

Is it time to do something about the way I feel about him? My heart thumps at the thought.

"It's nice out here," Jake says, filling the comfortable silence between us.

I watch the waves crashing on the shore, feel the soft sand underfoot, shiver at the slight breeze that brushes against us. It's more than nice, it's perfect. Like this moonlit walk on the beach was crafted especially for us, for us to finally speak our truth to each other.

"Here." Jake takes off his jacket and drapes it over my shoulders. "You're cold."

I pull the lapels of his suit jacket together, subtly sniffing as I do. *Yummy, it smells like Jake. My new favourite smell.*

"Thanks," I mutter, avoiding his eyes, which I can feel peering at me.

We continue walking without a destination, my thoughts still a jumbled mess in my head. Before tonight, my reservations about Jake and how to process what I feel for him were still up in the air, but after that dance, after the words he said to me, after the way he made me feel, well, none of my reasons for not being with him seem…well, reasonable, anymore.

My stomach swirls.

"Do you think we should talk?" I look up at him, our gazes colliding. He's giving me a soft look; a hopeful look and my heart takes off racing again at the sight of it.

"Do you want to sit?"

Without consideration for the fabric of my fanciest dress or what the sand may do to it, I sink down, grateful to be giving my shaky legs a break.

"So," he blows out a big breath. "What do you want to talk about?"

I stare at him, at his deep green eyes, which seem to see me better than anybody ever has, and my tongue promptly ties itself into a knot.

"My mind is a little muddled." I tap my forehead and roll my eyes at my absurdity. "Can we just sit for a bit?"

He picks up my hand again—I love holding his hand so much—and says nothing. His thumb draws lazy circles over the back of mine and I'm catapulted back in time. To a situation not unlike this, when he'd happily offered me quiet comfort.

I'd been dating Robby for only a short while—less than two months—and we'd gotten into a fight. It had probably been over Robby being selfish or carelessly cruel. I'd stormed out of his room in a huff, stumbling into his big brother. The one I'd been avoiding seeing.

"Are you OK?" he asked me, his voice deeper with concern.

I shrugged. "Not really."

His jaw had clenched, and he glared in the direction of Robby's room. "What did he do this time?"

I smiled at him, at his assumption that the fight had to be Robby's fault. That he hadn't even considered it could have been mine.

"He's just being Robby." I said this, knowing that if anyone was to understand how difficult life with Robby could be, it would be his brother. Jake grunted under his breath and disappeared into the kitchen, while I flopped down onto the couch.

"You need more paintings on your walls," I called out, unreasonably annoyed at the lack of any art or pictures in their otherwise comfortable house. Instead, there was just a large flat-screen TV and a whole heap of boy video game equipment.

"I'll get right on it," he said with a wry smile, putting a cup of tea in front of me. Made just how I liked it.

"Are you going back in there? To sort things out?" He gave me a curiously blank look, and I shook my head. No way was I going to make up with Robby any time soon.

"Want to watch TV out here then?"

I was shocked he offered to hang out with me, being more accustomed to him doing rapid about turns and leaving the room whenever I was around.

"Sounds good." I handed him the remote, as I was used to doing with Robby, frowning when he returned it to me.

"You choose."

Two simple words. A flood of warmth filled me upon hearing them, and I laughed at his appalled expression when I pressed play on the pilot episode of Gilmore Girls. And yet, he stayed sitting next to me, his mere presence offering comfort, and watched two full episodes.

"Why do they have to talk so fast?" he asked with a baffled expression as he tried to keep up with the rapid-fire dialogue. "And Rory is too young to drink so much coffee."

I poked him for being such an "old stick-in-the-mud" and laughing together, we settled back in to watch one more episode. For three episodes we sat close on the couch, not touching, but near enough for me to feel the warmth radiating from his body. And during that time, Robby had not come out of his room. Had not even deigned to look for me. To see if I was OK. Or even still around.

"He doesn't deserve you; you know?" Jake said, reading my mind. Not for the first time.

I sighed. I did know. And I also knew I'd probably do nothing to fix the situation, that Robby, for all his faults, was my guy. The one I'd chosen to be with.

"He's not so bad."

Jake opened his mouth to say something when Robby finally flounced out of his room, coming up short when he saw us together.

"Amelia? You're still here?"

I glared at him, shifting away from Jake and standing up to confront him. Only he didn't give me the chance. Instead, he flung himself on the ground in front of me, gesticulating wildly while he begged—literally begged—for my forgiveness. And me being the idiot that I was, I forgave him. In front of his brother, who had just told me I deserved better.

And he's still telling me this after all this time. Maybe it's time to believe him?

"I'm sorry," I say to him now, though I'm not sure what I'm exactly apologising for. Maybe everything that happened from that first meeting onward, from that first meeting when I should have chosen him?

"For what?" His eyebrows are drawn in confusion and his hand squeezes mine.

"For being such a hot mess that you have to keep picking up the pieces. For being the girl who you constantly need to say nice things to so I don't cry," I say while batting away tears. *I will* not *cry...this time.*

He exhales. Like it pains him to hear me say this. "Amelia, I don't say this so that you won't cry..." He trails off at the look I'm giving him, his beautiful mouth twisting into a wry smile. "OK, I definitely hate seeing you upset. But it's not why I tell you these things. I say it because it's the truth and I desperately want you to believe it. To believe in yourself."

His words floor me. *Has anyone ever spoken to me this way? Instinctively knowing exactly what I need to hear?*

I gather my tattered composure like a cloak around me. "That may well be true, but I'm sorry all the same. For continuing to put you in these situations."

"Don't you know I want to be here for you?" He says the words softly but with so much sincerity that I don't doubt him. I know he's the guy who wouldn't lie to me. Maybe the only guy who wouldn't lie to me.

"I made so many mistakes." I don't tell him what they are, hoping he'll know. Starting with picking his brother that first night.

He nods like he understands, and we fall back into silence.

"Can I ask you something?" His strained voice breaks the quiet surrounding us. I brace myself for his question, knowing what's about to come.

"OK."

"That night we met," he starts and stops.

I turn to look at him, his profile so perfectly silhouetted by the night sky behind him. His jaw is clenched and his eyes are narrowed as he stares straight ahead.

"Yes?" I give him permission to continue.

"Why did you choose to stay with Robby?" There, it's out there. The big, pink, sparkly elephant in the room is finally being addressed. "I mean, I get it, you guys were there to meet, but I thought, maybe incorrectly, that we had a spark, you know, before he turned up."

His vulnerability in admitting this urges me to give it back to him. "We did," I assure him, earning another hand squeeze. "From my end, the sparks were sizzling. I was 100 per cent sure you were there to meet me. That you were my match."

He turns to face me and our eyes lock. *OK, maybe he doesn't always need to wear his glasses.* Unfettered access to his green gaze has my heart ping-ponging around in my chest.

"So, what happened?"

I shrug, embarrassed by my choice that night. "Robby turned up, and I got…confused?"

"Confused?" he repeats my word back to me, slowly.

"I thought, incorrectly it turns out, that I had to trust the algorithm. That the people from the LIB app had picked the perfect guy for me, and that guy was Robby."
Jake snorts, and I let out a giggle. *Boy, was that algorithm wrong.*

"And then Robby said something about you…and I guess I got triggered?"

He looks so alarmed that I scoot in closer to him, linking my arm through his.

"What did he say?"

"He told me you were a workaholic, that you were married to your job, that he was surprised to see you out when all you do is work, work, work. And given my experience with my dad, this had all my alarm bells ringing. Dousing all those lovely sparks."

Jake digests this information and I wait. Thinking back again to that night, to that snap decision that I've forced myself to live with ever since.

"That's all it took? For you to choose Robby?"

I shake my head. "That's all it took in that moment, but I can't deny that I liked your brother. Really liked him, enough to date him for six months. I also can't deny that I was—am—pretty messed up and believed that the type of relationship I had with Robby was normal. Was what I deserved."

His already clenched jaw hardens further and I ache for the pain I feel I'm causing him. But if we're ever going to be anything, he needs to know the truth.

"Robby was who I thought I should be with; he fit my type exactly. He appeared to be fun-loving, spontaneous, a dreamer. And it's what I told myself I wanted. It turns out I've been choosing men who were the complete opposite of my dad." I stop and let out a small laugh. "It should have been obvious to me how I picked these types of men, but apparently I enjoyed having my head deeply buried in the sand."

"We all have issues from our past that shape the way we behave as adults," he says, excusing my behaviour. And I love him for trying.

"It's not just that. I was choosing men the opposite of my dad, true, but I was also dating men who I knew deep down I could never love, so that I'd never be truly hurt when they would inevitably leave me. Turns out I probably need some therapy."

"We could all benefit from therapy," he says, again chiming in with the most perfect comment.

"I think all of this played a part in why…" I trail off, not wanting to say more because it will reveal too much, anxiety at the rawness of this moment swirling through me.

"Why?" he probes, not letting me off the hook this time.

"Why I let you walk away that night. And why I've been going out on all these dates, instead of just letting you in."

I hear his swift intake of breath, turning my head away from him and focussing on the waves lapping at the shore in front of us.

"I started visiting the Love, Lilly café a week after you broke up with Robby," he says after a few minutes of charged silence, his tone now casual, like I hadn't just laid my heart out there for him.

"Oh?" I'm struggling to keep up with this swift turn in the conversation.

"I heard you talk about it with Robby so many times that I thought there may be a good chance I'd see you there."

Ah, now I'm following.

"I went in a few times a week, hoping to catch a glimpse of you. See how you're doing. Just see you."

My face flushes and my heart takes off racing so fast I fear it's about to escape my chest. *He came looking for me?*

"And then you were never there at the same time as me. But by that time, I was hooked…"

"On the brownies?"

We both laugh.

"Yes, the brownies. And the atmosphere. I enjoyed watching Bella and Lilly interact. It made me feel closer to you, as stalker-ish as that may sound."

"Very stalker-ish!"

He pinches my side. "And then when Bella and Lilly opened the gallery next door, I bought several of Bella's paintings, because *someone* had once told me in a huff that I needed to hang some art on my walls."

I flashback to the night of Bella's wedding, when I'd been slouched on his couch, staring at the landscape of the Melbourne skyline hanging on his wall. *That was one of Bella's paintings! No wonder it had looked so familiar.*

"You bought Bella's paintings?"

He nods. "Her work is exceptional."

His praise of my friend's work does little to stop my heart pounding in my chest. *Why must he be so perfect?*

"It is," I agree, not knowing what else to say. We'd both revealed a lot in this conversation, and I don't know where to go from here.

Jake, it seems, does know where he wants this to go. "That night, the night we all met?"

I smile at the use of the word 'all'.

"I'd been at the restaurant for ten minutes waiting for Steven, who is habitually late. He'd forced me to meet him at this 'trendy new place', the sort of place that Robby would love and I would hate, and from the minute I arrived my feet were itching to leave, to get home and work on a brief that needed to be done by the end of the weekend. And then you walked in."

I held my breath, dying to know what he's going to say next.

"It was like there was a spotlight on you. One minute I'd been lost in the document I was reading on my phone, the next my eyes were glued to you. And then my feet that had been wanting to leave were suddenly guiding me to the bar. To where you'd just sat down."

"And you said hi, and I was sure you were my match."

He hums. "Little did I know there was some sort of artificial intelligence who'd already set you up with my brother."

I frown along with him, equally disappointed in this technology fail as he seems to be.

"We can't blame just the supercomputer," I say to lighten the mood and also because it's true. The whole mess is purely my fault.

"I had to watch you with *him*." His voice is pained, tortured, and I lay my head on his shoulder, trying to get closer.

"I'm sorry." I can't say anything else. There's no taking back what had come before this. The only question is whether he wants anything with me moving forward.

"I waited for you," he says in a low voice, his head now resting on mine. "At the café and just in general. I waited for you to get over my brother and then you came to my door looking for him…"

I interrupt him, needing to make my intentions that night crystal clear. "That was to kick his butt."

He chuckles. "I know. But then after that…the whole dating plan…what am I supposed to do with that?"

I lift my head away from his shoulder, turning his face to mine with my forefinger. "I didn't know you wanted to do anything…with any of it. I didn't know."

He is solemn as he stares back at me. "Do you know now?"

My entire body tingles at this question, asked in that deep, deep voice of his. *I do know now, but am I brave enough to do something about it?* The trickle of anxiety turns into a river and I'm drowning in it. If I make a move towards Jake, I'd be risking heartbreak. Real heartbreak.

The weight of this decision forces me back onto the sand behind me, Jake's jacket doing its best to act as a blanket. Jake follows me down, lying next to me, our faces only inches apart.

"Amelia?" He says my name as both a question and a plea, and, my fears subside.

I don't think anymore. I just do.

Leaning over, I close the distance between us, pressing my lips against his. They fit perfectly against him and feel as firm and soft as I'd imagined they would.

How can lips be both firm and soft?

All thoughts leave my brain as Jake takes over, turning the kiss from a gentle exploration of each other to something more, something demanding. Something that feels like the best kiss I'd ever had. As he deepens the kiss, his hands sink into my hair, pulling me closer, closer and I comply, wanting to crawl under his skin and never leave.

"I've wanted to do that for so long," he mumbles as we come up for air, our lips swollen from the intensity of that kiss. "For so long."

I don't answer him, instead pulling his face back to mine, determined to get lost in the wonder of his kisses again. Forever this time. He rolls me over so I'm lying on my back and hovers over me, raining gentle kisses all over my face, his lips velvety soft on my eyelids, my nose, my lips, before moving to my cheeks, brushing his lips over them, once, twice, three times.

"I've wanted to kiss your freckles from the minute I met you," he says, his voice low and gravelly, stealing my breath away. "Every single one of them."

I melt at this. At the thought of him delighting in the freckles I painstakingly cover up every morning.

This. Being with Jake like this. I could do this forever.

Panic hits and I struggle to breathe.

What am I doing? Should I be melting into Jake? The one man with the power to hurt me should he choose to?

My head spins as the implications of what we've just done sinks in, even though I wanted to do it with every fibre of my being, and I sit up, pushing him away both literally and metaphorically.

"Amelia?" Jake looks at me, with a patient, almost resigned expression.

"I need a minute." My voice is breathless, like I'd just run a marathon. My heart certainly feels like I had, what with all the blood pumping that went along with that kiss.

"Take a minute. Take two, but please don't shut me out." He's reading my mind and can see that I'm scrambling. Away from him, it would seem.

"I think we should go back." His face falls. "Bella will be looking for me." This is true, but it was also true ten minutes ago, twenty minutes ago, without me giving her one single thought.

"OK." His voice is now devoid of any emotion. He stands up and wipes the sand off his pants. Leaning over, he offers me his hand, his big strong solid hand that seems to always be there to hold me steady. To help me up. To keep me up.

"Thanks." I take his hand and with some trouble, stand up next to him, brushing the sand out of my hair, my face, my dress, his jacket. I just know I'll be finding sand in places for days to come. "Let's go?"

He's no longer looking at me. His hand, which was holding mine, is now tucked into his pocket. With a muscle twitching in his cheek, he nods. Once. "Let's go."

The silence between us on the walk back to the Brighton Beach Club is no longer comfortable but instead is fraught with all the things I wish I could say. If my mind would just unjumble itself. I'm reeling from that kiss and all the emotion that came with it and I know I'm too emotionally stunted to put any coherent words together right now.

"I'm sorry," I say again. *For what, the hundredth time?*

"It's OK." His voice is dull, so unlike the voice I'm used to, the one that feels like a caress.

We walk side by side but now with a crater of unspoken words between us, up the stairs leading to the ballroom. When we get to the doors, I put my hand on his arm to stop him from walking in ahead of me. I need to fix this.

"I wanted that to happen!" The words burst out of me, earning me a quick flash of his dimple. "I need you to know that."

His gaze softens on me. "OK."

"OK?"

He nods.

"I'm going to go find Bella." I tilt my head towards the doors beside us. "But we'll talk soon?"

When my mind is less frazzled by your masterful kisses, I think but don't share.

"Yes, let's talk soon."

I stare up at him, memorising his face in this moment, the moment after we'd kissed for the first time. After we'd said so much. His lips are pink and rosy and slightly swollen—*I did that*, my inner voice whispers smugly—and his hair is tousled, the work of my fingers. He's delightfully mussed, and I wish I wasn't walking away from him. I wish I was walking away *with* him.

"OK, bye." My stupid brain says these words while my dumb hands give him a wave and my loser legs walk me away from him. *Why-oh-why am I not still out there kissing him? And how am I going to fix myself so I can make sure this all works out in the end?*

"There you are!" Bella huffs, appearing from nowhere to suddenly be standing next to me. "Where have you been?"

I touch my fingers to my also swollen lips and glance back to where Jake is no longer standing. "Oh, Bella. I think I messed up. Royally messed up."

She gives me a concerned look, taking the hand that belongs to Jake and squeezing it. "Whatever it is, we can handle it."

I look into her earnest face and want to believe her. But then I picture the sadness in Jake's and I wonder if there's any way to solve this.

"Let's go back to my place and talk this out. We'll come up with a plan. You'll see."

Another plan. I groan internally.

"This plan needs to be better than your last."

I must sound as bad as I feel, because she launches herself at me, hugging me tightly and whispering in my ear, "Whatever it is, we can make it better."

Returning her hug, I hope, on all the shooting stars, that she's right. That we find a way to sort out all my tangled emotions. And that in doing this, we find me a way back to Jake.

CHAPTER 14

Amelia

"YOU'RE KILLING ME!" BELLA SAYS through a mouthful of her breakfast muffin. "I need to know what happened last night."

It's been over twelve hours since the kiss to top all other kisses and I'm still processing. After vowing to come up with a plan to 'fix' everything, Bella had found Daniel and the three of us had left the ball (Daniel was happy to not have to be out socialising for one minute longer than needed). Once we'd returned to their house, Bella insisted I stay with them for the night, and I'd crashed in their spare room, the weight of too many emotions lulling me into a coma.

And now it's morning. Bella turned up in my room after the sun had barely made an appearance, a cup of tea in one hand, a plate of breakfast muffins in the other.

"I don't know where to start," I tell her, pushing away the food, all thoughts of eating making my stomach churn.

"When I left you, you were talking with Joe. When you disappeared, I was blissfully thinking the two of you may have hit it

off and you'd gone somewhere to get to know each other better."
She wiggles her eyebrows at me and I laugh. Like she knew I
would.

"Joe was…nice"—I cringe at the use of that word again—"but
then Mike turned up—"

"—No!" she gasps, crumbs spraying from her mouth. "Mike
the electrician, Mike?"

Her eyes are wide as saucers.

"Yes, that Mike. So, I'm introducing the two of them…"

"How did that go?" she interrupts again, gesturing with her
hands for me to tell the story faster.

"It was awkward and then…"

"What?" she screeches.

"Jake turned up."

She gapes at me. "He did *not.*"

"He did. I said hi, he looked at me and the two men, and he
turned and walked away."

"Hummph." Her muffin finished, Bella moves to sit next to me
in bed, her back against the headboard. "So, this is what we need
to fix?"

If only it were that simple.

"No." Despite my stomach telling me not to, I nibble on a
muffin. The smell of bacon and cheese too tempting to resist. "I
smoothed that over. We ended up chatting and then we danced."

In my mind I'm back in his arms, floating around the dancefloor, completely safe with his arms around me.

"I take it from that dreamy look on your face that the dance
was something special."

My cheeks heat and I wave my hands in front of them. *If this is
how I react to telling her about the dance, how am I going to get through
describing that kiss?*

"It was," I confirm. "And then we somehow found ourselves outside…" I decide to leave out the part where I hid from both of the men she'd been attempting to set me up with. Save myself that lecture. "And we went for a walk on the beach…"

"Hold up,"—her pointy elbow jabs me in the ribs—"you went for a moonlit walk on the beach *with Jake?*"

I nod and she squeals again, her face alight with excitement. "Tell me *everything.*"

With a deep breath, I detail everything that happened, from the honest conversation about that first night we met, to his feelings about me with his brother, to his visits to the café, hoping to see me.

"I knew that's what he was doing!" I give her a doubtful look. "Well, obviously not at first. But that day you were both there at the same time? I knew from the way he watched you that he came there for you."

"Actually, I think he came for the brownies."

She grins. "Why can't it be both?"

We sit in silence for a minute, while I let her digest all this new information. I can hardly believe all that was said between us, so she must be feeling a similar sort of way.

"None of this is a surprise to me." *OK, maybe not.* "When the two of you are together, you both have sparks flying off you."

There's that word again. Sparks.

"We kissed." I blurt it out, now physically unable to hold the information in.

She twinkles at me. "How was it?"
Mind-blowing, earth-shattering, life-changing.

"It was amazing."

She puts her arm around my shoulder. "So why do you sound so depressed about it?"

I sink into her, accepting the comfort she's offering. "I'm scared."

There. I'd said it. The reason I'd bolted away from Jake last night. I'm completely terrified of the way I feel about him. The way I feel when I'm with him. The way I desperately want him to feel about me.

"That's normal."

I can't help the snort that slips out from me. "Bella, I love you, but nothing about me is normal."

She huffs, a supremely annoyed huff. "Don't you remember how hard Daniel fought against his feelings for me? And how scared I was to stay here for him, not trusting in what we had together?"

I think back to the time when Bella and Daniel were not the solid couple they are today. When Daniel had been so consumed with his grief over the loss of his mum, that he'd pushed Bella away, repeatedly. And how, after they'd jumped over that hurdle, Bella had been the one to want to run away from their relationship, unsure whether he was worth the risk of uprooting her entire life for. *So maybe everyone is messed up in their own special way?*

"Yeah, but you guys had a deep friendship to fall back on when things got rough. Jake and I have barely a handful of moments together."

The muffin in my stomach flips at this. *How is it I'd spent six months wasting time with someone like Robby and have only had a matter of hours with someone as amazing as Jake?*

"The time spent together doesn't matter, Millie," Bella scolds me gently. "It is the quality of the time. And the connection between the two people. Let me ask you this: have you ever been this open about your family history and your insecurities with any of the men you've dated in the past?"

She's got me there. "To be fair, I only just figured out I had all this emotional baggage."

Bella tsks at me. "Not baggage, Millie. You need to reframe it. You've lived an experience that shapes your adult relationships. And that sort of trauma doesn't go away overnight. You are being honest about it now, working through it. And it sounds like Jake would want to work through it with you."

I think back to our conversation last night, how he'd supported me, excused my behaviour, cheered on my breakthroughs. None of his actions suggested he viewed me as damaged. As anything other than someone worthy of love.

"I messed up!" I flop over onto my front and moan into my pillow. "He's so amazing and I ran away from him. When he'd been so vulnerable with me."

"It's OK to have a freakout." She strokes my hair. "I pushed Daniel away after he'd flown to the other side of the world to be with me. If we can get through that, you two can get through a momentary freak out on the beach."

Her words, though reasonable, are not having their desired effect. I'd seen Jake's face, his disappointment, his resignation, like he knew I was going to do exactly what I did. I'm a walking cliché.

"I don't want to talk about this anymore."

She pouts as I peer up at her over the pillow stuffed against my face. "But we haven't come up with a plan."

"Please, Bella. I need to take a break from thinking about all of this..." A break from thinking about Jake. He's been running around in my head for too long now.

"OK." She brightens. "Let's stay in our pyjamas and watch Christmas movies!" She looks so delighted with her suggestion that I give in, even though every fibre of my being wants to sulk in bed, not enjoy movies filled with holiday cheer.

"I've got a whole DVD collection that I brought over with me from Italy." She bounces off the bed, a new plan to focus on. "You can choose the first one."

"DVDs? Really?"

She tugs on my hand, urging me to get moving. "It's the only way to make sure I have them all available to me when I want to watch them."

"Poor Daniel," I grumble as I follow her to the living room.

"I heard that."

"I meant you to."

She chuckles, not the least bit offended, and I take in the sheer volume of Christmas decorations surrounding us. I know Bella loves, loves, *loves* Christmas and each year since she moved here, she's upped her decorating game, but this is the next level. Every inch of space is covered in Christmas cheer. Daniel, the minimalist, must be losing his mind over this.

"Isn't it great?" Bella beams at me, watching me do a 360-degree spin, my mouth hanging open.

"It's…something."

"Daniel told me to decorate the place how I want…" she trails off, her head tilted, perhaps looking at it through my eyes and seeing that she's gone a little overboard. "And I think it's just right." *Perhaps not.*

"Your husband must have his love gogles on permanently to live with all of this." I point to a trio of life-sized elves standing next to us in the hallway, watching us with their dead eyes. It's creepy.

"They light up!"

"Of course, they do." I laugh and inch away from the potentially killer Christmas elves, flopping down on the couch, happy to have escaped their beady little eyes.

Bella drops next to me, pulling a tray from the coffee table over to us. "Pick one."

She's arranged what looks like fifteen DVD on a Christmas platter, like they're a dessert that you'd bring to a dinner party. It's confirmed: Bella is a Christmas lunatic.

"Ummm." I peruse through her selection, each one looking sickly sweet and so not what I need today. "No *Home Alone?*"

She bites her lip. "It's the only one I don't have, and it's also the only one anyone ever requests to watch." She looks aggrieved. "Back home, we don't see this little boy being left behind by his family as a Christmas movie. We see it as child abuse."

I hug her close, amused by her look of horror, along with her description of our cultural differences. She's so freaking delightful.

"OK, I guess we can watch *Love, Actually.*" She squeals. I guess I chose well. "I've never actually seen it."

She gapes at me for a full minute and I squirm under the intensity of her gaze. Had I known this was a prerequisite to be her friend, I would have brushed up on my rom-com watching.

"Right," she starts when she's pulled herself together. "You're in for a treat!"

Jumping up, she puts the DVD in the DVD player (where they found one of those, I don't even want to ask) and is chattering away excitedly about Hugh Grant and Colin Firth and "Oh, it's so good" when her phone goes off.

"It's my mamma," she says before answering, immediately launching into fluent Italian. "I'll be right back," she tells me, leaving the room, her voice louder when she's speaking her native language.

With Bella gone, I lean back against the couch and close my eyes. Flashes of Jake's face closing in on mine: Jake's lips on my freckles,

Jake's look of disappointment when I left him, have my eyes popping open. *Will I ever be able to rest in peace again?*

"Are you OK?" Daniel's voice startles me. "Sorry," he says as I press my hand to my racing heart. I hadn't even realised he was at home.

"I'm fine," I sigh, not even a bit close to fine.

"You don't sound fine." He sits down on the couch next to me, a kind look on his face. I've always liked Daniel, even before he gave in and fell in love with my best friend. He's a man of few words, but he's solid. A stand-up person you know you can depend on.

"It's boy troubles." I make a face, embarrassed to admit this to him.

He nods. "I figured."

We sit in silence. I fidget, picking at my cuticles while he stares at the rows of Christmas lights hanging around his window, appearing slightly baffled by them.

"So, I'm guessing it didn't work out with Joe?"

I leave my cuticles alone, tucking my hands under my thighs, and look at Daniel. "It did not."

"Was that because of Jake?"

I must look startled again because he laughs, a knowing laugh.

"How do you know about Jake?"

He gives me a look.

"Bella? She's got a big mouth."

"She's worried about you," he excuses her instantly. "And she's also sure that this Jake fellow is the one for you."

The breakfast muffin, which I'd thought would have been digested by now, takes another spin around my stomach. "It's not that simple."

"He's Robby's brother, right?" His mouth twists in disgust.

Not a big fan of Robby, it seems.

"Yes. See? Complicated!"

He doesn't argue with me, like all my girlfriends have done, instead humming under his breath and nodding. "It's not ideal." *An understatement.*

"But, not insurmountable, if you both want it? I guess that's the question; do you want it? Him?"

Yes! my brain screams at me. *Yes, I want him!*

"I think so," I say over my screeching brain. "But I also think that I've got a lot to work through before I let him, or anyone, in." I tap my head to show where exactly I'm messed up, and he nods again.

"I know exactly how you feel." And the funny thing is, I believe him. "Bella terrified me when we first met. I was scared of how I felt for her, scared to let her in, scared to have her leave me. I was in a permanent state of panic for months."

"So, how did you get over the fear?" I'm dying for him to give me the answers. To sort out this jumble for me.

"I didn't have a choice," he says simply. "I had to be with her. And that fear? That fear of losing the person you love? Of being hurt? It never goes away. It's just that all the good times, all the joy they bring to your life, all the love they pour into you, it drowns it out. Makes it easier to live with." He stops to draw breath and I wipe at the tears gathering in my eyes. "Being with someone, really being with them, doesn't suddenly make you all better, instead it makes you want to be better. For them. For her."

He smiles behind me, a look of pure adoration on his handsome face.

"You turning into a counsellor now?" Bella asks him from the doorway, her voice husky with emotion. She must have heard the bulk of his advice to me, and if she's anything like me, she must be melting inside.

"Just trying to help," he grins at her, the smile that's just for Bella. "Like Amelia did for us, when you were panicking and threatening to leave me."

A warmth fills me at this reminder of the minor role I played in the two of them getting together. Really, I was just a sounding board for when Bella was behaving like a crazy in love person, but I think it helped. They're married now, so it can't have hurt.

"You're a good man," she says, walking over and planting a soft kiss on his lips. "And I bet you're dying to spend the day watching *Love, Actually* with us, aren't you?"

He pulls her onto the couch in between us, tickling her while she giggles helplessly. "I think I'll pass," he yells over his shoulder as he makes a mad dash out of the living room, almost as if he feared we'd tie him down and force him to watch it.
Maybe Bella's done that to him in the past?

"So was his advice useful?" she asks once she's got her breath back. "Anything resonating with you?"
All of it.

"I think so. The part about feeling the fear and doing it anyway, that definitely struck a chord with me. I just need to get over myself and be brave."

She snuggles into my side. "It's not the easiest thing to do. Be kind to yourself, you'll get there."

"Thank you, Bella."

"You're welcome. You know I'm here for you always."

Her words warm my heart. "So, let's just watch the movie and forget about my boy trouble for a couple of hours."

She grins. "Done. You're going to love this movie."

And she's right. From the very first scene, I'm hooked. My attention is glued to the screen, watching Colin Firth fall in love through a language barrier, Emma Thompson's husband emotionally cheat on her (that scene almost broke me), Keira Knightly being serenaded with handwritten signs and the little boy learning to play the drums to woo his teenage crush. But it's the relationship between Hugh Grant, the Prime Minister, and his secretary, Natalie, that really has me enthralled. It's funny, and it's sweet and it's just so charming.

"I can't believe he had her fired," I mumble through a mouthful of popcorn that Daniel had thoughtfully delivered to us halfway through the movie. "What an idiot."

"Shush, just wait," Bella pats my hand and we resume watching.

I watch, hugging a pillow to me, as Hugh Grant's character regrets his decision to let the woman he loves go, how he sits down to read a bunch of Christmas cards and how one of them is from her.

"I'm actually yours," the voice of Natalie reads the words of her card to him in her delightful British accent and my body is zapped like it's been hit by lightning.

"What did she say?" I ask, my voice scratchy.

"Huh?" Bella's eyes are glued to the TV, completely ignoring the lightbulb moment I'm having on my side of the couch.

"The Christmas card? What did she say?"

She looks at me, her eyes widening as she takes in my nervous breakdown in progress. "Let me rewind."

We watch the scene going backward, coming to a halt when the Christmas card is in view. We listen to the voice of Natalie again, reading out the words written on her card: *"Particularly because (if you can't say it at Christmas, when can you eh?)—I'm actually yours. With love, your Natalie."*

"That's it."

Bella pauses the movie, turning her body to face me. "What's it?"

"All this time..." I mutter under my breath, the hamster wheel in my head turning furiously.

"All this time what?" She's impatient.

"All this time, I was actually his." I look at her, imploring her to understand.

She doesn't. "Actually whose?"

I think back on that first night, the way my heart raced when our eyes connected, the way I prayed he was my match, the way my brain stuttered to a halt at his mere presence. It was him. It's always been him.

"Jake. I've always been his."

Bella grins at me, a smile so wide it looks like it hurts. "Really?"

A smile grows on my face. "I'm so dumb. It's been him all along."

"This makes me so happy!"

My smile drops, panic replacing my joy. "I'm actually his." I repeat the words, absorbing the enormity behind them. It's not about a crush, or even just liking him, he's it for me. I'm his.

"OK, good, you're actually his." Bella runs a soothing hand over my arm, her touch anchoring me in place. "So, what are you going to do about it?"

I pick my phone up off the table, almost in slow motion, and tap on my text message chain with Jake.

AMELIA: Can we talk?

CHAPTER 15

Jake

*C*AN WE TALK?

These three words glare out at me from my mobile phone screen, replacing the other three words that had been plaguing me for the last eighteen hours and twenty-three minutes.

Amelia kissed me. Amelia kissed me. Amelia kissed me.

And now she wants to talk. Those three words together mean nothing good and I put my phone down on the highest shelf away from me, hoping if I can't see it, I won't have to deal with it.

For those brief moments when Amelia's lips were on mine—*finally*—everything was perfect. The stars were aligned; the angels were singing. I'd found my bliss. And then…she'd panicked. I could see it clear as day on her face. One minute we'd been lost in each other and the next she was withdrawing from me, running from me, like I've seen her do before. And now she wants to talk.

"It can't be good," I tell my TV friend Gina, a contestant on *Alone: The Australian Wilderness,* who's currently running naked into the freezing ocean waters of the Bass Strait, which are just south of where I live. "No one shares a kiss with a guy and then wants 'to talk' and it ends up being a good thing."

Gina continues on her delirious way to hypothermia, and I focus on the fact that I'm becoming a little nutty as well. Talking to a reality show contestant, instead of to the person I want to spend all my days talking to. I guess I'm just too afraid of what she might say, that she may declare us over before we'd even begun.

"Tea," I mutter, pausing the TV and walking to the kitchen. "That should help."

I fill the kettle up and get down the box of Melbourne Breakfast Tea Leaves I'd bought soon after Amelia started dating Robby. I'd overheard her asking for a cup of tea, only for Robby to make her a cup of coffee instead. He really is the worst. After that time, I'd casually asked her what sort of tea she liked the best, and she'd lit up like my taking an interest in something as small as her tea preference was a gift. She'd babbled on and on about her favourite tea shop, *T2*, which stocks all kinds of tea paraphernalia and after she'd eventually told me the one she likes the best—Melbourne Breakfast—I'd sought out this shop and bought a few boxes. For the next time she wanted tea, *not* coffee.

This is just one of the many details I'd learnt about Amelia during those awful months she was dating my brother. Some were obvious, like her deep love for that cheesy show, *Gilmore Girls* (which I secretly loved!) and her obsessive need to change her hair colour every few weeks. But others were only obvious to anyone who was actually paying attention (so, not Robby). I noticed she scrunches her nose up when she's listening to something or someone intently, and how she can't lie to save herself. Most people look to the left when they lie, but Amelia, she closes her eyes completely. And I don't think she realises it. Even if it's a small, white lie, she blinks for a really long time, until she's finished and then she just looks guilty, waiting to be caught out. It's incredibly adorable and speaks to how pure her heart is. Lying does not come easily to Amelia.

Other bits and pieces have imprinted on my brain, against my better judgement. Like how she mixes soft girly clothes with something edgy; dresses with combat boots or sweet floral tops with tight leather pants. She's always on time, obsessively so. She has a sweet tooth and will happily eat packets of Tiny Teddies all day long. She kills all her plants by over-watering them (I think she loves them to death). And she has the worst taste in men.

I've learnt these things just by being in her presence and paying attention, and I adore every single thing I know. I can't even imagine what it would feel like if she were actually mine and I could learn everything there is to know about her.

"It shouldn't be this hard."

My words echo off my walls in my empty house and I hazard a glance at my phone where it's taunting me from the shelf I'd left it on. I should just text her back and have the conversation, rip the Band-Aid off, so to speak, but I find this place of not knowing a bit more tolerable. If I don't call her, our relationship is like Schrodinger's cat—neither alive nor dead. The preferable place to be, it would seem.

And to be honest, if only with myself, I'm a little pissed off. Frustrated with how it all played out, how after being patient and earning her trust over so many months, she still ran away from me. She still doesn't feel safe enough with me to give me her heart. My wretched phone beeps at me again, and I send it an annoyed glance this time. *Is it Amelia wanting to force the issue? Wanting to get this part over and done with so she can go back to her dating plan? Man, I hate that plan.*

"Fine." I stomp over to my phone, well aware that I'm acting like a child and forever grateful that there's no one around to witness my behaviour. Gritting my teeth, I check my messages, letting out a relieved breath when I see the latest one is from Steven.

STEVEN: What happened to you last night? You disappeared.

What happened to me last night? Not much, except for the life-altering kiss followed by the swift kick of rejection.

She said she wanted that kiss, my inner voice reminds me, trying to lift my spirits and dampen my temper. And while she was in my arms, while *she* was kissing *me*, it had certainly felt that way. But then why did she pull away so suddenly? Is it because of Robby? Because if so, well, that problem isn't going away. I'm always going to be his older brother.

JAKE: Amelia happened.

STEVEN: Oh, do tell.

He really is like a teenage girl sometimes, loving to get in on the juicy gossip.

JAKE: There's nothing to tell. We kissed...

STEVEN: Congrats, man! That's awesome news.

JAKE: ...and now she wants 'to talk'.

STEVEN: Yikes.

JAKE: Exactly.

STEVEN: Want to go out for a beer?

I take a sip of my now lukewarm tea and think about it. Maybe a night out will help get me out of my head. Get me out of these four walls which feel like they're closing in on me. Or maybe a night at home to think about what's next, what do I want, is a better way to go.

JAKE: Nah, I'm good. I'll call you soon.

STEVEN: Call me anytime. And if I don't hear from you in the next 48 hours, I'm coming over...

JAKE: Is that a threat?

STEVEN: It's a promise.

A laugh escapes me. Although he's annoying and a busy-body who's all up in my business, I'm grateful to have him. Otherwise, I'd do nothing other than work. I'd never see the inside of a bar or a restaurant or a ballroom. I wouldn't have met Amelia that first night, before she met my brother.

Damn Robby for matching with her first!

It's not the first or even the tenth time I've railed against that stupid app for linking the two of them together. Though, in reality, Amelia was the one who made the choice that night. And even after she explained it, the wanting to trust the algorithm and being triggered by my description as a 'workaholic', it's a bitter pill to swallow. She will always be Robby's girlfriend first, and even though I'm completely crazy about her, it's a hard thing to come to terms with.

I put my phone on silent and back up on the top shelf—attempting to put it out of sight and therefore out of mind—and sit down to finish my episode of television. Then bed. I'll deal with Amelia tomorrow, when hopefully all my wayward thoughts have settled down.

I'm deep in the Tasmanian forest with Tommy, one of only two remaining contestants, as he sets yet another rabbit trap which will not be successful—he's going to starve at this rate—when the sound of keys in the door has me bolting upright.

"Robby?"

"Hey, big bro."

I watch, dumbfounded, as my little brother strolls into the living room, dropping his duffel bag and discarding his keys as he goes.

What is he doing here? He's supposed to be gone until February.

"What are you doing here?"

Robby gives me a lazy look, like he can't even be bothered to make a proper expression. "I live here."

Such a twat.

"I know that." I get up and round the couch, stopping a few steps away from him. "You were supposed to be gone all summer."

He shrugs, another lazy gesture. "I changed my mind."

Flinging himself on the spot I'd just vacated, he puts his feet up on the arm of the couch and changes the channel, like it's been six minutes and not six weeks since he'd flounced off on 'tour'.

I grab the remote, angrily putting it back to the show I'd just been watching, before pausing it and turning to face him. With supreme effort, I keep the annoyance off my face, needing to get to the bottom of his sudden reappearance.

"What happened?"

He sighs like talking to me is such a hassle. "Nothing 'happened'," he says, using exaggerated quotation marks and I want to punch him. "Things with the band were pretty slow, and I got over it."

This is typical Robby. He's always floating from one thing to the next, never committing, never seeing things through.

"So, you just left them?"

He makes another face, this time looking supremely annoyed to be questioned in this way. "It's not like they ever let me play." He sounds like a petulant child. So, accurate. "And I was bored."

This is so completely on brand for Robby that it takes my breath away. First, he jumps into a commitment with full enthusiasm and then he drops it when it all gets too hard. Or too boring, in this case. He does this with work and with jobs around the house. He does this with women. He did this with Amelia.

My blood boils.

"Didn't you expect this? You were the *back-up* drummer?"

He strokes the beginnings of the awful-looking beard on his chin. "I didn't really think about it. It just sounded cool. And Rebecca wanted to go, so I went."

The mention of his girlfriend has all the memories of that night, the one that had Amelia storming over here, note in hand, flooding through my brain. Without thinking, I fist the front of his shirt in my hand and pull him upright.

"Speaking of Rebecca." My face is mere inches from his. "What was with you leaving that note for Amelia before you took off?"

Robby's face flames red as he pushes me away from him. "How do you know about that?"

"Because she turned up here with the note, looking for you."

His face turns hopeful and I stalk away from him, the temptation to punch him getting stronger every minute.

"She did?"

"Yes, she was upset."

His face falls. *Good.* "How upset?"

I rub my face with my hands. "Actually, she wasn't upset. She was seething mad. What were you thinking?"

He flops back down on the couch, covering his eyes with his forearms, the very picture of dramatic. "I just missed her."
He is such *a twat!*

"You. Have. A. Girlfriend." I articulate each word, trying to get them to sink in.

"I know," he replies hotly. "And I really like Rebecca. But Amelia, well, she was special."
I know that! my inner voice wants to scream at him. *I've always known that.*

"So, what was the plan? You leave the note and then take off, expecting what...?"

He has the decency to look somewhat ashamed. "I left the note two days before I was due to leave. If she'd called me and wanted to give us another chance, I'd have stayed."

I'm floored by this information. *Does Robby still have feelings for Amelia? Please don't let it be so. We have enough obstacles in our way.*

"And now?" I ask through gritted teeth.

"Now what?" he has the audacity to look confused.

"How do you feel about Amelia now?"

I hold my breath as he ponders this, the time he's taking to answer the question speaking volumes.

"Eh, I think I'm over it. It was just an impulse thing, you know? I have Rebecca now and she's cool."

The air whooshes out of my lungs. *How can Robby speak about women like this? Like they're interchangeable and he can pick and choose as he pleases? And how dare he put Amelia in this scenario, like she's one of many instead of one in a million?*

"You're a jerk, you know that?"

Robby looks surprised that I'm speaking to him like this. Which is fair, because in his entire pampered life, no one had ever really called him out on his destructive behaviour. He's forever been the golden child who can do no wrong.

"What's up with you?"

I growl. A literal growl from deep inside my throat. "What's up with me? I had to deal with a furious, very upset Amelia when she came here looking for you."

"Well, sorry man." He doesn't look the least bit sorry. "But it's not like you have a busy social life. You have the time to deal with these situations. And Amelia always liked you. I'm sure you smoothed it all over."

I tuck that small piece of information away for later. Amelia told Robby that she liked me. My heart blooms, just a little. "So?

That's not the point. When are you going to grow up and learn, you can't mess with people's feelings on a whim?"

"Alright," he huffs, sitting up and glaring at me. "I get it. Enough with the big bro lecture."

It's not nearly enough, if his defiant expression is anything to go by.

"I'll call Amelia and apologise. She'll be cool."

The blood in my veins runs cold at the thought of Robby reaching out to Amelia. *My Amelia.*

"You leave her alone." My voice is low and threatening even to my own ears. "You've done enough."

Robby throws his hands up in surrender. "Whatever. It's all in the past. I'm sure you've fixed it and Amelia is fine."

Again, this is typical Robby. Happy to make a mess and equally happy to have someone else clean it up. Not that Amelia is a mess, even though she seems convinced otherwise.

"She is fine," I tell him, my voice now firm with authority. *I will make sure she's always fine.* "Just leave her alone."

He stands up, turning his back on me. "Fine. Geez, man. I just got home and you're already getting stuck into me. You know you're not my dad."

"I know that. I just wish you'd stop acting like a kid."

With a grunt as his only reply, he slinks off into his bedroom, muttering a 'happy homecoming to me' under his breath. Like the brat that he is.

"Should've stayed gone," I mutter in reply, then wishing I hadn't. There's something about Robby that brings out the worst in me. Makes me stoop to his level.

As his bedroom door slams, reinforcing that he's home for good and now a person I'm going to have to deal with daily, I turn off the TV, no longer in the mood to watch even my favourite show.

Switching off the living room lights, I pick up my phone, frowning when there are no new notifications, and walk to my bedroom. Once there, I sink gratefully onto my mattress, clutching my phone to my chest, closing my eyes and letting the events of the last twenty-four hours run through my mind. Amelia at the ball surrounded by admirers, Amelia swaying her body close to mine on the dancefloor, Amelia holding my hand as we walked along the moonlit beach, Amelia admitting she wished it was me she had let in, Amelia kissing me, leaving me, texting me. Me ignoring Amelia. And then to top things off, Robby. Back home and ready to cause more mischief.

If I thought things were bad just one hour ago, when I'd received Amelia's text, well, they are so much worse now. And with her message sitting there, read but not responded to, and Robby's presence looming like a dark shadow, for the first time in my life, I don't have a clue what to do next.

Or even where to start.

CHAPTER 16

Amelia

HE HASN'T MESSAGED ME BACK.

My 'can we talk' text message has been sitting on 'read' for a day now, just staring accusingly at me, like it's my fault for sending something so utterly offensive.

Why hasn't he messaged me back?

"It's not the best thing to send to a man after you ran away from him. After he laid out his heart to you."

This is from Andrea, who is firmly on Team Jake and is very cross at me for every action I took after the minutes our lips met. *I really shouldn't have gone into that much detail with her.*

"I just want to talk to him," I whine, combing my hair in front of my face, preparing to cut my own bangs.

"Don't do it!" Andrea snatches the scissors out of my hands and spins my chair around. It is past closing time at the salon and my idle hands are itching to do something drastic. To my hair, it seems. "Emotional bangs are not the answer."

I spin myself back around and glare at my reflection. *If I can't do bangs, then what colour can I change my hair to?* It's been this shade of blonde for over two weeks now, so I'm one week overdue for a new colour.

"Pink?" I ask my boss, twirling a strand in between my fingers. "Too much?"

She shakes her head at me. "I think you're distracting yourself with these trivial things, when really you need to be focussed on what you're going to do about Jake."

I know this. I just wish I knew the answer.

"It's up to him now, Drea. He needs to write back."

"You need to write something less scary." She points the scissors in her hand menacingly at me. "No one wants to have 'the talk' with a potential love interest. He probably thinks you're gearing up to reject him. Again."

That's what I've been fearing for the past twenty-four hours, clutching my phone and begging for a text message notification. Instead, it stayed so silent, I had to get Bella to text me, just to make sure my phone wasn't broken.

"I know, I know," I huff at her, pulling my hair up into a pony-tail, leaving the colour change for another day. "It's just that I'm scared too."

Her smile is sympathetic. "I know this is uncharted territory for you." I'd told her about my *Love, Actually* epiphany, after which she'd laugh hysterically. Rude. "But it's time for you to be brave. To put your heart on the line and hope that he looks after it."

Said heart hisses at the thought of it. It's been so badly mishandled by so many men in the past. In its battered and bruised state, it's begging for some care.

"He's a good man," I tell her, trying to convince us both that this is true. Though I guess it's a futile activity where Andrea is concerned. She doesn't think he's a 'good man', she thinks he's the 'best man'. For me.

"He is, so just call him."

No sooner have the words left her mouth when my phone pings, both of us lunging for it at the same time.

"Is it him?" Andrea asks holding the phone away from her face and squinting at the screen. I keep telling her she needs glasses, to which she responds that this is how everyone over the age of 45 reads their telephones.

I grab the phone off her, my posture deflating when I see who the text message is from.

"It's from Mike the electrician."

Andrea makes a face, like she's sucking a sour lemon, and goes back to closing up the salon. "What does he want?"

"He wants to go out again." *The man is determined. I'll give him that.*

"He's really keen, hey?"

"It's always the wrong ones who end up liking me the most."

"Or the ones who are interested in you, who you keep scaring away."

Touché. Andrea has a point.

I message Mike back, letting him know as gently as possible that I'm not interested in another date, and put my phone back down with another sigh. Only to pick it up again when it pings loudly.

"Is it him?"

I blink at the screen in front of me. It's a message from Joe the firefighter, who I don't remember giving my number to.

"Damn Bella." I send my bestie a rapid-fire text, demanding answers.

"It's not him," I report to Andrea, tapping my foot anxiously while I wait for Bella's response.

BELLA: Sorry! I gave it to him at the gala ball. When I'd THOUGHT you two had hit it off. My bad for not keeping up with the shenanigans of your love life.

Humph. That's a reasonable answer, but still. I don't want a message from Joe. *Why am hearing from everyone I know except for Jake?*

"This is getting ridiculous." I type another rejection text message, this time to Joe, the innocent firefighter who had haplessly wandered into my drama-filled love life. "I hate my phone!"

Determined to put it and thoughts of Jake out of my mind, I collect my bag from my locker, tossing my phone inside, retrieving it instantly when it pings again. This has to be him.

"It's not him." I feel the blood rush from my face as I read the latest message, looking up to see Andrea watching me with concern.

"Who's it from?"

I show her the screen, my hand shaking. "It's a message from my dad."

"What does he want?"

It's been two hours since I received the text message from my dad, out of the blue, while I'm at my most vulnerable. In true emotionally stunted fashion, I hadn't replied, instead calling my friends over for an emergency therapy/drinking session.

"He wants to see me," I tell them around the straw in my mouth. Lilly had turned up with ingredients to make strawberry daiquiris and had been keeping up my supply like a trooper.

"When was the last time you saw him?" Amy asks, taking my drink and replacing it with a glass of water. Which is a real grown-up move, given it's a Tuesday night and we all have to work in the morning.

I think back, counting the months, realising it's been years. "At least two years."

My friends give me matching looks of sympathy, and I gulp at my water. *Has it really been two years?*

"I wonder why he's reaching out now?" Bella asks in a soft voice.

"My mum told me his new wife is pregnant. Maybe he wants to share the news?"

Lilly frowns at this. "Do you really think so?"

Given that he hadn't contacted me the last two times his wife was pregnant, this seems doubtful, but what else can it be?

"Maybe you should just call him? Put us out of our misery?" This comes from Amy, the only adult in the room, apparently.

"Call him?" I gape at her like she's grown another head. "What are you? A Boomer?"

They laugh at my pain while I get up to hunt for some Tiny Teddies. Surely there's an emergency packet hidden somewhere in my pantry.

"Well, at least text him," Amy amends, her voice muffled as I dive deeper into the deep dark recesses of my cupboard.

Ah, success! I nab a packet that I'd tucked away for just such an occasion and happily tear into it. Chocolate chip, my favourite of all the Tiny Teddies.

"I don't know guys. My relationship with my dad is as bad as my relationship with all men."

"You have terrible relationships *because* of your relationship with your dad," Amy corrects me with the truth. "Maybe if you work on that one, the others will fall into place."

Huh, she may have a point. I look at my phone, where my message to Jake is still sitting there read and unanswered and wonder which relationship I should work on first.

"Is it a bit like the chicken and the egg?" I ask them, my three married friends who need to guide me through this. "Which one came first?"

"Your screwed-up relationship with your dad, of course. Everything after that has been a direct effect of what your dad did. And also, how your mum handled it."

I know what Bella is saying is true, but I also know that I really don't want to talk to my dad.

"I don't know if I can see him, guys." I've finished my cookies and I mourn the empty packet in my hand. No more Tiny Teddies.

"We know, Millie," Bella says. "But it really may help."

My emotional baggage, which I've been carrying around for so long, weighs heavily on me and I picture what my life would be like without it. Without the sadness of my dad abandoning me and my mum, moving on to a new family. A preferable family. A life without men who inevitably let me down. A life with someone like Jake. A life with Jake.

"OK," I give in. "I'll send him a text. See what he wants."

They give me an encouraging cheer and I quickly write a message, pressing send before I can change my mind.

"Done." I pick up my pink drink, having had my designated two glasses of water, wondering what happens next.

PING.

That was quick.

"Is it from your dad?" Lilly asks, the three of them scooting closer to me, offering comfort through their proximity.

I read the message through twice before handing the phone to Bella.

"He wants to meet you tomorrow morning, but gives no reason." She looks at me. "Are you going to meet him?"

Unfortunately for me, I work the late shift on a Wednesday, starting at lunchtime and finishing after 8 p.m., so I have no legitimate reason to say no. Other than, I really want to.

"You should do it. Get it over and done with," Amy says. "We can all be on standby for an SOS call, to get you out of there if you need."

Lilly and Bella nod along and I feel better. Supported. *I can do this.*

"OK." I send a quick message confirming the time and place for the next morning, stopping just short of inviting him to meet me at Love, Lilly café. "I'll do it. Just to see what he has to say for himself."

"At a minimum, you deserve an explanation for why he's been such a crappy Dad," Lilly says.

"And an apology as well," adds Bella.

"Yes," I nod, appearing confident while quivering with nerves on the inside. "It's just one meeting, and then I can move on with my life."

"Or," Amy speaks up, "maybe you could have some sort of relationship with your dad. A healthy one."

We all look at her. She needs to say more. To explain herself.

"It's just that I've got such a close relationship with my dad," she says, shifting in her seat. "As do you, Bella, and Lilly. And it's such an important one. If there's a chance to get it back on track, I think you should be open to it."

It's true, all three of my friends here with me tonight are close with their dads and maybe it's not such a coincidence that these are my three married friends as well.

"Is it that simple? Have a good dad, find a good man?"

"Gosh, no!" Lilly pipes up. "I don't think that's what we're saying at all." The other two shake their heads emphatically. "I think we just don't want you to miss out on that bond, if there's a possibility of making it work."

"You can totally be in a healthy, loving relationship and have a deadbeat dad," Amy clarifies, her cheeks flushed. "One doesn't dictate the other. But if there's trauma associated with your dad, it may be worth sorting through. Especially since you've kind of pinpointed that it may be a sore point for you."

She's right. They all are. I need to clear the air with my dad, not for him, but for me. To have some clarity and perhaps some closure. And maybe after that, I can work on getting Jake to call me back. Because it's my relationship with him I really, really want to work on.

"OK, you've convinced me. Pep talks over. Let's have one more drink before I kick you guys out so I can get my beauty sleep. Big day for me tomorrow."

They raise their half-finished drinks in the air and we toast. To being a grown-up and fixing relationships with people, even if they don't deserve it.

AMELIA: He's late.
BELLA: It's 10.01 a.m., give him some slack.
AMELIA: I've given him ten years.
BELLA: Fair. OK, give him ten more minutes, then bounce. Come to the café and I'll feed you cake.
I'm smiling at this message and scrolling through to find a GIF of a pig devouring cake when a shadow over me grabs my attention.

"Amelia?"

The question in his voice, like he doesn't completely recognise me, pierces my heart. *He's my dad. What's with the question mark?*

"Dad?"

I do it back to him, petty, but it puts us on equal footing. A better place to start.

His eyes race over me, taking in my carefully chosen outfit of a simple white t-shirt and boyfriend jeans (*thank you, Bella, for the advice*) and my white blonde hair with lavender tips. He looks baffled, like he's meeting a stranger and I'm grateful that my hair is at least similar to its natural colour and not the hot pink I was going to dye it yesterday—otherwise, he wouldn't have recognised me at all!

"You look great," he says with unexpected sincerity.

My heart jumps at his praise. "Thanks."

We stare at each other in a silence that is filled with so many unsaid words.

"Do you want to sit down?" I motion to the empty seat across from me, noticing that he too, has changed in the last two years. He looks older and...happier?

"What can I get you two?" I look up to see a server, pen and paper in hand, looking at us expectantly.

"Um," my dad scans the menu. "I'll just have a cup of tea."
Do we have this one thing in common?

"I'll have the same." I smile at the server, handing over both of the menus, watching her leave with some trepidation. Now that the logistics are over, we'll probably have to talk.

"So, how have you been?" my dad asks, his gaze still skirting over me.

"Since when?"

He winces at the hostility in my voice and I feel a little bad. *Keep it cool, Amelia. You're just here to hear him out, not to rake him over the coals. As good as that may feel.*

"It has been a while." He nervously runs his hand over his hair, which is thinning. Another sign of the many years of his life I'd missed. "I'm sorry for that."
Another loaded silence follows his apology. *How do I respond to it? What should come next?*

"For what?"

He gestures widely with his hands. "For everything. I don't know where to start."

We pause as our tea cups are placed in front of us, and I use the time to gather my wits. Now's not the time to fall apart. That will come later, with Bella…and cake.

"How about you start from the beginning?"

My dad nods, stirring a teaspoon of sugar into his tea before adding a splash of milk. One more thing we have in common.

"I'm sorry for all of it, Amelia. I know I let you down in so many ways, it's hard to know how to move forward."

"You could start with why you left me? Left us? Why you were never around growing up? And why you decided your new family was worth a better version of you than the one we ever got?" I'm panting by the end of this, my chest rising and falling rapidly. There's too much pain here; we won't ever be able to fix it.

My dad's face takes on a greenish tinge and he moves his hand to take mine, only to stop himself, uncertainty radiating from all over him. "I was a terrible father to you and husband to your mother. I know that. And I know there's no excuse for my behaviour."

"No excuse, but I'd love an explanation."

He grimaces. "Your mother and I got married young. I'd just turned twenty-one, your mother was only twenty. We were in love and impulsive and thought that life would just work out for us. That we wouldn't need to put in any work for things to be OK."

"You would have needed to be around to put in any work," I point out, tucking my shaky hands safely under the table and out of sight. "You didn't even try."

"That's where you're wrong. I tried in the beginning. When you were born, I was younger than you are now, a new dad who was terrified of being a parent. But I was also so in love with you."

My breath catches at this, at the look on his face.

"You were the best thing that had ever happened to me, the perfect baby who grew into a little girl who captured the heart of everyone you met. And things were good with your mum, too. We were happy."

He pauses, drawing in a deep breath. I wait.

"And then things like money and bills and real life started creeping in on us. Your mother wanted a bigger house, a newer car, she wanted to travel and have nice things for you. And I wanted to make that happen. So, I worked harder and travelled more for work. You probably don't remember it, but the first five years of your life, I was home all the time. I worked a nine-to-five job. I was home for dinner and to put you to bed."

I think back, trying to remember this. There are flashes of memories of him reading me a bedtime story, but I can't know for sure that they're real and not a figment of my imagination. Made up by someone so desperate to have a dad who loves them.

"And then what?"

"Then I got promoted. Your mother was thrilled. It meant more money, so she could be a stay-at-home mum. In that first year, I travelled once a month, trying to be home as much as possible and we made it work. But as with everything, the higher up you go in a company, the more you get paid, the more they own you. My job became more demanding. I needed to be in Sydney for two weeks out of the month. I didn't want to commit to that. I even started looking for another job, but your mum convinced me to try it. To see if we could make it work."

I don't remember any of the specifics of this, but I do recall in the early days my mum being happy with my dad's job, that she didn't complain when he was away a lot. That came later. When he didn't come home at all.

"How did it go from that to you leaving us completely?"

His eyes fill with tears and it's like a gut punch. *This is hard for him; why had I never considered that this hurt him too?*

"Time can make any situation seem normal," he explains. "At the start, it felt wrong to be away from you, from home so much. But then we all adjusted, and it became the new normal. It only developed into a problem when your mum stopped seeing the benefits and started seeing it for what it was. She had become almost like a single parent to you, and she was resenting it. Me, you, the whole situation."

This sounds familiar. Many times, growing up, I'd heard my mum complain bitterly to anyone who would listen about how she was basically raising me alone. And I'd agreed, having spent less and less time with a father who'd make only sporadic appearances.

"So why didn't you guys do anything to fix it?"

He shrugs, appearing deep in thought. "We were too far in it to find our way out. I was making a lot of money and this meant we lived a certain lifestyle, and though your mum complained, she didn't want that to change. We fought about it a lot. Do you remember that?"

I nod. Their arguments are etched into most my childhood memories.

"The longer it went on, the angrier your mother got, the more I dreaded coming home..."

"Until the day you decided to not come home."

He swallows hard, his Adam's apple bouncing up and down. "To a sixteen-year-old, that must have looked like a simple decision. But it wasn't. Leaving you was the hardest thing I've ever done."

My eyes sting. "It didn't seem that way. Especially after you met Penelope and started a new family. That seemed to come pretty easy to you."

"It may have appeared that way, but one thing did not equal the other. In your mind, my leaving and my marriage to Penny are linked, but it was two years after I left your mother that I started dating Penny. Two. Years. I was broken when I left."

I stare at him, disbelieving. "Mum told me you left us to be with her."

He gasps. "That's just not true, Millie." My heart squeezes at my nickname coming from him. "I sent you an invitation to the wedding. You know it was after you turned eighteen. You know how much I wanted you to be there, to be a part of our lives."

My knee bounces under the table, anxiety sky-high. "That's not how it happened."

He shakes his head sadly. "It is. When I left your mother—not you, your mother—she asked me to give you space. She said you were angry and didn't want to see me. So, I did what I thought was best. But I wanted to reach out. You have to believe me."

Looking at him, at his gutted expression, I think I do. *Had my mum been lying to me?*

"So, you wanted to see me? To be a part of my life?"

"More than anything. I tried with the wedding invitation, but I never heard back. I thought maybe it was too soon, maybe you needed more time and space. But then when you ignored all my calls and the birth of your step-sister, Juliet, I resigned myself to the fact that you wanted nothing to do with me."

Instinctively I reach over and take his hands in mine. "I never got your wedding invitation, and I think maybe mum intercepted some of your phone calls, because I don't remember receiving any of them. All I knew was that you were married and had a new family. That you didn't have any need for me."

My voice trails off as tears fall down my dad's cheeks, unchecked.

"Amelia, I've wanted you from the minute the stick turned blue and I knew I was going to be a dad. I should have tried harder to get in touch, to be a part of your life. I thought I was doing the right thing, staying away."

Regret courses through me at these words. Almost a decade has passed where we had believed the worst in each other, when we could have had a proper relationship.

"Can you forgive me for not trying harder? For not being there when you needed me the most?"

My own tears fall in sync with his. "I still need you," I whisper, because it's true. I think I need him now more than ever.

"Good, because you're not getting rid of me now."

My laugh is watery and I squeeze his hands, which are still in mine. "I'm sorry I didn't try harder to have a relationship with you. I guess I let Mum's feelings about you colour my own." And it's true, he's always been the villain in my story when I should have known that in real life, nothing is black and white. Nothing is just purely good versus bad.

"I don't blame you, and I don't even blame your mother. She was angry after I left and then she was terrified you'd leave her as well. She wanted to keep you close, I know that."

He's feeling more generous towards my mum than I am. The two of us are going to need to have a heart-to-heart, and soon, because this sort of behaviour needs to end now. I'm done with the toxicity.

"Can I ask why you reached out now? What made you ask for this meeting?"

He smiles, a sweet smile. "Penny's been dying to get to know you and with another baby on the way, it just felt like it was time. You have two sisters who know all about you, who look at pictures of you on Instagram and already idolise you. I didn't want to bring another child into the world knowing our relationship was so fractured. So, I messaged. And you replied. Thank you for that."

Thinking back on the emotional toll it took just to agree to this meeting, I'm grateful that my friends pushed me to do it. To face this conversation and find the answers to so many of the questions that have plagued me for so long.

"I didn't want to meet up with you," I admit with a small smile. "But I realise that our relationship has coloured the way I've entered all my relationships with men. And I wanted to fix that."

He looks stricken. "I did that?"

"It wasn't just you," I reassure him. "Mum played a big part. And I have to own my share of blame in it. All I know is that deep down I never felt worthy of anything real, because I thought that if my own father didn't want me, then no one else would."

My dad stands up so fast, his chair tips over behind him. People around us stare, but he ignores them all, reaching for me and pulling me to him. "I'm sorry I did that to you, that you ever felt for one minute that you aren't worthy of love. You've been loved by me for every second of your life, even the seconds we were apart. I love you, Amelia."

I hold on to him tightly, pressing my face against his chest, breathing in his long-forgotten scent, and my tears fall. The pressure loosens in my chest and I revel in letting go of all the pain, the rejection, the idea of not being good enough. My dad loves me, he's always loved me. Now it's just time to find our way forward.

"Thank you." I sit back, wiping my face with the back of my hand.

"Thank you," he repeats, picking up his chair and sitting down again.

I take a sip of my ice-cold tea—*ugh*—and smile at him. "So, what now?"

He returns my smile, looking younger than he had when he walked in thirty minutes ago. "Now? Would you like to come over for dinner? Meet Penny and your sisters?"

I thrill at the thought of it. The idea of his new family had always been a no-go zone for me, a place in my mind that I didn't visit because it hurt too much, but now I can make it a reality. I can make them my family.

"First let me talk to Mum." He makes a face that he can't quite hide, and I chuckle. "She's still my mum and I need to be careful with her feelings. But I want to meet them. And to get to know you better."

He beams at me like my words are a gift and I feel lighter than I have in years. "Sounds good."

"Yes."

"So, you'll call?"

I look into his hopeful face and take a mental snap-shot of it. After so many years of feeling like an afterthought, this new reality will take some getting used to. "I'll call."

He puts his hand out and we shake on it. And just like that, I have my dad back. And my outlook on life becomes just a bit rosier.

One broken relationship down. One more to go.

Jake won't know what hit him.

CHAPTER 17

Amelia

"**S**O, YOU STILL HAVEN'T HEARD from him?" Sammi shouts, trying to be heard over the rody noise in the bar where we've met for Thursday night after-work drinks.

I nibble on the chicken wing that has just been delivered to our table and shake my head. It's been four full days and Jake still hasn't messaged me back. The situation is dire.

"What you need is a plan," Madi says, making up our trio of single women who don't have yummy husbands to go home to at the end of a long day.

I close my eyes. "Not another plan."

If I hear that word 'plan' one more time, I'm going to scream.

"No, but seriously, what are you going to do?"

Madi and Sammi look at me expectantly, and I flounder. In the past twenty-four hours, I'd reconciled with my father after almost ten years of distance and had a breakthrough with my mother that was a long time coming.

After leaving my dad, with promises to visit him and his family soon, I'd dropped in to see my mum, hellbent on getting some answers. That conversation had been painful, but I'd entered into it with an open mind and open heart, willing to listen and to forgive. My mum wasn't trying to be a bad person when she kept me from my dad, she was just a person desperately trying to cling on to me, scared I would leave her, too. We cried together, and we really heard each other and by the end, we'd reached a resolution of sorts. She knows I want to have a relationship with my dad and my stepmother and sisters, and that I won't be dealing with her toxicity anymore, and she also knows that I will always love her and will never leave her. It was a moment of cleansing and clarity, and it was a long time coming.

And in amongst all this familial healing, my phone had remained resolutely silent. Not one word from Jake.

"I don't know, guys. Shouldn't I take his lack of answer as his answer? That he doesn't want to deal with me?"

Sammi immediately shakes her head, the eternal optimist, while Madi takes a little longer with her answer.

"You may be right," she says finally, earning a death glare from Sammi. "But he also may just be too scared to reply. You know that text message is like a walking red flag. No one wants to have 'the talk'."

"It's not 'the talk'," I say, frustrated. "It's just *a* talk. That's why text messages are the bane of my existence. There's no tone to clue one in on the intention behind the message. I just want to explain myself to him."

"Then it's up to you to make it happen," Sammi says. "You need to put yourself out there."

My stomach takes a turn in the tumble dryer. *I may be on my way to being all emotionally healed and stuff, but am I emotionally stable enough to put myself out there completely?* I'm not sure.

"Why me?"

"Let me count the ways." Sammi counts on her fingers. "One, you choose his brother over him. Two, you indulged in a dating plan when he was literally right there. Three, you kissed him and then ran away like a frightened mouse. And four, you sent him the death knell of all text messages. I mean, come on Amelia. 'Can we talk?' It's like the worst message to send to a man. Especially considering points one through three."

She has a point. Sammi, with her impromptu presentation of all the colossal mistakes I'd made with Jake, has really highlighted that the ball is in fact in my court.

"What should I do?"

Madi orders us a round of drinks, while Sammi rests her chin on her hand, a pensive look on her pretty face.

"It needs to be something that makes your feeling clear, while not being over the top," she starts, while I gratefully take a sip from the glass of wine that's just been placed in front of me. If we're doing this, I'm going to need some liquid courage.

"Something classy. That will tell him what he needs to know, but also give him breathing room to reply."

That sounds like mission impossible. I tell them this, worried that we've made this more complicated than it needs to be.

"No, we'll figure something out," says Sammi, patting my hand. "You'll see."

The three of us sit in silence. I watch their thinking faces, wondering why I can't just go to Jake's place and tell him how I feel?

"I've got it!" Sammi yells so loudly that I jump, spilling my wine down my shirt. Lucky it is black and not my favourite or else I'd have another thing to be upset about tonight.

"Tell us!" Madi looks excited, which makes me think the alcohol has got to her. She's usually the level-headed one in the group.

"I'll be right back." Sammi picks up her bag and dashes to the door, making a sharp right when she gets out onto the street and then disappearing out of view.

"Where's she going?"

Madi shrugs, looking as baffled as I feel, and we sit in silence together, watching the door.

"Do you think she's coming back?"

"Surely," Madi says, her eyebrows furrowed. "She walked out mid-sentence. That can't be it."

No sooner are the words out of Madi's mouth when we see Sammi prancing back into the bar, a paper bag in her hand.

"Where did you go?" I ask before she's even sat down.

She places the bag in front of me. "It's perfect. Look inside." Curious, I open the bag and pull out a pack of Christmas cards. *Huh?*

"Huh?"

Sammi sighs like she's disappointed in me. "Think about it. What made you realise Jake is the one? That you are *actually his?*" Her words jolt me. *A Christmas card? Of course!*

"You think I should write how I feel about him? Like Natalie in *Love, Actually?*"

Madi and Sammi give me matching grins, nodding enthusiastically. "It's perfect. Don't you think?"

I look at the card on top of the pile. There's a glitter-covered Santa Claus with the words 'ho, ho, ho,' coming out of his mouth in a speech bubble. It's the least romantic thing I've ever seen, and Sammi is right. It is perfect.

Pushing my hair behind my ears, I settle into my seat. "Do either of you have a pen?"

"You guys don't have to wait for me."

The three of us are piled into the back of an Uber, which has driven our tipsy butts from the bar to Jake's house. After we'd hunted down a pen, I'd gotten to work, pouring all my feelings onto the pint-sized Christmas card, telling Jake everything on paper that I'd been too scared to say to him in person.

"Are you sure?" Sammi has her face pressed against the window, looking at Jake's house, a wistful expression on your face. "I'd love to watch this all go down."

"Me too!" This comes from Sandra, our Uber driver, who is fully aware of the purpose of this excursion. And she's completely on board. "I won't even charge you guys. This is the most excitement I've had in the six months that I've been doing this."

In addition to learning all about me and my love mission, we'd learnt all about Sandra's life as an ex-school teacher who in her 50s has started down this new career path as a ride share driver.

"None of you need to stay." I'm adamant, pushing Sammi to open the door and let me out from my position, squished in the middle. "I'm going to do this, and hopefully, if all goes well, I won't need a ride home."

My friends love this idea, Sammi scrambling to get out of the way, while I hop/slide after her, trying not to flash my underwear as I go. Not the best day to wear this cute, but impractical leather mini-skirt.

"Love you, ladies. Thank you for your support." I wave to Madi, who's remained in the backseat, grinning wildly, before hugging Sammi tightly. "Thanks for listening and for coming up with this brilliant Christmas card idea. I hope it works."

"It will!" Sandra, my newest cheerleader, yells from the driver's seat. "He'd be a fool to turn you away."

Taking this confidence from Sandra the stranger, I straighten my shoulders and walk to the front door, remembering the last time

I'd marched down this very pathway, on my way to yell at Robby. *How much has my life—my love life—changed since the last time I was here?* My friends in their Uber yell good luck to me and Sandra honks the horn goodbye, and then there is silence. Just me and the front door.

Holding the Christmas card love letter in my sweaty hand, I take a deep breath, blow it out, and knock. Once, twice, and then a third time. And then I wait.

"Amelia?"

It's been five painfully long days since he'd been in his tuxedo, walking away from me to give me space, and in that time, he's grown even more gorgeous. More perfect looking. More perfect for me.

"Hi."

My word comes out as a squeak and I clear my throat. "Hi," I squeak out again. *Much better.*

He looks behind me before taking my hand and pulling me inside.

"Are you OK?"

My eyes are stuck on him; it's been less than a week and I've missed him. "You didn't message me back."

He looks at the phone in his hand. "I know."

Hmm, not off to a great start. I stop in the hallway, determined to get through this. To get through to him.

"Why?"

He runs his hand through this thick hair, making a mess of it as he goes. "Many reasons. Mainly, I wasn't sure I wanted to hear what you had to say."

Well, that's me stumped. *He doesn't want to hear me out?*

"Come on." He takes my hand in his—bliss—and guides me to the couch. "Let's sit."

I sink into the squishy couch cushions and take courage from Bella's painting staring at me from the wall. He had spent all those months at the Love, Lilly café waiting for me; those sorts of feelings don't just disappear in a week. Surely.

"I'm sorry." An apology is a good place to start. "About freaking out on you and panicking and then apparently sending the world's scariest text message the next day."

His dimple pops in his cheek. "Those are the three most frightening words a man can hear from a woman."

"So I've just found out."

"I'm sorry too. I should have called. There's just been a lot going on and, like I said, I'm not sure I'm ready to talk to you. In case…" he trails off, his eyes darting away from me.

"In case?"

"In case I don't like what you have to say."

And that's it. He's being vulnerable and laying his fears on the table. Perhaps he's been scared that I was going to reject him and he wanted to put it off for as long as possible?

"Did you think it would be bad news?"

His mouth twists. "I wasn't sure."

I feel a literal twinge in my heart that he'd gone all this time thinking that I'd run away from him and that my message meant I wanted to keep running.

It's time for me to be brave.

"I need to be clear with you." I pause, gathering my thoughts. It's now or never. "When I stopped all the lovely kissing." He lights up. "It wasn't because I wanted it to stop. It's because I didn't want it to stop."

He looks confused. *Do better with the explaining, Amelia.*

"The intensity of what I was feeling in that moment scared me."

There. That should be clear enough.

"It scared me too. Everything about you scares me." His voice is gruff and I shuffle closer to him. "But I had hoped you may have felt safe enough with me to at least stay and talk it through. I've never given you a reason to doubt me, Millie."

There is well-deserved reproach in his voice. "I know. And I know I messed up, but that's who I am. I'm the girl with a bucket load of emotional baggage who gets scared sometimes."

He smiles, edging closer to me. "I happen to be very good at carrying heavy loads. Maybe I can help you with that?"

"I'd like that."

Jake's handsome face, made more delectable by his two-day-old stubble, inches slowly closer to mine. So slowly that I want to grab it and plant my lips on his.

So, I do. After five days of not kissing Jake, I allow myself to get lost in the feeling of it. Of his lips moving against mine, so perfectly perfect that I can't hold in a sigh. A sigh of pure contentment, of being lost in the moment, of—

"What the hell is going on here?"

An angry voice tries to penetrate through the bliss I'm feeling and, determined not to let anything ruin this moment, I ignore it. And keep kissing this man who I love so much.

"Jake? What is this?"

Jake pulls his lips from mine, jumps to standing, and flushes a deep shade of red. I press my fingers to my lips, wishing they were still on Jake's lips, and turn to face the source of this interruption so we can get back to all the kissing.

Robby.

Oh no.

"Robby," Jake starts, backing away from me in small steps. "I—ah—we." He stops.

"Were you and Amelia kissing?" Robby spits out the last word with disgust and disbelief, and I gulp in a mouthful of air.

"I—ah," Jake tries again. And fails to say anything.

Looks like I'll be doing the talking.

"Hi, Robby." I wave to get his attention from where it's currently trained on Jake with furious intent. "Yes, I was kissing your brother."

Robby's face twists with fury. "What is going on? How long has this been going on? Were you two together behind my back when we were dating?"

That he would even think this, let alone ask this of the two of us, illustrates clearly how little he knows his own brother. And how he clearly never knew me.

"Of course not," I tell him while Jake continues to look on, frozen in place. "And I'm sorry you had to see that, but this just happened. And you and I? We've been done for a long time."

He shoots his brother another filthy look before stepping towards me. "Amelia, this can't be right. You and him? He's my brother..."

I give him a hard stare. "So?"

"So?" he splutters. "So, you guys can't be together. It's wrong."

My stomach flips as he articulates what I'd been grappling with for all these weeks. The obstacle I've finally gotten over.

"Robby, did you dump me? Out of the blue and then ghost me for six months?"

He doesn't respond, his mouth set in a mutinous line.

"And did you, or did you not cheat on me several times during our brief relationship?"

His face reddens and he looks down while Jake lets out a growl. *I knew it! What a cheating jerk.*

"And do you currently have a girlfriend? Who you were with when you left me that note? Proving that you cannot be trusted, not by me, and certainly not by the poor girl you're currently with."

Robby's mouth opens and closes, like he's a dead fish gasping for air.

"So, given all of this, do you think you have one leg to stand on when questioning me or your brother, who, by the way, is the most upstanding man I've ever met?" I ask this last question with an anger like I've never known swirling around my brain. My anger is so hot, I'm seeing red dots dance in front of my eyes. *How dare Robby ever question the integrity of someone like Jake? It's ridiculous.*

"It's still not right," he mutters, his tone belligerent. "Isn't there some sort of bro code?"

He's looking at his brother and Jake's lack of response has doubt creeping up my spine. *Why isn't he saying anything? Why isn't he standing up for me? For us?*

"Amelia," Jake finally speaks up, addressing me instead of his brother. "I think I need to talk to Robby."

His voice is flat, so I can't read into what he means. *Does he want space to talk to Robby to plead our case? Or does he want me to go, so he can make amends with his brother, effectively kicking me to the curb?*

"Um, ok?" I lock eyes with his, desperately trying to read his thoughts. "You want me to go?"

He gives me a pained look—finally, some emotion—and nods. "I think it's for the best."

What's for the best? my brain screams.

"OK," I say out loud. "I'll order an Uber."

The three of us remain standing in position as I order and then wait for my ride, the silence dripping with tension.

"It's here, waiting for me outside." I show my app to Jake, not knowing what else to do with my hands, and walk to the door.

Before I open the front door, I turn to look at Robby, who embodies everything I've been doing wrong in the love department for the longest time and something snaps in me.

"Robby," I start, my voice trembling. "You may think you have the moral high ground here, but you really don't. You treated me terribly when we were together and I let you. That's on me. But I know better and I will choose better." I glance at Jake whose eyes are shining at me. "You need to grow up and learn that actions have consequences. This is your consequence, you lost me. A loyal, amazing, funny, loving woman. And your loss will be another man's gain. I just hope that that man is your brother." I pull in a mouthful of air, my knees shaking. *Did I really just say all of that?* Jake's stunned expression suggests I did.

"And one other thing." My Uber driver honks the horn, and I open the front door and wave to him. "I am over you. And that my friend, is closure."

With my oh-so-excellent *Friends* reference ringing in my ears (*Bella is going to love this, we recently binged all ten seasons and loved this Rachel Green moment*), I flounce out of the house with Jake hot on my heels.

"I'm sorry about all of this." He takes my wrist in strong hand, halting all my fabulous flouncing.

"It's OK." I glance back to where Robby is still standing, his jaw on the floor. "I know you have a lot to sort through here. I'll go."

He nods but doesn't let me go. I look up at him and wait for his next move. *Has he changed his mind? Does he want me to stay? How does he feel about me? About Robby? About this entire mess?*

"I'll call you." He says nothing to assuage my fears.

Blinking tears away, my girl power moment well and truly behind me, I take a step away from him, only then realising what I still have clutched in my hand. *How had I forgotten the Christmas card?*

I hand over what is now a crumpled mess of red cardboard paper with some soggy, smudged writing on the envelope. "Here, take this."

He frowns down at it. "What is it?"

I shove it at him before I lose the nerve. My heart is written in that card, and it scares the life out of me to give it to him. Especially now, in light of the Robby debacle.

"Just read it. Later, perhaps. When you've dealt with all of that." I gesture to where Robby is standing, now glaring at us. "I've got to go."

Running down the path towards my waiting car, I refuse to turn back to where I know Jake is watching me. This has not gone as expected, but now that Jake has my Christmas card, my love letter to him, in his hands, the ball is well and truly in his court.

I just hope he's able to find his way out of the drama and come back to me.

CHAPTER 18

Jake

"WHAT THE HELL, MAN?"

I'm standing at the front door, watching the taillights of Amelia's Uber disappearing down the street, taking her away from me. *What just happened?*

Taking in a deep breath in, I turn around to start this difficult conversation with Robby, who's currently looking at me like I've just killed his puppy and told him that Santa Claus isn't real at the same time. *He's so freaking dramatic.* I put Amelia's Christmas card carefully into the back pocket of my jeans, feeling the weight of whatever she's written in there. I know I have to deal with my brother first, before I can deal with the contents of that card.

"Yes?" I straighten up to my full height and walk back to where he's waiting for me, still rooted in the same spot where he'd first seen me kissing Amelia. Kissing his ex-girlfriend.

I have to navigate this carefully. We've done nothing wrong, but in his mind, there has been a betrayal and I can't just ignore it.

"Care to explain what I just walked in on?" He looks sulky and I brace myself inwardly. This will not be easy; talking to Robby can sometimes be like talking to a five-year-old.

"What you saw is exactly what was happening." I take a seat on the couch and he follows me, sitting in the overstuffed armchair so that he's facing me. Glaring at me.

"You and Amelia?" he looks as confused as he sounds. "What? When? Why?"

I take in a deep breath, preparing to tell him the whole truth. "You know that first night? The one where we both met Amelia?"

He grimaces and nods.

"Well, that night I felt drawn to her in a way that I'd never felt before."

He looks so shocked by this that I'm impressed by my own acting skills. I had thought my feelings for Amelia must have been obvious for anyone to see, but clearly not. Though, come to think of it, Robby isn't the most observant guy with anyone other than himself, so it's more likely he just missed what was there to see, for anyone who was looking.

"When the two of you started dating," I continue, "I put all those feelings away. Believe me. I made sure I was only ever polite towards her. And then you broke up, and I still kept my feelings under wraps. But then you left the note, and she showed up here and…" I trail off, not knowing how to explain the events of the last six weeks. How we ended up here on this couch. Kissing.

"You had feelings for her the whole time I was dating her?" He sounds royally annoyed, and I don't blame him. The whole thing is…tricky.

I shake my head. "Once you started dating, I forced myself not to think about her at all. And if you'd stayed together, she would have only ever been my brother's girlfriend. But then you broke up. You have a new girlfriend and she and I…well, the feelings from that first night, they came back."

He's silent and I'm worried. A shouting Robby I can deal with; this version is unfamiliar.

"So, she feels something for you too?"

The Christmas card burns a hole in my pocket, begging to be read, so I can know for sure that she feels the same way I do.

"She does feel something for me, that I'm now sure of. We've grown…close in recent weeks. And I want to explore a relationship with her."

His skin has taken on a green tinge, and I worry he's going to vomit right here on my five-hundred-dollar rug. "But, but," he sputters. "Isn't that like…incest?"

I sigh again, a big, disappointed sigh. All my parents' hard-earned money wasted on Robby's high school education. "No, it's nothing like incest."

"But it still feels wrong."

Robby's stubborn nature is kicking in and it frustrates me. Getting up, I pace back and forth in front of him, prepared to argue him into submission. I'm a lawyer. It's literally what I'm trained to do.

"Explain to me what we've done wrong."

This simple question stumps him. "There's a bro code."

"Come on, Robby. We're not teenagers anymore. I get you feel weird about seeing me with your ex-girlfriend, but can you really, hand-on-heart, claim that you loved Amelia? That she was the one for you?"

His jaw clenches and he doesn't answer my question directly. "Are you saying that you love Amelia? That she's the one for you?"

Myriad of Amelia memories flood my brain and I don't hesitate "Yes, to both. Amelia, if she'll have me, is the one I want to spend my life with."

"What if I feel the same?"

I stare him down, knowing that Robby has loved no one other than himself. He doesn't have the capacity yet.

"I'd say, I don't believe you."

He deflates in front of me. The stubbornness from a minute ago now melting into the petulance I knew would ultimately appear.

"Whatever, man. She was mine first. This is all kinds of messed up."

And that's it. We've hit an impasse and there'll be no reasoning with him. Robby sees Amelia as his toy, the one he had first and then put down when he got bored. He doesn't want her, but he doesn't want anyone else to have her, either.

"Fair enough. I hear you and I'm sorry you feel this way. But if Amelia wants to be with me, I'm not letting anything—*anything*—get in the way of that. Do you understand me?"

"So, I'm supposed to live here with you while you date my ex-girlfriend?" He looks so appalled that I choke back a laugh.

"No, I would never ask you to do that." He lights up. "You are free to move out at any time."

And that's the moment when Robby realises that he has no more moves to play. He lives here with me, rent-free, because I allow it. Because my parents asked me to help him out. But if the choice is between having Robby as my freeloading roommate or a life with Amelia…well, there's no choice there, really. Amelia wins every time.

"I'm going to tell Mum and Dad about this."

This is his last card and I throw it back at him, utterly exhausted with his nonsense. "I'll save you the trouble," I tell him as I walk out of the room. *We're done here.* "I'll tell them myself."

With this parting shot, I leave my little brother to ruminate on his life decisions and hightail it to my bedroom. Now in the right headspace to read Amelia's Christmas card, I'm dying to know what she came here to share with me.

Dear Jake,

First, let me say I'm sorry. For so many things. For sending that scary text message, for running away after we kissed, for the whole 'dating plan' of it all, for picking your brother that first night. That's what I'll forever be sorry for. For seeing you and choosing him. Because what I've come to realise is that...I'm actually yours.
I have been and I always will be.

Yours,
Amelia.

My heart is in my mouth as I re-read Amelia's Christmas card to me. These are the words I've wanted to hear for so long, clearly articulated on the page in front of me, bouncing around as my eyes fill with tears.
She's mine?
She's mine.
The weight of what she's written lightens the pressure in my chest. The pressure that has been there for so long, I don't always notice it. But it's been a persistent sensation, this idea that, even if she chose me, I would only ever be her second choice. The option she took after choosing many others before me. Turns out, she'd

made her choice all along. It just took her mind a bit of time to catch up with her heart.

So, what are you going to do now? the nagging voice in my head questions me. Amelia has laid it out there and left the ball in my court. There are a couple of things left to juggle—namely Robby and my parents—and I know I will have to sort those out before I can fully commit myself to her. *Amelia, your heart is safe with me. And I'm going to prove it to you. Just give me some time.*

The next morning, after the most solid night's sleep I've had in months, I wake to find Robby shut away in his room. Refusing to talk to me.

"Very mature," I mutter to his closed door after he'd yelled at me to *get lost.* "I guess I'm going to have to be the adult here."

I spare his bedroom door one more glance before grabbing my coffee in my to-go cup and heading out the door. My plan is to see my parents before heading to Lilly's café. I need some advice about how to proceed with Amelia, and her closest friends are the best place to start.

On the drive over to where my parents live, two suburbs away (not too close, but near enough that mum can drop around food regularly) I ask Spotify to play Taylor Swift, happy for it to pick which song is going to fit my mood. Today I'm feeling anxious, hopeful and in love, so I'm sure Taylor has something appropriate for every one of these emotions. When a song I've heard on the radio over the decades fills my car, I hum along. The lyrics once again capturing perfectly how I feel about Amelia. How she's going to be the best thing to ever be mine.

Mine.

I park in front of the house where I grew up and take in a deep breath. I'm not sure how this will go. My parents are so protective of Robby, I can almost see them taking his side in this. Even if his side is ridiculous and without merit and will ultimately hurt me. *They've spoilt him for his entire life. Why should this be any different?*

"Jake?"

I startle at the knocking on my car door window, looking up to see my dad standing there, in his old dressing gown with the daily paper in his hand and a concerned look on his face.

Here goes nothing.

I open the door and let my dad take me into a tight hug.

"It's early," he frowns as he lets me go. "Come in, come in."

I follow him along the well-manicured pathway to the front door, which is tastefully decorated with Christmas decorations. I've been so caught up in this Amelia situation, the Christmas spirit has passed me by.

"Jake?" My mum's smiling face pokes around the corner from the kitchen. "Did we know you were coming over?"

"No, I just popped in for a quick visit." My parents look at each other, doing their usual telepathic communication. "And I need to talk to you both about something important."

My dad ushers me past him to where my mum has a cup of coffee waiting for me. *How did she have that ready so quickly?*

"Jake, you're scaring us," she says once we're all seated at our well-worn kitchen table. "Is something wrong?"

How to answer this? "Yes and no." I take a sip of coffee. "It's complicated."

"Why don't you start at the beginning?"

A very good place to start.

"OK, I'll do that." And so I begin, telling them about that first night with Amelia and Robby and everything that has happened since. I emphasise that it was never, ever my intent to pursue Amelia and that where we've landed, where we almost are, results from timing and the two of us giving into our feelings. And that we never wanted to hurt Robby, not that I actually think he's hurt.

"Well, maybe his pride is hurt," I finish up, taking in a gulp of air. *There, it's out there. The whole sordid story.*

"So, Amelia? Do you love her?" my mum asks, cutting through all the noise.

"I care for her a lot," I answer carefully. "And I know we can be something real together."

"Then what's the problem?"

My mum and dad look so confused, I doubt myself. *Did I not explain it properly?*

"The big deal is that Robby is currently at home throwing a tantrum because he doesn't want me with his ex-girlfriend."

"So?" This is from my dad.

Huh? Not the reaction I was expecting.

"Well, I don't want you to be upset with me, because I'm hurting Robby."

Mum smiles at me. "You always were so protective of him."

"We all were. We all are," I point out with a meaningful look. They're the reason he's the way he is. An entitled brat.

"Yes, but you took on the role of protector of Robby from the minute he was born. We barely got a look in. It was always you who wanted the best for him. Wanted him to have more and do less. We just went along with it."

That is not how I remember it. I tell them this with a frown.

"It's hard to recall behaviour accurately from when you're young," Dad tells me like a wise old owl. "But it's true. You had longed for a younger sibling, so when you got one, he was everything. To all of us, yes. But to you the most. And you've been babying him ever since."

"You think *I* baby him?"

They smirk at each other. "Whose house is he living in for free? Who cleans up all his messes? Who covers for him when he makes mistakes? It's not us."

"I thought it's what you'd want me to do," I splutter, floored by their account of our sibling relationship. "Didn't you want me to look out for him?"

My mum shrugs. "Sure, but he also needs to grow up and learn from his mistakes. He's not going to if you're always his soft place to land."

I look at Dad. "Do you both feel this way?"

"We're grateful that you're always there for your brother. It's what family should do for each other. But it should never be to the detriment of your own feelings."

I take a minute to absorb what they're saying. *Are they giving me permission to forgo Robby's feelings about me and Amelia?*

"So, you wouldn't have a problem with me dating Amelia?" I hold my breath.

Mum smiles brightly. "Of course not. We love her!"

"She thought you hated her."

"Oh no, I hated her with Robby. She deserved better. And now she has it." Mum pats my hand and I sit back, taking a minute to digest it all.

This is brand-new information.

"What should I do about Robby?"

Dad puts his arm around my shoulder. "You've always had such a kind heart. Don't worry about your brother, he'll come around. He has no choice. And if he doesn't…would it change how you feel? How you'll move forward with Amelia?"

I shake my head so violently my neck cracks. I'm getting old. "No way. Now that I may have a chance with her, there's nothing that will stand in my way."

"Then what are you waiting for? Go get your girl!"

With my dad's words ringing in my head, I hug them both goodbye, grateful for their support, and head out the door. Next stop, Love, Lilly café to make a plan to get my girl.
Finally, a plan I can get on board with.

The bell above the door rings as I enter the café, having covertly checked inside to make sure Amelia isn't there. I know that she's working today—I stalker-ishly know her schedule—but I didn't want to risk her accidentally showing up and ruining any surprise in the making.

"Jake?" Bella is frowning at me from the counter. "What are you doing here?"
My mouth fills with saliva as I look at the brownies proudly on display and lecture myself not to get distracted. *Treats are for later, there are more important matters to focus on.*

"Are you looking for Amelia?" Bella asks when I've been silent too long, waging my internal no-brownie battle.

"No, I came to talk to you. And Lilly, if you have some time?"

She looks rightfully confused. "Me?"

"Yes."

"You sit with Jake," Lilly says, coming out from the kitchen. "I'll come over when things die down here."

I send her a grateful smile and walk to a table by the window.

"OK, mister. Spill it." Bella is giving me a stern look, and I wonder what Amelia has told her.

"What do you know?"

She narrows her eyes. "Amelia told me about Robby busting in on you guys last night. And that she gave you a Christmas card telling you how she feels and that you haven't contacted her since."

Oh. So she knows *everything.*

"Yes, well. That's all true," I agree as Lilly sits down next to Bella, both of them with their arms crossed. "There's been a bit to sort through, you know? With Robby..." I trail off when their expressions don't shift.

Hmmm, what to do to get them on side?

"It's really quite simple, Jake," Bella says, unknowingly answering my unspoken question. "Do you care for Amelia? And if so, are you going to do anything about it?"

This I can answer. "I do and I am."

Lilly grins at me. "Right answer. So, what are you doing here? Waiting for Amelia?"

"No!" They both jump. "No," I repeat in a softer voice. "I came to talk to you both. You're her best friends, and I want to make all of this up to her. The not returning her text, the whole Robby situation. All of it. I want to let her know how I feel in a way that she deserves and I want to do it right."

They're both silent, watching me with wide eyes.

"I need your help."

"Well then." Bella's face is shining with happiness. "Our help you will get."

"Starting with brownies!" Lilly bounces off to get us some treats, and I let out a relieved sigh. *Part one, done. Friends are on my side. Now, we need a plan.*

"What are you thinking?" Lilly places three plates filled with brownie and vanilla ice cream in front of us. I dig in immediately, chewing through my muddled thoughts.

"Amelia told me about the grand gesture Daniel did for you when the two of you started dating." I swallow a big bite. "Maybe something like that?"

When Bella and Daniel were finding their way to each other, Daniel had copied a scene from Bella's favourite TV show, *Dawson's Creek,* and had won her heart with this gesture. Amelia had spoken of it often while dating Robby and I'd paid attention. I was always paying attention to Amelia.

"It was pretty romantic," Lilly says while Bella blushes prettily. "Are you thinking something like that?"

I nod. "Amelia deserves to be wooed. Don't you think? A grand gesture all of her own. She gave me what I needed with that Christmas card. I want to do the same for her."

Bella's face turns thoughtful. "That's it. The Christmas card!"

"He can't just give her a Christmas card back, Bella. That's lame," Lilly argues, while I silently agree.

"No, not the actual Christmas card," Bella clarifies in a huff. "But where did the Christmas card idea come from?"

Lilly's smile grows wide with recognition while I sit in the dark. "Where? I'm confused."

"Jake, have you ever seen the movie *Love, Actually?*"

I search through the recesses of my brain. It sounds familiar. "Maybe?"

Bella scoffs. "You men can't ever remember anything important. It's only the most iconic Christmas movie ever. With Hugh Grant playing the role of the Prime Minister of England?"

This is ringing more bells and the image of Hugh Grant dancing on the stairs to some old 70s songs floats through my brain. "Is that the one with all the different storylines happening at the same time?"

"That's it!" They both look proud of me and my chest puffs.

"And it was while we were watching this movie that Amelia came to the realisation that it has always been you. Hence the Christmas card."

I'm confused again. "Huh?"

"There's a tiny scene where feelings are expressed with a Christmas card, Jake. Come on, keep up!" Bella looks annoyed again, so I nod, even though I'm lost. "And now we can use the same movie for your grand gesture."

I keep quiet, not wanting to irritate her further. But I honestly don't know what she's talking about.

"Bella, give the man a chance to catch up," Lilly chides. *Thank you!* "The boy brain doesn't have immediate access to all the essential romantic knowledge like we do."

Oh, OK.

Bella picks up her phone and starts typing. "Here!" She thrusts the screen in front of my face. "Watch."

I take the phone from her. On it is a YouTube video where a young Keira Knightly is standing in front of a door, while the guy from *The Walking Dead* is expressing his love to her on giant pieces of cardboard paper. *Ah, now it's making sense.*

"You think I should...?" I give Bella her phone back, pointing to where the scene is paused. "Do that?"

They both nod enthusiastically, hearts floating in their eyes.

"Do you think it would work?"

They look at each other and then back at me. "Oh, it will work. As long as you know what to say on the cards. She will eat it up."

Huh? Declaring my feelings on large pieces of paper is not how I thought this would go down. But I wanted it to be a grand gesture, and what is bigger than this?

"Will you help me?"

They smile at me.

"Absolutely," Bella says. "But the first thing you need to do is message Amelia. She's dying a slow death with that Christmas card out there and you not responding."

I nod. I can do that. "So, send her a message and then what?"

"You pour your heart out on six to ten large pieces of cardboard paper and leave the rest to us."

My stomach clenches at the thought of putting myself out there in such a big way. But Amelia deserves it and hopefully, with the help of her friends, I can pull this off and we can be together. Properly, with no barriers or miscommunication between us.

"Done. I'll message her now."

Amelia's friends hug me one by one.

"You won't regret this, Jake," Bella whispers in my ear. "Just trust us. After this stunt, you will have won the girl."

I squeeze her back and hope that both Bella—and Taylor Swift—are right. And this is how I get my girl.

CHAPTER 19

Amelia

Thank you for the Christmas card.

I've read Jake's text message so many times it no longer holds any meaning. The words make little sense, it's like I'm reading gibberish.

"Thank you for the Christmas card?!"

I thrust my phone in Bella's face, not for the first time, hoping she will provide some clarity. "What kind of rubbish message is that?"

She smiles at me, looking serene. I'm going to need her hot Italian blood to fire up soon and get on the same page as me, so we can both explode together.

"I think it means that he's thanking you for the Christmas card."

Helpful, Bella. So freaking helpful.

"I can see that." Sort of. My eyes are going crossed from re-reading those five simple words. "But what does he mean?"

Bella pushes a plate of cookies towards me and I take the biggest one. It's been two days since I left my heart on Jake's doorstep, and all I've gotten from him is this one lousy text message.

"I'm officially done with text messages," I tell her through a mouthful of cookie, spraying crumbs and not caring one bit. "They have caused me nothing but angst."

"It's true, people run into trouble when they communicate without actually talking."

"So, do you think I should go and see him? Just talk this out once and for all?"

"No!" she yells in sync with Lilly, who's standing behind the counter, listening to our conversation.

"What we mean," Lilly says as I look between them, baffled, "is that you need to wait for him to come to you."

Bella nods and I sit back with a sigh. This is not what I wanted to hear from them, given that the waiting for Jake to make a move is killing me.

"Do you think Robby has convinced him to not pursue something with me?" This thought has plagued me every minute since I left the two of them to hash it out. "I should have stayed and helped Jake plead our case. It shouldn't have been just on him to fix this."

Lilly sits down at our table, her forehead wrinkled with sympathy. "I think you did the right thing. They're brothers. You had to leave them to sort out their relationship."

"It's true," Bella agrees. "You don't have any siblings who you're close to, but that dynamic isn't always smooth sailing. It's like having a best friend and your biggest rival all in one. And you will love them even when you hate them."

Their words go some way to soothing my concerns, but the fear gnawing at my stomach just won't go away.

"Maybe I should just bow out?" I offer half-heartedly, because I really, *really* don't want to do that. "You know? For the sake of their relationship?"

Lilly shakes her head, an adamant no. "You just need to give it some time and some space. And trust Jake to make it all OK."

I picture Jake now, with his serious green eyes behind those sexy glasses, his protective and solid nature, the way he asked me to trust him, to know that I'm safe with him. I need to remember this now more than ever.

But why hasn't he called me?

"He's most likely just sorting through the whole Robby situation," Bella says, once again reading my mind. "You know Robby, he's a man-child who won't make this easy. That's what Jake is dealing with right now. Just be patient."

Patient. I can do that.

"I don't think I can do that," I whine into my cup of tea. "It's been two days. What's taking so long?"

My friends look at each other, a long, loaded look that has my spidey senses going off. Before I can question them, though, the bell tinkles over the front door, announcing a group of new customers.

"Amelia, I know you're going through an existential crisis right now," Lilly says, standing up and moving away from our table. "But are you able to do that over by the window?"

Great, I can't even wallow in peace. Picking up my cup of tea and plate of half-eaten cookies, I move to a table in a corner up the front of the café, pressed up against the window.

"Way to rub it in," I mutter under my breath as I take in the table set for one.

They ignore my irrational rumblings, too busy serving customers to deal with my tantrums. *Fair.*

"Just distract yourself with some people watching," Bella calls from behind the counter.

Hmmm, people watching. Usually, this is one of my favourite pastimes, watching people and mentally changing their hairstyles to one I think would suit them better. It's something I could do for hours, but not today. Today my mind is too distracted to focus on hair.

My phone pings on the table in front of me and I lung for it. This has to be him. I open my messages app, which has had quite the workout this week, and…

"It's not him," I tell my friends who I know are watching me expectantly. My phone notification is so loud, every person in the café is watching me with the same expression. "It's my dad."

In the past week, since we met up for our long overdue father-daughter chat, he's been in regular contact with me. Sometimes just a text message, asking about my day, and other times he's actually called and we've talked for several minutes. It's been weird but also delightful. Having him back in my life, and really trying, is filling a hole in my heart I hadn't known existed until now.

I type back a response to his question, letting him know that I'll be joining him and his family for Christmas brunch next week. He invited me the day after our initial meeting and after a long talk with Mum, I've decided to go. I want to be a part of his life, his family, as much as he seems to want to be a part of mine.

AMELIA: I'll be there. Looking forward to seeing you all.

I press send, surprised that I actually mean it. I have two sisters, with another one on the way, and a stepmother, who all want to know me. And on my path to healing, I realise I really want to know them as well.

"All OK?" Bella asks. I look up to see her standing next to me, concerned.

"It's better than OK. I'm spending Christmas morning with my dad."

She leans down to hug me. If there's anyone who knows the value of family, it's Bella. Last year, her dad had been very unwell after a stroke left him in hospital with life-threatening injuries. During that time, Bella had to make the tough decision to either stay in Italy with her parents or follow her heart and move to be with Daniel in Melbourne permanently. I know how gut-wrenching that had been for her, but luckily, she ended up with the best of both worlds. Her dad is well enough to travel Down Under to be with Bella and her husband, which they've done several times in the past eighteen months.

"That's wonderful, Millie. I'm so happy for you."

"Me too." There isn't much enthusiasm in my voice and we both know why. I need to sort things out with Jake before I can feel much joy in anything else. "I think I'm going to go home now and wallow in private."

Bella looks at her watch, her gaze bouncing to Lilly. "How about one more cup of tea before you go?"

There are my spidey senses going off again. "What's going on?"

They exchange a look. "Nothing," Bella lies. She's so bad at it. "We just don't think you should be alone."

That's fair. I've spent way too much time alone with the *Gilmore Girls* thinking about every missed turn I've made in my life that's landed me in this position.

"OK, one more cup of tea. Then wallowing."

Bella gives Lilly a thumbs up, which isn't very covert, but I let it go. I don't have the brain capacity to explore this strange behaviour.

"A cup of tea coming right up."

She skips back to the kitchen and I watch as she bumbles about, not even close to making me a cup of tea. *Come on, Bella. I'm on a deadline here. My couch is calling my name.*

I'm just about to call it quits and cancel the cup of tea that I didn't want in the first place, when a flash of activity outside the café window catches my eye.

"What in the world?"

My full attention now on the footpath outside the window next to me, my breath catches in my thrat when I see who is standing out there.

Jake.

And he's grinning at me.

I get up to go to him, only to be pushed back down into my seat by a surprisingly strong pair of hands.

"Bella?" I frown at her. "I need to get out there!"

"Just trust me," she whispers in my ear, holding me in place.

Giving in, I turn back to where Jake is still standing, now with a portable bluetooth speaker in his hand, his brow scrunched up in concentration as he looks between the speaker and his phone.

"For goodness's sake," Bella hisses from behind me. "Lilly, go help Grandpa out there."

"I'm on it!"

Baffled and mildly amused, I watch Lilly walk—no *bounce*—outside. She says something to Jake, making him laugh and then takes his phone from him. Two minutes pass and she hands it back to him, patting him on his arm and then walking back inside.

By now, the entire café is looking between me and Jake, and I hold my breath for what is coming next.

Jake puts the speaker on the ground in front of him and I hear *Silent Night* blaring from it.

"Excellent attention to detail," Bella murmurs to Lilly, who has joined us at the window.

"What?" I ask, trying to get up again.

"Just wait!" This time, Lilly presses me back down into my seat. "And watch."

My gaze returns to Jake, who's staring at me intently, his glasses glinting in the sunlight. My heart thumps painfully in my chest as he bends over to pick something up. Pieces of cardboard paper. *What's going on?*

"He's really doing it!" Bella squeals.

Jake holds up the first one and I read what is scrawled across it, in his neat handwriting.

AMELIA, I'M SORRY THIS HAS TAKEN SO LONG.

He flips to the next one.

THAT IT'S TAKEN ME SO LONG
TO TELL YOU...

I feel the entire café hold its breath as he pauses before flipping to the next card.

TO ME, YOU ARE PERFECT.

"He didn't need to copy the movie exactly," Bella grumbles before being shushed by Lilly. *The movie? He's* Love, Actually*-ing me?*

Jake holds up the next card.

I'VE LOVED YOU FROM THE MOMENT WE MET.
AND I'VE WAITED FOR YOU TO BE READY TO LOVE ME BACK.

Tears fill my eyes and I wipe at them frantically, not wanting to miss a thing.

AND SO I CAN TELL YOU THIS...
WITHOUT FEAR OR HESITATION...
THAT I'M ACTUALLY YOURS...
FOR AS LONG AS YOU'LL HAVE ME...
SO, FOREVER?

Jake ends on this card, his face hopeful, imploring me to answer. I nod, tears now running freely down my face.
He loves me? He wants to be with me? Forever!
"What are you waiting for?" Bella's hands, which had been holding me down, are now pulling me up. "Don't leave him standing there."

Jake's expression has turned from hopeful to worried and I galvanise into action. Without seeing where I'm going, who or what is in front of me, I bolt to the front door, slamming it open and racing towards him. To where he's waiting with open arms.

"Do you mean it?" I ask as he pulls me into him, his arms like steel closing in around my waist. He's not letting me go.

"I mean every word and more, Millie," he whispers into my ear as hot tears continue to pour from my eyes. "I should have fought for you that first night. And I should have fought for you every day since. You've had my heart for so long, it no longer belongs to me. It's yours now. If you'll have it?"

He looks down at me, uncertain, and I kiss his worries away. With my lips on his, I tell him everything that has been locked away in my heart. And he kisses me back with the same intensity, the two of us lost in the wonders of just kissing each other with no barriers in our way.

"We can swap." I press a damp kiss on his lips. "Because you've got mine. You've had it for some time now."

He leans down to kiss me again, stopping when a group of kindergarten children, holding hands in groups of three, plough into us.

"Maybe we should move away from the middle of the footpath?" I suggest not moving away from him. Now that he's mine, I'm not letting him go.

"Come inside for celebratory brownies," Lilly calls from the doorway, where she and Bella are standing with tears in their eyes.

Jake lets go of me to pick up the cardboard declaration of his love for me and, in a daze, I grab the Bluetooth speaker. Only now is the full force of this grand gesture hitting me, and I can't believe that he did it this way.

"How did you know to use *Love, Actually* to woo me?" I ask as we enter the café to an embarrassing round of applause. We both stop in our tracks and give a little bow before snagging a table in the back, away from the prying eyes of the amused customers.

"Bella and Lilly told me about your *Love, Actually* moment and may have suggested I could draw inspiration from the movie," he tells me.

We sit down, Jake pulling my chair closer to him and snuggling his face into my neck.

"Oh, really? So, this wasn't your idea?"

"The idea, no," he admits honestly. "But the sentiment and the words on the cards? That was all me."

I let out a contented sigh and cuddle in closer to him. "Well, I loved it!" I look up into his beautiful green eyes that captivated me from the very first minute I met him. "And I love you."

He presses a soft kiss on my lips. "I love you too."

These words reverberate through my mind. *He loves me. He loves me. He loves me!*

"Why did it take so long for us to do this?" I grumble after he's pressed yet another kiss on my lips, nibbling them slightly, causing a spray of shivers down my spine.

"We had a few obstacles to work through. Our path to each other has not been easy."

"Speaking of easy, how did things go with Robby?" I'm dying to know. "Is he OK?"

Jake makes a face. "He will be."

He sounds so confident and yet I'm not convinced. "He's the reason it's taken you a couple of days to do this? To respond to my Christmas card."

At this, Jake pulls me even closer until I'm almost sitting on his lap. "Reading that Christmas card was the best thing ever to happen to me. And I wanted to respond, but only when I was free to love you like I've always wanted to love you. So, I waited. And I spoke with Robby, and my parents, and then those two"—he points to Lilly and Bella, who are watching us with beaming smiles on their faces—"and once I had all the loose ends tied up, namely making sure that my parents were OK with what this—us—may do to my relationship with Robby, then it was all systems go. I just needed to get you here and in the right place for the grand gesture."

"And what a grand gesture it was," I compliment him.

He bows his head, that charming dimple popping in his cheek. "Why, thank you."

"But," I start, unable to shake my unsettled feeling, "I don't want to come between you and Robby."

Jake sighs and kisses my temple. "That's not for you to worry about, Millie. Robby is my brother and we'll sort it out, but there's no way I'm letting you go just to soothe his ego."

I argue and he stops me, putting his mouth on mine. *Yummy. I hope this is how all our arguments end.*

"Robby will be fine," he repeats after we've come up for air. "He just needs to grow up a bit to realise the world doesn't revolve around him."

I agree with this and so I let it go. Their relationship is for them to fix. I'm not letting Robby stand in the way of my happily ever after. *Not again.*

"So, what now?"

"Now?" he smiles at me, a pure smile that fills me with joy. "Now I'm going to ask you if you'll go out on a date with me?"

My heart thump, thump, thumps in my chest, and I pretend to think about his question. "Hmmm, a date, hey?"

"Yes," he growls, squeezing my waist with his arm that's glued to my body.

"I'm not sure..." I trail off, tapping my finger to my mouth.

"Amelia," he warns.

"It's just that I still have to go through letters H, I, J, K before I can date you. L is for lawyer..." I squeal as he lunges at me, pulling me to him and effectively shutting me up with another kiss.

"That damn dating plan," he mutters as we break apart.

"It's done now." I run my fingers over his furrowed brow, smoothing his worried lines away. "You are the only man I want to date for now..."

"And forever," he finishes for me. His voice was confident and sure.

I lean into him, feeling safe and content in his arms. Finally.

"And forever. After all, I'm actually yours."
He smiles and kisses me again.
"Actually mine."
Forever.

The End

EPILOGUE

Jake

Six months later

"**M**ILLIE, ARE YOU HOME?" I hear a thump, followed by a grunt, and then see a flash of pink hair and a bright smile hurtling towards me.

"You're here!"

I catch Amelia in my arms and she wraps her legs around my waist, kissing me like it's been weeks instead of the mere hours that have passed since I last saw her. Not that I'm complaining. After wanting her in secret for so long, I relish every minute of the affection she so freely gives me.

"We're getting better at this!" I laugh, planting one more kiss on her mouth before letting her slide to the ground.

"Our best run and jump yet," she agrees. Having watched all seven seasons of *Gilmore Girls* during our first few months of dating, Amelia has moved us onto watching *The Bachelor* and now has us practising 'the run and jump.' It's what the contestants do on this show every time they see the lead: hop, skip, and jump into his arms, where he's waiting to catch them. It's ridiculous, but it also means that whenever I see her, she's launching herself at me, so I'm not complaining.

"How was your day?" She moves away from me, pulling her hair into a messy bun on top of her head. This week her hair is a light pink colour, reminding me of an Easter egg. *Who knows what colour she'll opt for next week?*

"Boring," I tell her while I loosen my tie. My hours in the office have taken a drastic hit since I started dating Amelia, something my bosses have been grumbling about. But what I don't get done in the ten full hours they demand that I stay in the sterile, fluorescent-lit office building, I finish up after hours, cuddled up on Amelia's couch. It's a win-win in my book.

"I'm glad you're here." I follow her into her small kitchen, watching as she lovingly waters her cactus plant. The one she calls Callie.

She's so adorable.

"Why is that?"

"Because we're not eating here tonight," she says, garnering a groan from me. Although we've been together for just over half a year, she still hasn't dragged me out of my introverted ways.

"What have you committed us to tonight?"

She gives me her very best puppy dog eyes. *Oh, I will not like this.*

"We're meeting Robby and his new girlfriend for dinner at that new Thai restaurant down the road."

So, that's why she's got her pleading face on. She's agreed to go out with my brother and whichever girl he's tricked into dating him this month!

"Do we have to?" I pull her into my arms and nuzzle my nose into her neck, using my own ways of persuading her to stay in. "Wouldn't you rather have a night on the couch?"

I feel her resolve weakening before she rallies. "He's trying, Jake. We need to meet him in the middle."

I sigh. She's right. In the weeks after we first got together, Robby's behaviour had been as expected. Tantrums, silent treatment, blow-ups. But once he realised that me and Amelia were here to stay and he was the expendable one in my life, he came around. Somewhat. Amelia has been amazing through it all, playing peacemaker, trying to get us both to be reasonable, and I know it's because of her that my brother and I are on decent terms, even if I had to end our roommate agreement. It was too difficult having Amelia and him thrown into the same space constantly. Robby had to go.

"Fine, let's meet them early so we can get home early."

She laughs, wagging her finger at me. "I can see right through you. You're pretending it's because you want to get away from your brother, but really you want to get home in time to watch *The Bachelor.*"

Busted. I don't trust us to not get spoiled if we don't watch it live. A fact that amuses Amelia endlessly.

"Well, it's your fault for getting me hooked," I grumble. "I need to know who Zac picks."

She throws her head back with laughter and I marvel again that she's mine. This shiny, glorious woman in front of me, who lives her life in multi-colour, actually wants to spend her life with me.

"Fine, let's have a quick bite to eat and then get you home in time for your reality TV fix."

Decision made, I make my way to her bedroom, where most of my clothes are hanging in her small closet. Everything about Amelia's place is small, meant for just one petite woman, and I'm more than ready for the day we can move into a place that we own together. So far, we've been happy having our separate places to retreat to, and when I say we, I mean Amelia, because I'd move in with her in a heartbeat. In fact, that's something I need to talk to her about. I just need to make sure I sweeten the deal a bit.

"Are you busy tomorrow?" I yell the question down the hallway while I change into a casual pair of blue jeans and a green cashmere jumper that is suitable for the cooler autumn climate. Amelia loves it when I wear green, something about my eyes looking like emeralds when I do.

"Nothing much," she replies. "I'm working in the afternoon. Why?"

I don't answer her, hoping to keep my plans for the morning a secret. Over the last six months, Amelia has grown so much emotionally. She's now closer with her dad and his family, has worked through a lot of her issues with her mum and has started therapy. I've gone to a few sessions with her, knowing it's important for our relationship for me to be a part of her journey to healing. Her ability to open up and trust in herself, her feelings and emotions, and most of all her trust in me, have only gotten stronger with time. So much so that I think she's ready for the next step. The next two steps, in fact.

"I've also been busy making secret plans."
She lights up with pleasure and she sashays over to me, a determined look on her face. *Uh oh, she's going to get the information out of me. I'm a sucker for this woman.*

"Tell me." She purrs at me, her face inches away from mine.

I shake my head, rolling my lips into a tight line.
She brushes her lips over the pulse point on my neck. *Oh, she's playing dirty.*

"Please?"

I pick her up and move her away from me, seconds away from cracking and telling her all my plans.

"Come on, Jake. You know I hate secrets!" She pouts at me and I can't hold back my smile. It's a known fact that she hates secrets, surprises or anything where she can't have an input. It's one of the many things I love about her.

"Fine." I make a big show f giving in, when in reality I knew that I was going to tell her everything the minute she asked me. "Ruin the surprise, why don't you?"

She pulls me to the couch and turns her body to face me, an empty packet of Tiny Teddies on the coffee table next to us.

"Go!"

I take her small hand in mine, marvelling at how something so delicate holds my whole life in its palm. "I've been thinking…about our future."

Her expression grows serious, and she scoots closer to me until our knees are touching.

"What about it?"

"We've been together for how long now?"

"Six amazing months," she answers instantly.

"And it's been the best six months of my life."

She plants a soft kiss on my lips. "Mine too."

"So, I've been thinking about us taking the next step."
I stop and she looks bemused and a little scared. *What does she think I'm about to say?*

"The next step?" she stutters.

"Yes, I think we should…"

Her hands are trembling in mine and I forge ahead, putting her out of her misery. "We should get a cat together!"

Her pretty mouth falls open. "A cat?"

I grin at her, pleased that I've caught her off guard. "Yes, a cat."

"Together?"

"Yes."

She shakes her head slightly, trying to get her bearings. "But I can't have a cat. I kill all things I look after."

And this is the reason we need to do this. Even after all the therapy and every piece of evidence to the contrary, Amelia still thinks she is incapable of giving enough love to another person. Or animal.

"That's complete rubbish, and you know it."

She shakes her head, more firmly this time. "I can't have pets in this apartment, Jake."

I put my arm around her, tucking her into my side. "That's where the 'we' comes into it. I said we should get a cat. As in you and me…"

"We'd share custody?"

OK, this is getting annoying.

"Yes, we'd share custody because we'd be living together."

She squeals, and a laugh is torn from me. That's the reaction I'd been hoping for.

"You want to live together? With me?"

I want to do more than just live together, if the diamond ring I've been hiding in my bedside drawer is anything to go by. But with Amelia, I know we need to take baby steps. Adopting a cat and living together seems the most natural next step.

"I do."

She thinks about it for so long, a trickle of sweat runs down my back. *Is there a chance I misread this, and she's going to say no?*

"Yes!"

My heart sings in response to this one word.

"Yes?"

"Yes, Jake, I want to live with you and get a cat. Maybe we can get two…?" Her brain is off and running, filled with thoughts of running a feline hotel if what she's saying is anything to go by.

"Let's start with the one and go from there."

She nods and snuggles back into me. "So, should I move into your place…?" She sounds uncertain again.

"How about we get a place that's just our own? A fresh start, somewhere we can make new memories together?"

She bites her lip; a sign of relief and I know we're doing the right thing. My place, while having so many wonderful memories of our time together, is also shrouded by memories of her time with him. With Robby.

"I've been looking online for a while." *About five and a half months.* "And I found a place close to your salon, and Love, Lilly, and it has a cute enclosed yard out the back for the one cat we're getting." I emphasise the word *one*, pulling out my phone to show her the real estate ad for a place that I've already fallen in love with. I can just picture the two of us living there together, making a life and raising a family. It's a crystal-clear image in my mind.

"Oh, Jake. I love it!" she exclaims as she scrolls through the photos. "It's perfect. Look at those bay windows and that little front porch. It's exactly the sort of place we should get."

With my nerves gone, I reach into my back pocket. "I'm glad that you think so, because it's ours."

I hand her the keys to this place, which I'd bought with our future in mind, my heart racing as her eyes fill with tears.

"It's ours?" her voice is trembling with emotion.

I nod, too choked up to speak. It may not be the ring I'm so desperate to give her, but giving her this key is like giving her my heart all over again. And I know, as she's done every day since we first said I love you, that she'll take care of it.

"You bought us a place?"

"We need somewhere that's just ours. Just for you and me."

She throws her arms around my neck and holds on tight. "I love it, Jake. And I love you."

My eyes close and I hug her back, whispering back how much I love her too.

We sit like this, in our own bubble, and I think not for the first time how grateful I am that we found our way to each other and that we now have a future that is wide open with possibilities.

A future for the two of us.

A future that is actually ours.

ACKNOWLEDGEMENTS

To my husband, my best friend and my partner in life, this and every book is for you. Thank you for the countless hours you give to make my dream come true. For encouraging me, and sending me positive Goodreads reviews out of the blue. For finding me editors and designers and every little thing in between. For standing next to me at that book signing and proudly wearing your 'assistant' lanyard. For smiling at me like you think I'm cute when I tell you what my characters are up to in my head. For never letting me give up, even though you know I've wanted to. You are better than all my imaginary book boyfriends combined, and I'll love you forever.

To my beautiful Hunter and Sienna, who help pick character names and tell me they like my book covers. You two make everything worthwhile. Thank you for sharing your mummy with her laptop on the weekends. I love you more than you'll ever know.

To Sarah, my wonderfully efficient editor, whose real time reactions in the margins make my day. Thank you for helping me shape this story to where it is now, and for letting me know when I use that one particular word way too many times. To my amazing beta readers, your ideas and encouragement had me squealing with joy. This story is better for having had your eyes on it. And to my wonderful cover designer, Elin. What can I say? I'm in love with this cover and the work you did to get Amelia and Jake just right. I can't wait to work with you again soon.

To my family and friends who have remained my fans since the release of Love, Lilly. When you buy each book and then send me a message to say you loved it, it means the world to me. Thank you for your never-ending support.

And finally, to my readers who show up for me every day. From the bottom of my heart, thank you. To Melissa, Hayley, Emma, Patty, Rachael, Kristin, Sam, Beth, Heather and so many more that I can't mention you all, thank you for your messages, your posts, your love of my words. I write these stories for you.

LOVE, LILLY

He's her best friend's brother and completely out of her league...

Twenty-three-year-old Lilly is the quirky girl, the one with the c-c-curly hair. She's always late, is rarely neat and does not have her life together. She will never be that girl, the one who gets the perfect guy. But hopefully, this is about to change. It is a new year and Lilly has made some resolutions to get her act together.

Her best friend's brother Oliver is the reliable guy, the one who rescues Lilly from all of her disasters. He's organised, makes lots of lists and has a strict five-year plan in place to get ahead in life. He never makes rash decisions, unless it relates to Lilly, and then he can't seem to help himself.

With this in mind, it would seem that these two friends have little in common. Except perhaps a secret pining for each other that has gone unspoken for too long.

Can a weekend of fake dating convince Lilly and Oliver that they are actually perfect for each other? And that opposites really do attract, after all?

AVAILABLE NOW ON AMAZON

ALWAYS, AMY

Can two people go from being enemies to lovers to...just friends?

Twenty-five-year-old Amy Harlow has read every romance trope that exists and she loves them all. She's very familiar with the fictional archetypal bad boy characters, and sadly, she has dated quite a few. And so, when she meets the suave, arrogant, but oh-so-good looking Lucas Mancini, the new doctor working with her in the emergency department, she knows exactly where to put him. As public enemy, number one.

Unfortunately for Amy, Lucas is determined to evade his role as the bad guy in her story, and before she knows what's happening, he has moved from enemy to lover and now to friend? How had that happened? And now that he has put her in the friend zone, Amy cannot focus on anything other than getting herself out of it.

With the help of an anxious puppy, her friends in a raucous romance book club, and a weekend of fake dating (it works in all the books she so happily devours), will Amy be able to overcome her preconceived notions about love and Lucas, and finally write her own happy ending?

AVAILABLE NOW ON AMAZON

CIAO, BELLA

He's just her new roommate...nothing more!

Twenty-six-year-old Bella Mancini is moving to Australia! She's leaving behind her small Italian village on a mission to find a new job, to find new adventures, and maybe even to find love? What she didn't expect to find was him.

Daniel Richardson was not looking for her. Still grieving the death of his mother, he finds comfort in being alone and is determined to not let anyone too close to him, to not get hurt again. So, when Bella turns up on his doorstep, he has only one thought: he wants her gone, and fast!

Lucky for Bella—not so much for Daniel—she gets to move in! And as the summer progresses, her sunny personality begins to melt his icy exterior and soon they find in each other everything they didn't know they'd always wanted.

But when their newfound love is challenged, Daniel worries that Bella will leave, that he will be alone again. And Bella is left to wonder if Daniel is healed enough to let her stay forever...

AVAILABLE NOW ON AMAZON

NOTICING NATALIE

What happens when the boy you crushed on in high school—the one who crushed your heart—turns up 6 years later...and he needs your help?

Natalie Henderson was that girl in high school. The invisible one lost in her books; going unnoticed in the hallways. Until he paid her attention. Matthew Barkly was that boy in high school. The star of the soccer team and all-round Mr Popular, and he'd started noticing her. Under the guise of studying together, Natalie was swept into his spotlight and started believing that perhaps she wasn't invisible after all. But turns out...it was all a lie.

Six years later, Natalie is taking her first steps into adulthood. Leaving behind the shy, awkward girl from high school and embracing her new role as a nurse in a busy hospital, she has everything carefully planned out. Until her one and only crush comes barrelling back into her life, disrupting everything.

Matthew is a national soccer hero and has the world at his feet. He's also wondering if any of it—fame, attention, money—is worth it. And then he sees her again. The one he always wanted, the one he can't forget. Grasping at any opportunity to spend time with her; he begs Natalie to pretend to be his girlfriend to help fix his playboy image. Unbelievably, she agrees to play along, and soon the lines between what's fake and what's real are blurred and all those long-forgotten feelings are flaring back to life.

But as Natalie navigates the pitfalls of fame and media attention that follow 'dating' a celebrity sports star, will the distrust and uncertainty from their past stand in the way of them becoming something more in the present? Or will Natalie have the courage to believe that Matthew could possibly notice her…for real this time?

AVAILABLE NOW ON AMAZON

ABOUT THE AUTHOR

Belinda Mary is a long-time lover of all the books, and with her first romantic comedy series out in the world, she is thrilled to find readers out there who connect with the characters that have been running around in her brain for so long now. When she is not reading or writing, she can be found spending time with her family who she adores, watching all things Bravo, eating anything chocolate-related, or listening to true crime podcasts. Belinda writes the kind of stories she loves to read; filled with laughter, longing and love.

You can find out more about Belinda and connect with her online and on social media.

If you'd like to be part of Belinda's newsletter, you can subscribe through her website www.*belindamary.com* and get the latest news, information and bookish insights.

@belindamary @belindamary

@belindamary.author @belindamary.author

www.ingramcontent.com/pod-product-compliance
Lightning Source LLC
Chambersburg PA
CBHW020911130726
47904CB00006BA/1813